DEATH OF THE DEMON

THE PHOENIX'S ASHES, BOOK FIVE

REBECCA ETHINGTON

Published by Imdalind Press

Production Management by Imdalind Press

ISBN (print) **978-1-949725-27-8**

ISBN (e-book) **978-1-949725-22-3**

Printed in USA

This Edition, April 2019

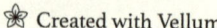 Created with Vellum

CONTENTS

For My Kids
Always.

1

CALLAY

EVERY PART of my body felt disconnected, like I was a Barbie doll that had been pulled apart by some treacherous older brother with anger issues. I was sure if I looked I would find my pieces scattered around me, the white rubber nubs sticking out so that we could connect them back together.

Not that I could move even if I was in one piece. Something which wasn't caused by the heavy rope that tied me to the post or the gunk that was still coating my hands after being captured by Fallon and her real best friend, Parris.

Last time I tried to be fake best friends with a wicked little girl who turned out to be a bird-shifter. I would probably wring her neck first if she wasn't holding me in place with her mega voodoo.

Her icy breath wrapped over my face and through my mind, muddling my focus on the cave until it was just her. Staring at me with those damn violet eyes.

I had spent years keeping this bitch out of my dragons' beds which I admittedly failed at, and keeping her out of their heads, which I also failed at. To be fair, Killian was not someone you can control. Either way, I had spent hundreds of years attempting to keep her away from them and succeeding from keeping her away from me, so still a win.

Until now, when homegirl decided to get all up in my business.

"Don't speak like that, you sound like a fool." Dabria's voice rattled around inside my head, reminding me how close I was to the ultimate massive failure.

I needed to keep her out of the important bits of fluff I had been hiding for a few centuries and I would be good. Except that task was proving near impossible. Everything was fuzzy and I kept feeling like I needed to go to sleep. Just close my eyes and drift away into nothing.

The beautiful nothing that probably included flowers and trees and...

"No!" The word snapped through the fog, breaking through the gag that was still stuffed in my mouth with a noise that kind of sounded like what I had meant it to. It was hard to tell as the snap of sound echoed through the cave, bringing both cold air and the ugly tittering of a certain blood sucker right along with it.

Parris slowly stepped toward me, his burned face melting down the side of his neck in a bubbling, boiling, mess. I wasn't sure how much of that was my delusions and how much of that was his run-in with Ellie.

Humor and hate boiled, my magic trying to break through before the world started to swim again, my vision shifting as the ice dragon duplicated herself, littering the cave with the same violet stare and long coils of black and lavender hair.

Because the world needed more than one of her.

Whatever she had done to me was equal to the worst acid trip of my life.

"Have you really not been able to take control?" Parris slurred, or rather my brain slurred seeing as his wobbling steps around Fallon made him look like he was trying to engage in an interpretive dance competition.

I totally snickered. Or drooled. Not sure.

"She's fighting me, Parry," Dabria pouted with a stomp of her foot that I could have sworn sent the entire cave jiggling like Jell-O. "There is something there, like a barrier."

Dabria sounded pissed, even though she was swaying to the jiggling cave like a hula girl. Parris, however, began laughing with a sound like he had swallowed a kettle drum. It was shaking the Jell-O walls as bad as Dabria's mini fit.

"Of course she's guarded. She's created by a goddess and you think this will be easy?" Fallon's voice danced from somewhere in the jelly shrine, Parris joining in on her tittering.

Dabria's scowl furrowed into her forehead, her eyes flashing blue as she turned to Fallon, shooting ice or something at her.

She could have peed on her for all I knew.

Now it was my turn to laugh, not that I could help it. Maybe I was on an acid trip. Dabria could be trying to infect my mind, or I could be drugged, or both. Or, I could be really, really hungry. The last time I had felt this uninhibited and perhaps a little crazy was when I had been starving to death. When I had met...

I stopped myself right before I got there, but Dabria still spun back around to face me. Damn it, she had heard the end of the thought. Her eyes narrowed as she stepped closer, pursing her lips and blowing an icy breath over me. Maybe that was the drug, her foul-smelling ice breath.

She gave me another glare and I laughed harder, pressing against the ropes in an attempt to get closer to her.

I doubt that I moved more than a few inches, although everything was spinning as though I was taking a whirl on my spaceship through the stars.

Like that time I tried to eat the fish from the pond, and the stars skittered over the surface like the long-legged skeeters the frogs ate. Maybe I could eat them too.

Star bugs.

I bet they would give me magic powers.

"We are close," Dabria whispered through the memory, her face swirling over the water as she came back into focus. "She needs to give in. Go to sleep or something..."

"You need her unconscious?" Parris whispered from somewhere to the left, his icy breath as vile and chilled as Dabria's. No wonder they liked each other, their breath both smelled like a corpse in defrost.

"Stinky." I mumbled through the gag, laughing at myself. I don't know why they weren't laughing. That was funny.

"I can fix that," Parris continued, oblivious to my very well-placed insult.

Instead, he placed his fist against my temple. Dabria's squeal followed me into the dark, into a life from hundreds of years ago and the scattered stars of the pond as I laid next to it, watching the fish twitch beneath the thin layer of ice. His shimmering scales cut through the frost, dancing with the stars that reflected in the shimmering ice as they swam together.

I wondered if he was cold too. If he felt the bitterness of the ice. Spring should have come more than a month ago, it should be warm for him to be swimming like that. So carefree. So happy. He hadn't run out of food like we had.

I scooted closer, my joints aching as I hovered over the ice. My bare hand curled over the frozen bank, my blackened fingers clutching what I hoped was a big enough rock to break the ice and clobber the fish before he had a chance to swim away. It didn't matter if it wasn't. It was the biggest I could lift, my starving body and frozen limbs barely able to grip the stone.

One swing. One swing and he would be mine. Perhaps it would be enough to last a few days, perhaps the spring would come by then and we could replenish the food that the Turks stole in this asinine war.

The snap of my grunt echoed over ice and frozen trees, the hollow iron clang of the rock skipping over the surface of the ice and into the middle of the pond shattering my heart into a million frozen fragments.

"No!" I could barely force the word out. It was more of a sob as I watched the fish swim away.

I collapsed into the snow, as the damp soaked into my dress and my socks. I didn't even have my old leather boots to keep my feet warm. After the food ran out, they were the first to go. Boiled down to something that could pass as food.

We might as well have eaten stones, which is what my baby brother had done in his desperation. I had left him screaming with my little sister Danna while I went to find food. Same as mother had done a fortnight before. Same as father days later. They hadn't returned. And with the ache in my bones, neither would I.

The fish was gone. The rock was gone. Warmth was gone. Hope had gone along with it.

"I can't leave them. Please don't make me leave them. Please. Someone. Save us."

Collapsing to the ground, I placed my hand and two blackened fingers against the ice, pressing with every last bit of strength I had. It didn't budge. There wasn't even a creak as the chill of the pond bled through me, making me as cold as everything else.

Cold. So cold.

So cold that there was nothing left, nothing but the stars as dancing high above me.

I lay still, watching them fade.

Fade to nothing.

Nothing but black.

Nothing but death.

The ice cracked with a loud snap that burst through the trees, swaying the snow covered bows away from a blast although none of the inches of snow that covered them fell. As they froze. Nothing moved, not even the bird that had been drifting through the starry sky, the white face of the owl staring down at me. Perhaps he thought I was food.

Perhaps I was now.

Nothing more than food.

"Not yet, but you can be if you want, I guess. I stopped it. For now." The voice was too perky for the gaunt Prussian wilderness I had crawled into in my search for food. Too perky for the Turks that fought my country in war, ripping everything to shreds and leaving only death behind them.

The Turkish soldiers also didn't look anything like the girl that was hovering over me. Her almond shaped eyes shimmered, just like her sheet of hair the color of night, her face spread into a smile that I didn't think was possible anymore.

I sure as shit wasn't smiling. But she seemed happy about something. Soup maybe? And not because she found some, but because she was going to make me into some.

Okay, so maybe I wasn't dead yet, but I was hallucinating, either that or the witches in the forest had found me. Great.

"Are you going to curse me?" My throat burned with each word, a weird sensation considering everything was frozen. I was surprised my fingers hadn't fallen off yet. Danna had already lost two.

"It looks like you are already cursed, child." She smiled and sunk down in the snow next to me, leaning over me in some jewel covered thing that looked like what royals would wear. Red velvet and stones that looked like glittering blocks of clear ice. She was dripping in sparkle, and not nearly enough clothing to survive the harsh cold of the tundra.

Like I was one to talk. I was hallucinating witches as I prepared to become another frozen body in this endless winter. I had passed a few on my way here, and someone would pass me in the future.

"Oh, don't be so dramatic," the girl said, leaning over and pressing a finger to my forehead. The touch was hot, like a branding iron that was burning straight through me. Through my nerves, through my bones, over my skin like liquid heat. I must be really cold if I thought one touch from a kid was enough to warm me up right to my bones.

Either that or I really was dead. It was hard to know considering I stared at the stars as I lay on my back in the snow. Snow that was getting warm and melting around me, pooling around my hands and tingling against my blackened fingers.

Yep. Totally dead. I had felt nothing from those fingers in a few days.

"Again with the drama," the girl said with something that I could have sworn was a giggle. A giggle when the whole world around us was dying. Okay, she might have a point.

Either that or I was losing it.

Because if I wasn't mistaken she could hear my thoughts. Yeah, that was normal and certainly not something that would happen to a dead person. I was going to accept that drama, even the kid's smile was widening. I was totally right. And totally dead.

"You are not dead. Nor am I a witch, well, not the crazy old women that eats children that you are thinking of. And I certainly am not going to make you into soup. You're what? Fifteen? Too old for me. Your soup would be too tough. Gross."

I should be horrified, but I was too lost in the warmth as it continued to melt through my skin, like the snow. Heat tingled over me, just like the water that was everywhere. So warm. Even my dead and blackened fingers felt warm, and not so much like they were going to pop off. I flexed the dratted appendages, amazingly nothing snapped off.

"If I'm not dead, and you aren't a witch, then what is going on?" That burning rasp in my throat had left. Even my lungs didn't ache on the inhale.

"You asked for help, so I came." The girl held out her hand in an offer to help me sit. With how warm and nimble I was, I was sure I could do some sort of jumping jack into the snow-covered tree above me. Instead, I stubbornly lay in the snow and crossed my arms over my chest.

Stubborn? I preferred to think of myself as superstitious. But I was a Prussian serf in the middle of a war, living in a barren wasteland, starving to death. It was kinda our thing.

"A little girl. Dressed like a princess or some shit. I'm not sure how you can help me, or even how you got here." I gripped the dirt and brambles around me, suddenly afraid she was going to pull me up and force me into her witch's cave.

"Again with the drama." She rolled her eyes and jumped to standing, sending a shower of snow over me. Warm specks of white fell over the blanket and the exposed part of my neck. Warm snow? Because that was possible.

Well, unless I was so cold that everything around me felt warm. Again, I was clearly dead.

"You have been told the fairytale about the fish in the pond, correct?" I stared at her. "The fisherman catches a fish and brings it home to his wife who goes to cut it open and it offers to grant her a wish in exchange for its life." She stood above me now, jutting her hand out at me again.

I might have taken it that time if I wasn't so dumbfounded by what she had said.

"The fish in the pond? That was you? Are you going to grant me a wish now?" My mind was already buzzing of all the things I could ask her for. My family alive and safe. A warmer home for my siblings. A never-ending supply of food.

I knew how this worked, however. Fish were slippery creatures. I had heard the story, and that wish-granting fish twisted the fisherman's wife's words until they meant nothing and her wish was as lost as she was.

There was only one thing that I would ever wish for. My family, alive and safe. I didn't see a way that could be twisted, and I wasn't about to ask for anything else. No mountain of gold could ever replace that. Replace my parents. Replace that safety.

I opened my mouth to ask, but her offered hand shifted to a single finger, stopping me before I could get a word out.

"Do I look like a fish to you?" That was a little bit harsher than the smiling kid she had been a minute before. "No, I am not some silly fish. I am so much more than a fish. While I might grant you a wish, it would be in exchange for your life, not mine."

"I don't understand." I was seriously regretting my stubborn choice to remain flat on my back in the snow, having a non-fish-witch hovering above me in the shape of a nine-year-old girl was making my confusion feel like something closer to stupidity.

"I created the fish." She smiled again, as if that somehow answered everything. "You have good in you, and it's been so long since good has asked for help that I couldn't help but answer. You found my pond. Your heart is pure, so I will give you one wish. One wish in exchange for your life, like the fish. If you choose this path, your life will be tied to mine, until my task is complete, and only then will I release you and give you the full strength of the good inside of you. After that I will create your nemesis. Do you accept?"

I would have to understand enough to accept, but while most of that was gibberish to me, one thing was clear. She would save my family if I consented to be her slave. I was already owned by the lord of our province. I would be losing nothing by changing a master, but my family would be gaining everything. If I could save them, then all of this would be worth it.

"What is your task?"

"I must put the world back to where it was. I must bring my sister home before the demons she released into our world take control."

"Huh?" All of that sounded way too ominous to be real.

"I cannot tell you more than that, child. But it will take many years. Many more than your mortal body can handle, so I will have to change you."

"Change me? Wait... *child*?" What in the world was she talking about? She was younger than me, but she seemed to think she was not only older, but capable of 'changing' me.

She was acting like some wise old crone now too. There wasn't a drop of giggle left in her eyes. Just something dark, something that felt like the whole world in one color, a color that was ready to swallow everything whole.

Death? Hallucinating? Which one would I go with this time? Perhaps we had moved on to pure unbridled insanity.

"Yes, change you into something a bit closer to me. Something with more power."

With a smile that big, full of so much foreboding darkness, there was no way she wasn't a witch. "Power, like...?"

"You'll be better than a wish-granting fish," she winked. "But you'll be able to do that too."

"Turn into a fish?" Yep, definitely the old witch that I had been warned about my whole life.

"If that's the future you wish for joining me, sure, but I was thinking something more along the lines of granting wishes and using the power that is already inside of you to improve the world. Much as I will do for you if you choose to join me. A wish, in exchange for a little bit of work."

A wish. I had almost forgotten about it in the nonsense that was melting around me, like the snow.

"Will you grant me anything?" I was very careful with my wording, if I was going to do this, I would make sure to get what I wanted. It didn't help that I was sure she was reading my mind, I wasn't about to trust in any witch not to double cross me.

"Anything." She smiled, holding out her hand again. This time I was sure it meant more than helping me to my feet. "But be aware. That your wish, your hope for now, will impact your future in years to come. For you. For your family. For the dangerous fate that will always be waiting for you on the other side of this icy winter. Be very careful about what you desire, child. But I have a feeling you already know that."

The little girl waited, her hand unwavering as she

watched me, as my mind buzzed with a million wishes, and a million dangerous outcomes.

"You say you are magic…"

"You will be too if you choose to follow me," she interrupted me and my next question went right out the window.

"Magic?" I couldn't get out more than that one word.

"What do you say, Callay? What would you wish for? What would you do for this gift?"

It was much harder to think of a logical way to ask this now that I had a promise of magic in my mind, but there were more lives at stake than my own. More that I needed to save. I had to be careful, luckily, I knew what to ask for.

"When all this is over, when I have served my time with you and your task is completed, I wish for you to send me back to this forest. Back to my family from the summer before now, so that I may save them."

"Are you completely sure?" I didn't even hesitate before I nodded, before I reached up and grasped her hand and allowed her to pull me up from the soggy mud that the melted snow had revealed.

I knew exactly what I would see, the glittery trees of the girl's magic, the world in shimmering crystal as it was when I first received my magic. When I first made a deal with a Unicorn. Sold my soul for the chance of saving my family.

Nearly two hundred years had passed since then. I wasn't sure we were any closer to completing her mysterious task, or if going back to save my family was what I wanted after all this was over. There was so much more pain in what the world had become, so much more that I could help.

The glittering forest was replaced by the blurred lines of what I was sure was Dabria and Parris.

"I'm in," a mumble that I was sure belonged to Dabria

echoed through my head, as if the sound was a weight pounding against skull and spine. "She belongs to me now."

I wanted to scream at her, to rant and rave and yell about how crazy she was and fight against the binds.

But I did nothing more than lift my head and smile, the blurred lines of the vampire and his posse coming into focus as they smiled back, as Parris stepped forward.

"To me, you mean," he hissed, the icy chill of his breath assaulting me as he leaned in, his nose running down my jaw, breathing me in. "She belongs to me."

I couldn't stop him as he ripped off the gag and kissed me. I couldn't even bite his tongue as it slipped between my lips, as his hands pulled me from the post.

My arms wrapped around him of their own accord, my lips kissing him back even though everything inside of me was screaming.

Screaming as I tilted my neck. Screaming as I felt his tongue drag over the protruding vein there, his fangs digging into my skin. Drinking. Feasting.

Everything inside of me was screaming, even as Dabria laughed and clapped her hands.

"Perfect," Parris moaned as he pulled away, a drop of my blood drizzling over his chin. "Let's stow her away, we need her for later, and I don't want to make it too easy for any would-be rescuers to succeed. We still need her."

They all laughed as I was forced away, staggering from blood loss toward where Ceres was, and the room I could already tell they were going to hide me in. I was trapped inside a mind that was no longer mine, same as the whimpering King in the corner.

The King who, as I was dragged passed him, had more life in his eyes than they had a moment before. As if our keeper was stretching herself too thin.

2

ELLIOT

"I don't understand why you can't let me go in on my own. I can kill the guys who need killing, while you wimps save the ones who need saving and be done with it." Lilly barked as we raced down another tunnel, Killian and Zoe leading the way to the throne room, and what should be a hostile takeover of a Vampire and a Dragon in an attempt to rescue Callay.

If we could get there.

Zoe and Killian were supposed to be leading us there, instead they were arguing about which way we needed to go next. It seems the last collapse had changed the map of tunnels, and neither Zoe or Killian were content to let the other one lead.

"Because, *Lilly*," Zoe snapped, pulling us to a stop as we reached yet another dead end. Figures I would be the only one that was limping after all the barefoot running we were doing. I wasn't tired, too much circus for that, but damn my feet hurt. "We have faced this enemy before, and we have all been in messes like these enough to know that if we go in there guns blazing it's going to end badly. We need to make sure we have the right information. The right plan and..."

"The right boring-ass, mindset," Lilly interrupted, causing Zoe to jerk as if she had been punched.

"Excuse me?" Oh shit. I knew Lilly had balls, but it also appeared she had no common sense whatsoever.

I stepped back out of habit, right into Drake who was as shocked as I was.

Jarron, however, was ready to bust a gut, the quick-made torch he was holding flickering as he swallowed a laugh.

"I don't know who put you in charge anyway. We have been wandering in these tunnels for hoooours." Lilly dragged out the word like the punk kid she was. Talk about an exaggeration, it had been maybe ten minutes, tops. "Just let me pop in there, kill them all, and pop out. Won't take me more than a few minutes."

"If you can find the place," Jarron snickered, although not loud enough for anyone else to hear.

Lilly took one big step toward the dragon who I half expected to light the cave on fire. A shared thought considering that Drake, Jarron and I all took another large step back.

"Pop in?" Zoe stepped closer, towering over the kid as she slowly folded her arms.

I had seen the blood red flames in her eyes enough to know what was coming. I was willing to settle in and watch this showdown from the other side for once, except the scarlet fire was gone, replaced with something a little more opalescent, a little more white and glowing.

A little more like something I had seen before.

The memory traveled with the blink, but all I saw was a glimpse of another type of white fire before it was gone, leaving me staring at Zoe and wishing that my memories would fully plow into existence.

"What the hell?" I whispered to myself, taking a step toward her in an attempt to see, but Drake pulled me back, right into his chest, his arms wrapping around my waist as he shook his head no.

"I already told you, you can't go in on your own. You are lucky I have let you come with us this far. You're a kid. We should have left you back with The Forgotten." Zoe stepped forward, away from Killian who was taking the opportunity to lead our makeshift charge. Zoe's fire might have been gone, but Killian's was flowing in spades. He looked ready to spontaneously combust and take us all out.

"Correction. I'm a kid trained to fight by a demon. I'm more skilled at this than you are. Killian thinks so." Lilly was smiling now, her chin up as she followed Killian who was now charging down another dark tunnel, leaving Zoe fuming.

Damn kid was going to pit those two against each other even more and make this whole journey to Rydaim even longer.

"Technically he was a fallen angel," Jarron said from the back, herding us all after Killian who had already been swallowed by the dark. Thank God, someone was all for getting this complain train moving again.

"Doesn't matter." I cut in, picking up my pace as I caught up to Killian, the guy focused ahead, his eyes were as black as the cave. "I killed the demon, pretty sure I have the power to kill the vamp too. I don't care much who goes in first, as long as we get there."

"You say that like it makes it any better," Killian said with a growl as he backed us up from yet another dead end. "I'm sure there is something worse waiting for us up there."

"If you are talking about the all you can eat buffet..." Jarron began, cutting himself short with one dark look from Killian.

Time for me to take another step back. I may be a badass Phoenix with a demon slicing knife still strapped to my hip. But the darkness in Killian was scaring the bejesus out of me.

It was like he had soaked his soul in tar and all his emerald light had been sucked away.

I liked that light, even though it managed to piss me off while simultaneously enrapturing me in a blanket of lust and silken need. Need like when he held me against him in the bathroom, his fingers running over my bare back, his fingertips counting each rib as they tip-toed...

And it was time for a change of subject. Luckily, he chose that moment to turn and stare at me, his gaze burning black and freaking me the fuck out.

Maybe we should send Killian and the kid up there, they both looked ready to devour them all anyway.

"Something worse?" I said doing my best to keep my voice even. "What could be worse than a poor excuse for a vampire and his idiot whores?"

I winced as we turned another corner, the stone rough and prickly under my feet. I was sure we had started running on knives.

Fitting for a masochistic vampire, this better be the right way. I was going to have to fart rocket out of here if we had to make a return trip, the sharp stone was cutting into my feet.

"I met Suvi's brother in the Himalayas." Killian's voice lowered as he pulled to a stop. Creepy. "He sent his familiar, a falcon, to collect what I can only assume is Callay or Elliot. Seeing as Elliot is here, that can only mean..."

"Hold up," I interrupted with a snap, pressing my palm into the air like some late 90's gangster. "I thought you said you were fighting off your own demon?"

"I was." His voice was still dripping with that darkness that made him sound like a grim reaper come to collect my soul.

"I did. I won. I lost." Was he trying to freak me out more? I was already running on knives toward a room full of Vampires, Dragons, and I guess a bird?

Sorry, that was officially out as to the 'scary things we were about to go kill' list.

"But Suvi isn't a demoness, is she? Because we were fighting off a real demon. Like I am pretty sure he had smoky wings and his face was all fiery and, you know, demony." I gestured to Jarron and the kid, who was no longer listening and was instead leaning against the rough stone wall of yet another dead end, changing the color of her camo pants to some weird bubblegum pink color. Because that will help you to stealth your way into battle... in the bubble gum forest.

And she thought she was ready to fight vampires and mind reading dragons.

That's it! I'm sending her in!

"You were probably fighting off some man with a cane and got confused," Zoe wasn't even trying to disguise her laugh.

Given how old Suvi was, it was probably the only option.

"No cane, trust me, and not someone we should barge in on." Killian's brow furrowed, shooting his own brand of eye daggers at his sister who had chosen this dead end as an opportunity to take the lead.

I half expected the two of them to duke it out at some point, the intensity of their glares was getting dangerous.

"The bird or the brother? Or the demon? Or are we back to arguing over who is going to take out the Vampire? I am starting to lose track of the villains." Drake asked as he came up behind me, hooking his arms behind my knees and swiftly swinging me into his arms.

I must have been limping worse than I thought, either that or he could smell the blood that was coating the bottom of my feet.

His worried half smile was giving him away. That and superpowered Dragon smell receptors.

"Thank you handsome," I whispered, my stomach swooping as he planted a kiss against my cheek, close enough to my lips that both me and Phoenix nearly lost it all together.

I was fully willing and able to fart rocket out of the tunnel of knives, but this was so much better.

"You are a fool if you think there is only one villain." Killian snapped as he turned to face us, the torch in Jarron's hand reflecting off the stone walls, deepening the shadows in Killian's three-day scruff until he looked like he was turning into an angel demon himself. "We were all fools to think there was only one villain before this. Ceres was the first, but he has already fallen. Dabria and Parris have been controlling him for who knows how long and that kid at the circus..."

"What?" Zoe stopped in place, turning in the middle of yet another cave intersection and sending us into twisty bumper cars, me being the bumper, right between Jarron's back and Drake's chest.

Oof!

"There is no way Ceres would have fallen to that blood sucker."

"Strange things happen when you have a mind reader on

your side," Jarron said, the light twisting his features as bad as his brother's. "Dabria is more of a menace than we thought. Which means she should probably be the first to go. Kill her, Ceres falls for good, and then there is the Vamp..."

"And his crew. Don't forget. One whistle and that throne room is full of the icy demons." Killian cut in, stepping toward Jarron, but the guy didn't even flinch. He was cool and collected, like he was on some beach and not one step from war. "I'm telling you, we need to get rid of the falcon first."

"It's a bird, Killian. I doubt it's a risk, and focusing on it is going to put us in danger." I would have given anything to agree with Zoe right then, except that my Phoenix was back to her bipolar tango, her claws digging into my heart. I cringed, snapping my eyes shut and giving myself one flash of some weird room and a man with a bird on his shoulder.

A falcon.

The man laughed, the bird's feathers rustling as he stepped closer, the knife balanced on the palm of his hand as he extended it to me.

Shit. Creepy little Xi said I had sold something to get that knife... I really didn't want to put that together. Seeing as my Phoenix was ready to go all bat-shit take down after that display, I wiggled my way out of Drake's arm before I flame farted all over him. Thankfully the floor wasn't as stabby.

"I didn't expect you to get fixated on someone's pet, Kills." Zoe kicked some loose rock as she peered into one of the two tunnels that flowed from this annex.

"It's not a pet. It's a falcon familiar of a warlock, Zoe. Ignoring that there is power there is dangerous." Killian stepped closer, his voice so dark that it was sucking away all the light.

"And disregarding the danger you know? If I didn't know better, Killian, I would say that you are wanting to join them." I didn't know how two people could be so loud, and so stern, without yelling. But it appeared to be a skill that both Zoe and Killian possessed.

"I'm half tempted to get out of here and let those two figure out their woes on their own," Drake whispered, pressing his cheek against mine, holding my hand between us as his thumb ran over the back of my hand in a calm motion that was so counterintuitive to the verbal assault ground we were in that I tensed more.

"Don't be a fool! I'm here to save them. To protect my mate. To protect..."

"Protect what, Killian?" Zoe roared, stepping even closer to her brother. "You know what you are, you know you aren't fit to be around her anymore. Step down and let the others take that role."

"Woah! What the fuck, Zo?" Talk about going from zero to sixty. I wasn't about to let Zoe go back to her lord over me attitude. "I am the only one to decide which one of my mates I don't want around, and right now the answer is none of them. I want them all."

"You don't know what you are saying, Elliot."

Fuck that! I wasn't going to play that game. I was going to rip her head off.

Well, I would have, if she hadn't turned to me with eyes full of a white flame.

Because that was normal. She looked possessed and I fell back into Drake. I really didn't want to get any closer to that nonsense.

My Phoenix was screaming, Drake was growling, and

Jarron was extending his hand as he stepped back from protector mode and into burn my sister's face off mode.

Great. We were going to have a showdown before we even reached the damn vampire.

"She is my mate, Zoe, not yours." Killian stepped between me and Zoe, his shoulders straightened as he towered over her, his hands tightening into fists that looked able to smash her into the ground like a villain in a video game.

"Will you suck the life from her too, Killian, when you let the darkness take control?"

Had I stepped into some sub-dimension? What the hell was going on?

I was ready to pull them apart with the full strength of my five-foot-tall phoenix shifter self and pull out some fire javelins up in here.

Too bad I didn't get there first.

"That's enough!" Jarron's booming voice ripped through the cave, sending a crack over the wall behind us. That wasn't a good sign.

Downside of being bonded to three brothers as well as being best friends with their sister, the eternal family showdown. Thankfully, Killian and Zoe weren't spitting fire at each other like they had at the circus.

Yet.

"You both are acting like toddlers," Jarron continued when the two had stopped growling at each other enough that he could get a word in. "I don't know what has gotten into the two of you, but you need to knock it off. We are running in circles, and at this point I have no problem blaming the both of you. Your battle for control is getting us nowhere. Shit has happened, and it's going to keep happening unless we go take some shit down. And if we keep sitting in our own shit we are going to do nothing more than drown in the smell."

Okay, so I hadn't left behind all of my juvenile tendencies, because I totally giggled at that. I wasn't alone, even Drake was covering his mouth in an attempt to hide a smirk.

The one among us who I had expected to outright laugh at that however, didn't.

In fact, she didn't make a sound. Probably because she was nowhere to be found.

Lilly had vanished. We had been ready to rip each other's heads off, and she had taken the opportunity to go do some head-ripping of her own.

"Speaking of shit," I shrieked, pulling everyone's focus as I gestured around us and the lack of mouthy kid. "We are about to be covered in a whole bunch of it if we don't head off the super-freak before she reaches the throne room."

There was no way this was going to end well.

3

ELLIOT

"WHAT KIND of kid takes off after a vampire?" Drake mumbled from somewhere near the back of our rampage through the tunnels and backstreets of Rydaim, his low voice bouncing off the stone and rubble of what I thought used to be a back alley. It was hard to tell, so much of the city was destroyed, and we definitely weren't stopping for a tour.

It had taken a punk kid rampaging off on a suicide mission to get us really moving, but they were moving, and Killian and Zoe were too distracted to rip each other's throats out, even if they were still bickering like an old married couple. Super weird as that was.

"A masochistic weapon raised by a demon. That's who runs after a vampire," Jarron rumbled over to Drake from the other side of me, and was instantly met by a few disgusted gasps or grunts. Either that or Drake was orchestrating a Dragon-growl concert back there.

I might get in on that. This demon raised kid was also going spoil the only thing we had going in this fight; the element of surprise.

"Say we don't get there in time," I sighed as Zoe took a sharp left. I would have missed the turn if she hadn't grabbed my arm and practically towed me after her.

Well, before Killian overtook her and she raced after him, leaving me to bring up the rear with Jarron and Drake again, not like either of them were concerned.

"We will get there in time," Jarron huffed as he came up beside me, his response easily drowned out by Zoe and Killian who were once again arguing over who everyone was going to follow and who was the better tracker. Because screaming at full volume wasn't going to give us away. Cue the eye roll.

If Lilly didn't get there first... damn it. Damn it. Damn it.

There was no way this was going to end well.

"We will get there in time," Jarron repeated, that time it was more for him. His eyes were golden, thin tendrils of smoke drifting from his nostrils, the same fear I felt looking back at me.

My phoenix shifted in my chest, pushing me forward as we turned another corner, through something that looked like an alley, before darting back into yet another cave.

"Well, say we don't," I heaved, pushing my Phoenix down as she pressed against my heart. "Say she gets there first, and faces that vampire that 'sired' her..."

"Don't say it like that," Jarron interrupted with a growl and gave me a look like I was chewing cud.

"Hey it's her own words, you know, when she was gushing about how powerful he is and how like him she is."

Oh god, repeating it was so much worse. I was really starting to question why I had let Jarron convince me into bringing the kid back with us. Yes, I had seen the change in her after Henry died, like she had stepped out of a fog. That didn't make her any less of a liability.

"She's going to get there and bow down at that damn blood sucker's feet and then it's all over," Drake said from the other side of me, he wasn't looking at either of us, and he wasn't smiling. Neither of those things was a good sign.

"She's not going to go over to Parris' side," Jarron grumbled, the three of us picked up our pace in unison.

None of us believed that. Even Jarron, whose jaw was tight enough I was surprised that smoke was still making its way out.

"I want to believe that, too." And I did, truly I did, although the closer we got to wherever we were going and didn't run into her the more hope I lost. "But just in case... Say she gets in there, with Dabria and a smooth-talking Vampire and she could turn on us, and if she turns on us..."

Jarron gave me a look, his dragon growling in a low hum that vibrated the stone. And my bones. If we weren't all out running I probably would have jumped straight into the ceiling.

"Damn it, Elliot! I love you, and I hate that you are right." Jarron's growl picked up, Drake chuckling behind me as we turned another corner.

I was really starting to get weirded out that we hadn't run into anyone yet. Dragon or Vampire. I mean we had to be close by now. And I doubt everyone was waiting for us in the throne room for some kind of welcoming party.

"She's Callay's daughter, and I needed to bring her home," Jarron cut through my internal rambling, and the heated panic that was building right along with it. "I didn't expect to be chasing after the obnoxious child through tunnels full of vampire ash, while wearing a totally smoking outfit from the 1970s."

"You do look pretty hot," I gave him a wink and almost ran smack dab into a wall as everyone turned and slowed.

"Gee, thanks. Just let me handle her. *When* we find her."

I wasn't paying enough attention to catch the turn, but thankfully Drake had long arms, climbing hands, and the good sense to make sure I didn't face plant against stone.

"Thanks," I mumbled, ready to take off running again, but everyone had slowed.

"Almost there," Killian's grumble echoed as he tried to turn one direction, Zoe peeking around the corner like we were in some spy movie.

I had never felt so scared of my mind. But it might have been just me, my soul was rumbling with excitement as she began to purr. Yes, she was fucking purring.

Thank god no one else noticed that, because the sound felt and sounded weird enough in my own head.

Although, with the way Killian was looking back at me, maybe they were pretending not to hear.

Zoe waved to us once, pulling us around the corner and into a tunnel that looked more finished than the rest. The tall grey walls of stone even appeared to be carved with something resembling a worship scene, tons of people bowing toward something that was carved into the doors at the end of the hall.

It was only after I noticed that one of the figures no longer had a head that the worship became a genocide. The same as the glass eye above the city.

"Lilly," Jarron gasped from beside me, dodging between Killian and Zoe who were still playing a game of Parcheesi for the top spot.

The kid was as haunting as the carving in walls. Except she was real, and thankfully hadn't lost her head.

"Lilly, come back," Jarron was almost to her when she turned, her blood-soaked hands and shirt swinging into view as she smiled at us, taking one step back, toward the door where a few familiar voices were bleeding through.

I could recognize Dabria's whine anywhere.

"Let me finish them off," Lilly said with a smile, that same twisted voice blazing through her. So much for being released from some kind of demon spell. The demon appeared to still be part of her.

"Lilly, don't--"

"I'll finish them, then I'll come back for you." She cut Jarron off, taking a step back as her smile stretched, as the door swung open without her so much as touching it.

Shit. Bringing her back to Rydaim in a conscious state had been a terrible, terrible choice.

"Lilly..." Jarron was almost to her now, walking slowly, his hand outstretched like he was going to grab her and hold her down or some shit.

Even with what little we had seen of her I knew that wasn't going to happen.

He didn't even get close enough to try. She had slipped into the door and slid it shut silently behind her before Jarron could take another step.

I guess we were really going for the element of surprise.

"Fucking great," Zoe hissed in a whisper, rounding on the rest of us as though we had something to do with this. "Next time you show up on my doorstep with a kid like that you best believe I am going to smack some sense into you all."

"I already told you that she isn't mine," I threw my hands up, smoke and sparks flinging from my fingertips in agitation. Luckily Drake was able to get out of the way, one of the screaming rock martyrs wasn't so lucky. I guess the scene needed another headless contribution.

The sound of my flames was like a whip, a crack that

mixed nearly perfectly with the cackling laugh from the other side of the door, muffled voices coming right behind.

"It's only going to take a few hundred to clear them all out, Fallon, you finish that job and then we can finish the job down below. Bam! They are all gone!" We all jumped as something hard hit against something harder, the booming impact rattling the doors.

Ice and lust twisted down my spine at his voice, his snide face infiltrating my mind with a thousand new memories that were pounding on my head begging to be let in. I didn't even have to blink to remember.

Parris was sitting at a table with another man, the solid wood surface covered with piles of ashes, my ashes. A line of children was pressed against the wall, each one handed a spoonful of the dark gritty stuff to swallow. Thank god this Vampire's experiments involved little more than forcing children to eat a tablespoon of reincarnation dust, which was already bad enough, really. Here, eat the burned bits of my body.

Gross.

There wasn't a wire, a beaker, or a floating head jar in sight. Didn't mean he wasn't any less psychotic, if only for who his table mate was.

He knew Henry. Of course the wicked Vampire would know the Demon. I was sure they had picnics together, and phones calls where they gossiped about the latest torture techniques and ate ice cream.

Parris was going to be really pissed when he learned that I killed Henry.

I clung to the knife, the cool metal strangely comforting against my sweaty fingertips.

"Parry. We have a problem," Another voice I recognized cut through my memory and brought me back to the tunnel, where Killian and Zoe were creating some kind of battle plan against the now headless man's chest.

So much for battle planning.

Dabria's shoes clacked closer to us, I could practically see her step behind the vampire, probably removing his shirt with how much sex and booze was in her voice.

"What is it!" The vampire snapped, okay, maybe no shirt removal. Damn it, I really thought walking in on an orgy would have been a cool opening to a totally epic battle, one that involved naked villains being burned to a crisp.

"Speak, bitch!"

Everyone exchanged glances, Zoe's eyes narrowing in question before they grew very wide.

We apparently forgot one very big piece of this disaster. You couldn't sneak up on a mind reading ice dragon and expect to come out on top.

"The boys are here." The ice dragon was practically laughing. Zoe swore loudly and muscled passed Killian to dart her way into the room, leaving him fuming behind her as she strode into the battleground like some badass queen.

"I don't know what boys you are talking about, but I'm sure I can finish you all off without their help."

"Holy shit, Zoe's alive?" That was all that I was able to make out before the room exploded.

Zoe's fire ignited over the ceiling as I plunged myself through the door, Lilly popping up right behind Parris with a laugh that sent him screaming, and her into the wall with one well-placed punch from the blood-sucker.

Poor kid didn't stand a chance. That's what she gets for taking off, I guess.

Her bubblegum camo pants sure didn't do her a lot of good.

I guess my rescue of Callay had turned into a twofer.

Lilly would have to wait, though. I needed to find the mom first. I pushed my way passed Jarron who was trying to fight off both Dabria and Parris while Drake and Zoe fought their way past some grungy looking girl I had never seen before.

Killian spit dark fire onto the ceiling, watching the flames move as he fought against Dabria's ice, probably trying to track down that damn bird.

Ice, fire, and some weird black smoke was spiraling through the air, making it hard to see, let alone spot the spunky blonde Fae.

Considering that I had met the girl only once, I was already in over my head. Blonde hair, good fashion sense, and a tongue like a whip. Should be enough to go on. Even then, how many captives would they have in this place?

None, seeing as there didn't seem to be anyone here other than the fire-spitters behind me.

It was almost like being back at the circus in the middle of Zoe's act, except that then fire didn't shoot right at you.

I was only barely able to get out of the way of Jarron's blast, swan diving toward what looked like a burned pyre in the middle of the floor. I had an inkling that Jarron's fire wasn't going to do anything to me, but I wasn't about to test that theory out. I hid behind the large wooden spike as the golden lines of his fire dragged over the dark stone like dragon drool, following the lines of blood that made a jagged line between my now smoldering hiding place and a stretch of bare stone.

Now that I was looking at it, the blood was everywhere. It was soaked into the wood, dripping from the stone wall. It reminded me of that hotel room, when Stacia had vanished. Everything had been soaked, because, you know, I lived in a horror movie now.

A really, really stupid horror movie.

Only Dabria would be dumb enough to leave a blood trail right to the hidden door that they had supposedly hid Callay in. If I had to guess whatever was behind there was full of Vampires ready to feast on super powerful Phoenix blood. Not going to happen.

"Idiots," I grumbled, peering out from behind the pyre. Both Dabria and Parris kept glancing at me from where they were battling. Did they really think that I was going to fall for that?

"Double idiots."

I skittered away from the pyre, making a beeline towards the wall, taking a slight detour near where Drake and Ceres were fighting.

My skin prickled as another wave of golden fire shot overhead, this time impacting against the floor and sending everything rattling, including that gaudy mural at the end of the hall.

The bloody scene was familiar. Like something I had seen before.

Like everything else in this damn twisted world.

The horrified glass faces pulled at me, and even though the battle was everywhere, I took one slow step forward. Stepping through the smoke and renegade fire, toward the glass genocide, and the owl faced man that stood in the back.

The man I had last seen in the mirror back in the demon's cave.

"Holy shit!"

Flyaway eyebrows, pointed nose, and dark eyes stared straight forward, unseeing. After everything, I half expected that man to wink and move through the glass people to reach me, but he stayed still, carved into the glass like everything around him.

Didn't make my heart beat any less though.

I was really starting to question why so many things from my past were appearing in very villainous happenings.

I took one more step, fire exploding around me as something hard collided with my back and I flew forward, wrists scraping against the stone and I was effectively turned into a human pancake.

Phoenix scream rattled my skull, fire blazed through my veins, and I rolled up like a ninja baby all ready to go into full-on attack mode. Instead, I came face to face with Callay, a weird looking bat in her hand, the spiky thing lifting above her head in preparation to strike.

"Wait, Callay!" I shrieked, smoking hands flinging forward like a shield. At least I didn't shoot fire at her, that would have made the whole thing worse. "It's me!"

"I know."

Oh shit. I was only barely able to roll out of the way in time. The spiked bat rammed into the floor, intersecting with ice and stone and showering me with bits of both. Pebbles rattled against my skin as I tried to crawl away, which I guess would logically be what ninja babies would do.

Super slow ninja babies, I was barely able to escape clubbing attempt number two by the deranged Fae, my bare feet slipping on ice as I pushed myself up to face her.

With the way I was slipping, I wanted to beg for the spiky stone floor back.

"You are exactly who I was looking for," Callay said with a snarl I never would have expected from her, her lip curling as she took a step closer, swinging the bat by her side.

Seeing as that thing just ripped apart stone, I really didn't want to know what it could do to me. I took one giant step back, which she quickly countered.

"Your rescue team? Because we are here! You can stop trying to beat the shit out of me now."

"No," she grumbled. "I don't need to be rescued. I'm right where I want to be."

"Hogshit," I snapped, dodging yet another swing of her medieval weapon. Although this time I wasn't quite fast enough. The spikes caught on the fluffy fur lining on the front of the robe I was still dressed in, throwing me off center and right toward the red and brown fire that was soaring through the air beside me.

Damn. This place was getting dangerous.

"You don't want to be here, especially not with the melty vampire."

"Yes. I. Do." Each word was punctuated by a swing and a miss, well, all but the last one that slammed into my shoulder with the force of an angry rhinoceros. Might as well have been with the way robe ripped, the skin underneath shredded and bleeding.

Heat pooled under the skin as my Phoenix screamed, as I screamed. Pain ripped over me before my shifter began to heal the cut.

"What the fuck?" I said between clenched teeth, the two words ground between agony and anger. The once spunky Fae, however, smiled. Her purple tinted eyes glittered in the fire that was filling the cave.

Purple eyes. Yeah, I had seen those before.

Fucking Dabria.

"Shit. Why'd you have to go and get yourself mindbuggered? Damn it, Callay, I really didn't want to hurt you."

Blood wasn't pouring down my arm nearly as bad now, which was good, because Callay was back to swinging her club like a caveman, and I was trying to land a punch on her pretty little jaw.

I already felt bad about it, but it's not like I had another choice. My fire might kill her, and she wasn't bad, just under the influence of some.

She swiped, I dodged, she sidestepped, I lunged, and my fist hit solidly against her temple with as much force as I could muster.

Which, might have been too much.

She slumped against the stone, her eyes fading in and out of focus before they closed. Her head lulled forward so severely that if she wasn't breathing quite so deeply I would have thought she was dead.

I was still impressed I had knocked her out with that hit. I didn't think I could land a punch that well.

I wasn't going to stop and ask questions, I had bigger villains to broil.

"Stop wasting time, Killian, you are going to get us all killed." Zoe's shout echoed behind me as I stood, ready to walk back into the fight and deliver some ass kicking.

One pseudo villain down.

My sexy strut into battle was ruined as I dodged a ribbon of Jarron's fire, only to be smacked in the side by the icy chill of Dabria's. So much for powerhouse battle number two, I was officially tumbling end over end.

From this twisted pretzel I had landed in, everything looked even worse.

Fire exploded over the ceiling in a growl that was clearly dragon, my phoenix lifting her head as I untangled myself. As if the scream was some kind of plea.

Some kind of panic.

I saw the attack a second before it happened, saw Drake fall to his knees as he tried to stop his shift. Saw his father take one shaky step forward, smoke drifting from his jaw as he prepared to end him.

"Like hell if I'm going to let that happen." My bones were rattling, my chest was screaming. I forced out one shaky exhale before I let my soul take control, hand flying forward in an attempt to stop Ceres fire. I screamed as the dripping grey flame rolled from his jaw. And bright yellow fire ripped from mine.

Battle number two was back on.

4

KILLIAN

"Holy shit, Zoe's alive?" Parris' shout was all it took for the room to explode in flames.

Killian's brothers rushed in behind him, Jarron already spewing his golden flames over the Vampire and the ratty girl beside him. The girl's dark eyes narrowed at Killian from behind the greasy strings of her hair before she went back to fighting.

Zoe rushed right to Parris to finish him off, the vampire weak enough from Jarron's attack that it wouldn't take much effort. Or, that would be the assumption, the two were already fighting back, the Vampire zipping around and dodging both her and Drake's fire. Killian took his own target, their father. Although the man was little more than a weak pile of bones against the floor.

Fine by him. Finish him quick and then he could get to the important stuff.

The bird. It had to be here somewhere he knew it. Although he didn't see a sign of the beady eyed bugger anywhere in the room, he didn't have much time to check.

Dabria was sauntering her way towards him, jaw hard, ice already coating the ground around her.

Shit.

It had been years since he had fought Dabria, and it may have been the only time, sans Zoe, that he had come close to losing. Zoe should have been the one to take on the dragon-climbing-whore but she was still locked in a battle with the vampire that the unconscious kid had failed to end. Poor kid didn't know what hit her.

"Why, hello, Killian. Come to watch me be crowned Queen?" she crooned, ice spreading over the stone floor as the violet light in her eyes grew darker and brighter all at once. The color flashed dangerously as his head ached with her prying fingers.

Her tricks would never change. His, however, did.

Ash and hellfire were swirling through his soul, filling his veins and swelling through his muscles. It didn't take much to redirect it to his mind, building the same shield that had blocked Mattia from devouring his heart, and blocking this bitch from his mind.

The pain of her infiltration lessened the more of the wall he built, her face falling from that damn smug smile to bitch slapped shock.

"What did you do?"

Killian laughed, the booming sound cutting through her with as much chill as the ice that was dropping from her fingers like icicles. It trailed up his legs in their attempt to both freeze him and lock him in place.

Again. Could she seriously not think of anything better to do? She hadn't spit her *fire* at him yet, that was the real danger.

"I didn't do anything Dabria, I just kicked you out of where you don't belong." Smiling, Killian built the ashen shield up more and stepped towards her, the ice cracking and falling away from him.

Black smoke billowed, flowing like liquid as it lapped around his ankles. Dabria's eyes grew, her pupils shaking in a beautiful fear as she watched the stuff. Her fear darkened as his laugh slapped against her, the sound audible over the screams, grunts, and sparks of fire that were surrounding them.

"I have power of my own, Dabria. I have a darkness, and as you swallowed me for years. It's my turn." Killian took one quick step forward, pressing his hands forward and sending ribbons of the thick magic right toward her.

The smoke was thick, heady, and smelled like sulfur and death, probably because he was drawing it right from hell.

The thought was becoming normal. The existence of hell and darkness and all that consumed him was normal, not that he would ever admit that he was connected to hell. Or that he enjoyed it.

Dabria stared slack-jawed at the smoke with that same dumb expression, dodging away right before the smoke would devour her. As if it would be that easy. Instead of continuing forward and smashing into the stone wall behind her, the smoke turned, sending Dabria shrieking before she got her wits about her and encased herself in ice.

Looks like she had a shield of her own. Perfect. Nothing like playing with a cat in a cage after decades of her doing the same to him.

He was going to enjoy this. And then he was going to find that damn bird.

Killian took one slow step toward her, Jarron's golden fire smashing into a wall behind him as the shrieks and shouts picked up. He didn't even turn, he just stared at the dome of ice, his smoke knocking against it, cracking into it with each step he took.

"Come and play, Dabria," he crooned when he was close enough he was sure she could hear. "Isn't this what you wanted."

Killian's arms were pocked in gooseflesh, his back prickling as the start of scales made their appearance, but he kept his monster at bay, letting only the dragon's full howl escape. The sound filled the cave, rocking stone and glass into a groan as Dabria's pathetic dome shattered, as the floor rocked, the whole thing feeling as though it was going to give way.

His beast roared long after the cave stopped shaking, the sound grumbling in his chest as his skin pulled and stretched, his bones ached in want of escape.

What he wouldn't give to let the beast free, to swallow this menace in one gulp, feel her slide down his throat like an ice cube. Refreshing. Dead. Transforming in here, with this many dragons would be a mistake. There were too many of them, shifting into the bulky forms would limit their movement and give Parris, Dabria, and whoever the dirty girl was, the upper hand.

"Come play, Dabria," he taunted, the woman twisting on the floor until she faced him, the icy streams of her fire ripping from her without so much as a warning.

Killian side-stepped, howling as a tiny wisp of flame impacted with his arm. It didn't take more than that. The coils of her flame wrapped around his arm, threatening to freeze and pull the appendage from his shoulder.

Killian lept back, Dabria's lavender eyes glittering as her ice raced over the floor toward him.

"What were you saying about playing, Killian?"

Killian was ready this time. Smoke snapped back to him

like it was on a whip, his magic flowing behind him like wings as his dragon's ebony fire ripped from his jaw to devour her. To eat her soul.

He had possessed that ability for centuries, his dragon's gift of eating souls. Of devouring power. Now it was time to blend the masterpiece with the darkness, to devour both her and her ability.

Even her ice couldn't stop his blackened flame as it rushed toward her, whipping around her until there was only the sound of her scream in the air. Killian's dragon roared in delight, the creature sucking the life from the bitch, the darkness eating away her power.

Killian had done this hundreds of times before, but it had never felt like this, never felt this strong. The two powers were joining together and becoming something more. Something he wasn't sure he could control. A tornado of smoke and ice whirled around the dying dragon as her power, her ice, moved into him.

Becoming his own.

Power filled him like a geyser, swelling through each vein as his feet left the ground, as the demonic magic and icy power became something dangerous. Lifting his arms, he waited for the climax, for the power to connect with his soul and become his.

So close... the tether snapped with a scream in his ear, his body tangling with the limbs and sparks of his sister as she slammed against him, sending both of them into a wall.

Dabria's power slithered into the air as he slid to the floor, shoving Zoe off of him.

Dabria was crumpled on the ground, lifeless, powerless. The magic that should have been his lost in the blood-soaked air of the cave.

"Fucking Hell, Zoe," Killian roared, slamming a fist into

Zoe's jaw and sending her right into the stone wall to their left. "Do you have any idea what you have done!"

"I'm killing a vampire, Kills. So, maybe if you could stay out of my way..." Zoe jumped up from where she had landed, turning on him, the white fire he had seen in her before blazing behind her eyes, digging into him.

Igniting something that boiled in him, pulsing with each beat of his black-smoke heart.

"I could say the same for you." His voice was little more than dragon now, the grinding snarl of the creature burning stronger as the white in Zoe's eyes sparked like opaline lightning.

Something weird was happening. The tunnels had been bad enough, but now it was getting dangerous.

Murderous.

"Stop wasting time, Killian, you are going to get us all killed."

How dare she? She gave up her role nearly fifty years ago. She walked away from the crown, from the family. He had given her enough slack over the past few months, but not anymore.

Killian wanted nothing more than to rip her limb from limb and feel the warmth of her blood spill over his hands. He wanted it, more than he had ever wanted it before.

Something about the light in her eyes tugged at his darkness, screaming that there was a connection there, something that he had done perhaps. He wasn't so sure, and he couldn't remember enough of that sparkling beach to know. There were gaps there, gaps that he was starting to think would be better left hidden in the glittering memory.

"I am the only one doing the killing," Killian's dragon roared, fire ripping from him, plunging through the air, right toward the woman who was made of lightning.

The fire never reached her, but a low sardonic laugh did.

The Vampire's laugh grated against Killian's spine, pulling at his dragon until the bones snapped, threatening to pull him into his dark scaled monster. He would have to end this bastard. As he had Dabria.

"Well, well, well. Isn't this an interesting turn of events," Parris said with a laugh that grated against Killian's spine.

He smiled brightly, stepping between Zoe and Killian. Fool's move. It wouldn't take much for Killian to end the bloodsucker at this range. Yet, he couldn't get himself to move. He stared at the Vampire, his mind trying to wrap around what he had said.

"I was shocked enough to see that the horned bitch created another light," the pale faced man continued with a nod to Zoe, sending the girl's face into a scowl.

Something was familiar here...

"But to have her darkness right beside her. The two sides of your power, right here, where only one that can defeat the other. This will be a battle larger than I have seen in centuries. Wonderful." He clapped his hands and stepped away, as though he was starting the battle himself. "I think I'll let the two of you finish each other off. The hatred in the air is palpable, don't you think?"

"Why would I fight my sister, when I have a bastard like you right before me?"

Parris turned to Killian slowly, his motions controlled as he clasped his fingers under his chin, his distorted face twisting awkwardly as he smiled.

"Because your sister holds what you lost. She stopped you from using your power, just as you stopped her. Your powers cannot exist together. One must die, and the other must be the one to do it. Didn't the unicorn tell you that?" Parris laughed at his own joke, clapping his hand like a deranged child, Killian stepped back as more pieces of that beach fell into place and his soul twisted in understanding.

No. It can't be true. He can't have done this.

"The Unicorn said..." Zoe began, her own pieces falling into place as her eyes widened, shaking in fear as she turned to him. As she scowled at him.

As she understood him.

Shit. He had done this. First act of villainy, indeed.

"You feel it don't you?" Parris said as he backed away, neither Killian or Zoe moving to stop him. "The need for blood. For victory. You can't deny it, can you? I have seen it before.

"He's right you know. The need for blood. I feel it. I need to end it so that we can win this fight. So that I can take my crown, you are in the way of that." Killian had never heard his sister talk like that, and it chilled him to the bone, as cold and powerful as the ice that he was sure he could still feel flow through his veins.

"We need to end this now," she continued, her hands dripping something that looked like a mix of fire and lightning. Her eyes flashed white, pulling at the black inside him, igniting that need again.

The need to kill her.

The need to devour her soul.

Damn it! This was wrong, he knew it was. But he couldn't hold onto the thought long enough to stop himself. His hatred toward his sister was growing too strong to think past anything.

But he had to try.

"No Zoe!" Killian roared, scales ripping over his skin in shadows. "That is not our purpose. We need to end this. But not with us, with them."

He said the words, but the darkness still wanted to attack her instead of the vampire. What was going on here?

"You are as bad as them. You stood by their side and killed thousands in mass genocide. I cannot forgive that." Her dragon rattled her voice, rippling over the black smoke that Killian had summoned. Billows of ebony surrounded them as though they were in a demonic snow globe.

"Be realistic, Zoe!" He was getting truly angry now, the fury raging as the black smoke closed in, tendrils lapping at his sister. Ready to strangle her.

It was getting harder to convince himself that that wouldn't be a good idea.

"I was only a child when the Fae were enslaved. You were a hundred years older than me and you didn't stop it."

"But I didn't agree with it. I didn't stand by them. You did. I need to make you pay," she continued, sparks of white lightning shooting from her fingers as she clawed at him, much the same as her dragon would have. If her dragon was made up of some kind of magical lightning. White lightning. Black smoke.

Light and Dark.

Two powers ready to intersect. Ready to explode.

Zoe quick-stepped forward, swiping through the air with her dripping fingers as though she was wielding an ax. The white sparks of her magic went everywhere, lighting through his smoke and zapped into his chest with a burn as though he had been electrocuted.

White-hot flame ripped over him, screaming through his throat and igniting every muscle. His dragon screamed, the massive head rearing and roaring as the beast threatened to break its way through and end the agony that she was ripping through him.

His mind screamed for him to stop, but his dragon and

the other beast that was now taking up residence in his heart was not having that. Fire spewed from his mouth as smoke rushed from his hands, both colliding as they ripped through the tiny space.

They didn't get very far.

Zoe stopped them in a flash of white, rushing him, wrapping her hands around his biceps and attempting to throw him to the ground. She wasn't able to move him more than an inch, if only because her touch was filled with the same fire and agony as the electric sparks of before.

He screamed as she did. Her roar mixed with his as she jumped back, staring at her hands in pain and shock. He looked at the bright red outline of her hand against the sleeve of his suit, as though the touch had burned it all away.

This was about to get interesting and it would start with one well-placed throw, and his sister's head impacting with the throne she loved so much.

5
———

DRAKE

CERES WAS ALIVE.

Drake had been hoping that the Vampire would have already had done in the old man given what Killian and Jarron had said about him being controlled by Dabria. But the frail old dragon was still alive, curled up against the wall, his decrepit body shuddering to stand the moment the door to the throne room flew open and everyone streamed in.

Screams, fire, and ice filled the air in seconds, everyone running to the closest available target. Their attempt at battle planning was worthless.

Drake wasn't supposed to go to his father. He was supposed to take out Dabria. Taking out Dabria had a high chance of taking out his father, after all. That was, if the bitch was controlling him as they said.

But the image of his frail father gripping the wall, knees clacking together, changed his target. Someone else could take care of Dabria.

He was going to face his father.

Dabria was coating the cave in ice, facing Killian as he

foolishly looked for the bird. Good, the stubborn "heir to the throne" could take her on.

"This time I won't back down," Drake said to himself, sliding his stockinged feet out of his sandals and bolting toward the old man, his steely gaze boring into him.

That stare had pushed into Drake's soul for his entire life, he had cowered and whimpered and cried over that stare and all the implications behind it for nearly a hundred years.

"No more." After the last twenty years, after cowering to the loss and paying that price, he wasn't going to do that anymore.

He had lived for this. And he would live through this.

"Why I am not surprised to see you alive, you little bastard? You were always a disappointment. You were never good enough."

The old king was supposed to be under Dabria's control, not that you could tell. The words were perfect echoes of what Drake had been told his entire life. The hatred and malice was so familiar that he almost backed down.

Almost.

Not anymore.

"No more!" Drake's voice was all Dragon as he roared, the old man smiling as he reached him, as the murky red and browns of his flames ripped from him. His chest and throat felt as though he had swallowed a white-hot iron that was attempting to turn him inside out. The fire was agony, but it was worth it to watch his father coated in his flames.

Instead of screaming in pain at the flames, however, the old man laughed. The hollow sound drifted over everything, seeping through the last of his flames as they vanished.

Drake was ready to take him down, to finish him off, but he was gone.

Not ash. Not dead. Just gone.

"Shit." He said, just as a stone impacted with the side of his head.

The jagged edge of the rock pressed perfectly into his temple, turning the dark stone cave into blossoms of bright red flowers.

It took far too much effort to keep himself upright, but he managed, stumbling toward the stone or whatever had hit him.

It was his father.

The man's steel grey eyes narrowed as his face pulled into a smile, his teeth flashing behind the crook in his thin lips. Smoke twisted from nostrils and mouth, pulling around him as the light in his eyes flickered.

Drake's dragon growled, desperate to emerge and bite into the old man. To taste his blood and feel it as it stopped pumping through his veins. If only he could. A shift would incapacitate him.

Fire from the battle surrounded them on all sides now, licking against walls and ceiling as it threatened to box them in. The old man stepped closer.

Something crashed overhead, ribbons of Jarron's fire slicing through the air. The crackle and screams blended with the glimmering blaze until their war zone had become a hell.

"What was that about, boy? I'm sure I have trained you better than that. You thought that weak attack would work? Pathetic." Even Ceres' voice was something out of a nightmare, twisted into something from an especially bad beating.

Too many. Too many things for the bastard to pay for.

Drake stepped forward, letting the spark filled smoke of his breath roll over his father's face. It was only this close that he could see the clouded mask of Dabria's magic over his eyes.

It should matter. It should lessen this moment. But it didn't. Drake smiled, reaching to curl his fingers over his father's shoulders, his strong climbing fingers pressing painfully into the muscle and bone there.

The man winced, his brow pulling together as his shoulder jerked. Drake dug in harder.

"You should have stayed dead," Ceres hissed, his own smoke spreading over Drake's face, chilling the stubble that was trying to take over his chin.

"Naw, that position is waiting for you."

Smoke was everywhere as Drake opened his mouth as his tongue coated with the first sparks of his flame, his father doing the same. This close, any fire would only end in death.

Time for plan B.

Drake dodged as Ceres' black flame exploded from him, grabbing the old man's legs and throwing him down to the ground. He looked like a geyser that the humans would visit for fun, the image masochistic and twisted as the fire continued to eat away everything around him.

Too bad a dragon's fire could never harm themselves, or this would have been a lot easier.

His dripping flame spread, mixing with the black smoke that appeared to be everywhere. The heavy mask was thicker than the smoke from dragon fire. Thick, and dark, and sparkling. It stuck to the walls until everything looked like the City of Soot that the damn Sphinx had called home.

He didn't have time to dwell on that. He had an old man to finish.

The geyser fire slowed and Drake grabbed the King's

legs, dragging him over the rough stone floor to where he kneeled, fist at the ready.

"This is for Gayl," Drake snapped, pushing all of his fury into the fist as it impacted against the pointed nose of his father.

The bone cracked with a snap, the flesh and cartilage collapsing underneath his knuckles as blood sprayed over them both. Hot, wet, and mixing with the sulfur of the smoke in a bouquet that Drake never thought he would love.

This time was different, this time he smiled.

"This one is for Callay," Drake wound back again, ready to smack the broken fragments of the old man's nose to the back of his skull.

Instead, Ceres kicked up, his feet impacting against Drake's hips, throwing him up and into the throne of bones and stone that had stood in the middle of the room for as long as he remembered.

Bones cracked in the impact, although if the cracking was from the throne or where his spine had crumpled against the knobby structure, he could not tell. Everything hurt enough that it could easily be both, however, the sharp pressure that moved into his shoulder as he slid to the floor was making him think it was more him.

Shit.

"I won't stop," Drake growled from behind the clench in his teeth, his mouth filling with blood as he pushed himself to standing, his arms attempting to collapse under the weight.

"Not this time." His dragon pushed and pulled against the ache in his back, the creature trying to force its way out. To devour the man who was slowly walking their way.

"What? Winning. You are quite right. You won't be winning this time. Not ever."

Ceres' voice had deepened, his eyes had darkened, even his grin was the same as he always had before a kill. The man was so sly and demonic that he was clearly in control. He had pushed passed Dabria's power for this. And no wonder, he had always wanted Drake dead. Now, he would get his chance.

Not that Drake had any plans in letting him.

"Not anymore," Drake screamed as he pushed his way to stand, rushing the old man with another punch.

That missed.

"No," Drake gasped at Ceres smile, at the impact of his hand against his shoulder as he fell to his knees. He hit hard, rattling through his bones as another crack of bone and stone hit his ears.

"You are nothing but a weak mortal, son. I'm ashamed of you."

Pain was everywhere. Agony was everywhere. Each bone pulled and twisted in pain as his very mortal body threatened to succumb. With his dragon injured and locked away, injuries that would barely affect a dragon were incapacitating him.

Which was why his dragon was forcing its way out of him. Scales pressing against his arms, his bones cracking and lengthening.

To shift was death, but his body was broken, he didn't have the strength to fight it.

"No." The word was more of a sob as his limbs stretching towards a shift that he knew would be the end. There was no one to stop him, no way to stop the flame from consuming him.

The burning lines of gold peeked through his human

skin, eating him away as the shift grew closer, the agony taking over.

"This is not your victory," Drake gasped, looking to his father with tears running down his face, watching the smoke and flame drip from his jaw as he prepared to end him. "I still lived. I still conquered you. I still loved."

"Love made you weak," Ceres voice ground against Drake's bones as the shift grew closer. "Perhaps it should be what kills you, then."

"Like hell if I'm going to let that happen." Ellie's snark echoed through the painful rattle in his mind, his dragon relaxing as her sunflower flames ripped over his head, smashing right against the iron fire of his father and sending him back to where Jarron and Fallon were fighting.

The cave was shaking in the battle, everything covered in flame and ice. But as Ellie's and Ceres' flames intersected, the floor shifted, a large crack snapping between where Drake's hands were pressed against the floor.

"Holy shit," Drake mumbled, scuttling away from the growing crevice. With the way the floor was rattling he half expected the entire cavern to give way and send them all raining over the ruins of Rydaim.

"You okay?" Ellie asked, stepping between him and his father, her robe hanging on her shoulders.

"Yeah, baby. This one I've got," he whispered, leaning closer to her, his back not aching as much anymore.

Thanks to the powerful goddess protecting him, Drake had been able to press his dragon back into his heart, thankfully taking away much of the pain with it.

"This one I am going to end," Drake finished, his Dragon's growl rumbling through his voice as he leaned closer to his mate, winding his hand over her waist and pressing his lips against her cheek, never looking away from the heaving King.

Drake left her behind as he postured the old man, ready to rip him limb from limb. Before he could reach him, they were all treated to Zoe streaking through the air like a rocket, screaming and swearing before she slammed against the throne and floor.

Ellie went running after her, leaving Drake to face the ancient dragon that was already heading for him.

Fire ripped between them, hands flying, punches pressing against gut and jaw, adding grunts and groans to the vampiric screams from the massive wall of vampires that had joined them.

Drake swung high, landing his fist right against Ceres' temple, sending the man stumbling back. His eyes faded, his head swaying and the old man stumbled.

He was close to death.

This was it!

Drake rushed the old man, ash filling his mouth. He swung his fist.

Fist met temple as the hot fingers of his father wrapped around Drake's throat, the grip stronger than it should be.

Strong as the dragon he was. Not the icy woman that controlled him.

The icy woman that now lay lifeless on the floor, blood trickling from her mouth.

Shit.

His father. He was looking at his father.

"You have always been scared, boy. You have never been what was needed to rule, to be part of this line." The king's hand gripped harder, lifting him and swinging him against the roughhewn wall until his back was flat against the stone his throat compressed between rock and hand.

It was fitting that the stone that had hurt him, the rock that had saved him, the mountain that had changed him, would swallow him whole.

"You had a chance to be everything, you could have controlled the world with a few words. Instead you chose to be nothing. Instead you squandered your power. You will always be worthless."

'Power.'

Drake's dragon pressed itself against his chest, against the kings hand that was blocking his air. It was so hot, so strong, if only the beast could stop this. Drake could feel him, right there, pressing right against him, pulling at him.

'We don't need his power. We have our own.'

That voice was so familiar, even though he had never heard it before. It had always been there. His dragon. For once, Drake didn't fight the power of the beast, he didn't cringe against it. He let the beasts words and power flow through him with the last gasp he could suck in through the pressure of his father's hand.

"*Let go*," Drake said simply, gasping as Ceres hand fell from his throat, the old man's eyes glazing over in shock and fear.

"*Say goodbye*," Drake said again, his father's forced response shattered by Drake's own scream as he pressed his dragon to the surface, transforming his hand as he had so often before.

The tiny shift was agony, the pain of his brothers' fire ripping through everything, but it was enough for this. For the feeling of his father's blood as it pooled over his claws, the flesh of his gut and throat underneath his talons.

"Goodbye," Drake heaved, the pain almost too much, and he collapsed as his father did, their bodies tangling together in pain and death.

6

ELLIOT

CERES WAS DOWN. Dabria was down. Were they dead? I had no clue. Everything had turned to all out Mayhem.

Fire was licking against the walls, ice dripping and coating the floor until it looked like we were visiting Satan's ice skating rink.

Sans demons, because I was all over demons. So last week. Or tomorrow. Who the fuck knew anymore? I had worse problems at the moment than to crack the timeline.

Problems like whatever the hell was going on with Killian and Zoe. Snaps of electricity ate through the consuming black smoke, obscuring the mess of limbs that was inside of it as two sets of arms and far too much hair went at it like they were locked in a cage fight.

"You don't get to lord over me!" Zoe screamed from behind all that hair.

"You gotta be shitting me."

"Really guys?" I sighed to myself, sure no one could hear me over the war zone. "You choose now to do this?"

If I had to guess, this had something to do with the Vampire that was laughing sadistically beside the cloud of aggression and what I could have sworn was magic. You know, if either of them had magic.

I would have to worry about that later. I had officially found my target.

That vampire was going down.

Fire buzzed through my veins, heat roaring over my skin as my arms and legs pricked up in gooseflesh. Everything was coming alive as my Phoenix screamed and I charged at the Vampire, lifting my hand to launch a line of fire toward him. He turned at the scream with a smile, thinking himself invincible.

Well, until he saw who was racing toward him.

Yeah, bitch, you are going down!

Or maybe not.

He side-stepped the flame, racing toward me in a zig-zag that no matter how many times I tried to attack him, I missed.

I only took one shaky inhale before he was right before me. His nose was inches from mine, his colorless grey eyes boring into mine as the air drenched with the ice of the undead beast.

I fought the shudder, stepping closer as I let my Phoenix peer at the guy from behind my eyes.

"Nice try," he hissed, tiny drops of spittle flinging over my face. "But I know better than to fight you. I was waiting for you, Elliana."

He lifted his hands, snapping his fingers with a loud pop that echoed over the screams and flames, reverberating off of walls and everything else.

That was all it took for the door to the left to open and streams of vampires to flood in.

Welcome to my circus. It's a real shit show.

Bring on the fart cannons and fire burps. I was going

all in.

Phoenix cries filled the tubular cave as my skin caught fire, waves of gold and scarlet rolling over me as my hair fanned into wisps of flame and smoke, and flesh and form melted away in the flash of flame and feathers. My hands twisted into claws as my back lengthened, as the robe disintegrated. I remembered the knife concealed there one second before it clattered to the ground. Snatching it from the air with a twist of my mutating finger talons, I tucked it into a notch of wings and feathers that I was pretty sure I had used for this purpose before given how normal it felt.

And some point I would remember everything, but right now all that mattered was remembering how to take down the dozens of vamps that were zipping toward me with blood-red hunger in their eyes.

Good thing I was already a pro at Vampire melting fire.

Twisting my neck, feathers bristled over my back in angry hackles, I screamed a line of red and gold flame toward the horde of vampires. The mob didn't stop running, they laughed and plunged forward, toward my flame. Parris screamed in warning, but not one deviated. Fine by me, he could add more melted vamps to his family.

'I thought you said you were ready, you little twerp.'

The second my flame hit them, the screams began. High pitched shrieking pulled everyone's focus, giving Jarron the upper hand from where he fought that grubby girl and what appeared to be Parris, giving him one clear strike against her chest. It was a good hit, and he might have had another if he hadn't become distracted by the horror show opening up before him.

Vampire death was officially my least favorite thing ever.

Flesh melted off the vampires like candle wax, dripping to the stone floor in great grey drops that immediately turned to ash and drifted over the floor like snow. Snow and wax, and not a drop of blood to be seen.

I didn't know if that made it better or worse. My stomach was definitely twisting.

"Jarron!" Drake yelled as he ran all out to the Vampire leader, the sudden panic threatening to pull my focus as more vampires began running through a second door.

Those boys would have to take care of themselves, I was quickly being overrun. Vampires: Wave Two, the musical was as screechy, out of tune, and obnoxious as wave one. It went down nearly as fast, the string of snarling undead melting like crayons on the sidewalk.

What I hadn't expected however, was wave three to come barreling at my tail feathers, weapons in hand.

Cold metal sliced through the feathers I had always thought to be impenetrable, plunging into my side and filling my mouth with the taste of salt and pain.

I screamed out, the agonizing shout echoing over the rock and rattling the glass mural, pulling the focus of the two rampaging siblings to my left. Well, the focus of one of them anyway.

Zoe turned, but that was mostly because she was sent flying as a second blade pierced my side. Killian's roar mixed with my own as he ran to my side, throwing vampires away like matchsticks. Even going so far as to break a few in half. Drake was only steps behind him, leaving Jarron to Parris and the dirty girl and ripping the bastards to shreds as he attempted to reach the door. His burnt ember flames worked to mold the rock and stop the incessant flow of pale skinned blood-bastards.

Fire burst from Zoe as she ran back to us, although not to burn the vampires, to herd them towards Killian and I. To help us finish them off.

Which was proving so much harder than I expected, seeing as I had been stabbed in the mother-fucking ass by what I was starting to think was another demon blade. It sure as shit hurt like one.

Everything burned with a pain that I was sure I hadn't felt in centuries, my bones twisting as though they were about to shatter. I could barely move, I could barely see straight. The intensity of the pain was crippling in its own, forget the fact that I was gushing glittering blood all over everything.

I let out one last scream, forcing myself past the pain and shooting a fire javelin right into the last of the vampires, the line of sparking fire ate through them like a bomb, turning them into the wax monster blobs. Fire and flesh dripped to the floor, melting away the last of Dabria's ice as I collapsed in the pool of fury, phoenix screaming, blood dripping, and feathers melting away into pools of ash.

I didn't know what they had hit me with, but I knew that this was not good. I was turning into a wrinkled prune, everything twisting in on itself. The gash in my ass and side were weeping what looked and smelled like rot as I reverted back to my human, and very ash covered, form. I barely caught the knife from where I had stowed it in what I guess was my armpit. Sexy.

Normally at the end of a shift there was this powerful calm that was generally accompanied by an overall feeling of badassery.

The badassery this time had made way for an intense wave of pain that rippled up my spine, rattling each vertebrae in a heat that was nothing like the fire and smoke of my Phoenix. This was the heat of pain, the heat of my blood as it poured over my back.

"Elliot," Killian growled, lifting me against him, his hand

fanning over my back as if holding the skin together would be enough to stop the flow of blood from whatever had sliced me.

Because it certainly wasn't going to stop on its own. Normally my phoenix's heat would fuse skin and heal bones pretty quickly, but this just kept coming.

This just kept flowing.

Like the demon's blood from my knife. Damn it, it was a demon blade, but for Phoenixes or some shit.

If this blood flow kept up I wasn't going to last long. But, I also wasn't going to let that stop me.

Fuck this. We needed to finish this. Now.

"Ellie?"

I needed to finish this, and the dragons weren't going to be able to help. They needed something stronger. Something... godlike.

Damn it, Drake. He was always right.

The guy was still working on closing the stone door, his eyes continually darting toward me, a weird mix of fear and expectation coloring the honey in his eyes.

Like he was waiting for something. Like he had already seen what to expect.

I didn't need the flash of some ancient battle to know what was going to happen this time around. I got it anyway, the last time covered with about as much blood as I was now.

"I'm fine." I finally answered Killian. Knowing I was lying right to his face. "I'm going to finish this."

Well, that last part wasn't a lie. At least, I didn't want it to be.

Killian took it as such anyway, trying to hold me tighter in what was going to be some kind of emergency escape plan.

Which would have been great if I had any interest in, you know, escaping.

"Killian stop," I snapped, forcing myself away from him. Pain and fire rippled over my skin with every movement. It heated against my hair, beaming from my eyes.

He stepped back, and you better believe I gave him a smug little smile.

"I've so got this." It was then I lifted the knife, flipping it end over end.

"Is that...?" I had never heard Killian so scared before.

He stared at the silver as it shone in a blast of red fire that broke over our heads, the room erupting around Killian and me again. Zoe had joined Jarron in his attempted takedown of the stubborn ass bitch and her brown stringy hair.

"Go find your bird. I've got a vampire with my name on it."

He wasn't going to let me go that easy. You know, for being so obsessed with his bird before, he certainly didn't seem too concerned now.

"You are injured, Ellie. I need to get you out of here." He was so ruggedly handsome when he turned on the charm, and I knew he had a point, but I wasn't having it. Yes, I had been stabbed. But I had every intention of finishing this fight.

Besides, I had been in worse situations, one slow blink confirmed that yes, battling against what appeared to be a smoke dragon with my wings torn from my body would indeed be a worse situation.

"When we are done, and we aren't done." I snapped as another ribbon of fire broke over head, "Stop thinking I am the only one who needs your help Killian. You pulled your head out of your ass long enough to end your fight with Zoe and help us. So help us."

This would have been that epic movie moment when I threw him a gun and ran into the dark tunnel toward the secret chemical lab of our arch nemesis, my leather clad bottom glistening in the light that came from nowhere. Unfortunately, I had no gun, and I was naked and covered in ash. A smug grin, a swear, and a smack on Killian's ass would have to do.

"Go kick some villain ass." I smacked him once, kissed him once, and ran away from him before he could stop me. Right to where Jarron was battling Parris and the girl.

They could take the girl.

The Vampire was mine.

7

JARRON

A FUCKING VAMPIRE stampede was coming through the open doors in the cavern, hundreds of the pale skinned blood suckers making a bee-line right for Elliot. Their teeth were already gnashing in need of a bite.

Jarron didn't want to think what her blood running through their veins would do to this fight. The night dwellers were already bad enough when drunk on Fae blood, and with how a few of them were darting and weaving through the crowd it was clear they had already found a buffet of their own.

He didn't want to think about where that blood had come from, or what state Callay was in. At what would happen if they added Phoenix blood to their binge.

Jarron needed to get there. He needed to be fighting by Ellie's side, pulling the bastards off her. But he was stuck, fighting an unknown enemy who was a tad more irritating than he had expected. She looked like some kind of conceited homeless woman, stringy hair, grungy clothes and all.

In some ways, the bitch was as powerful as Lilly.

Although, she didn't appear to be immune to his fire. Just wicked fast and having more than a few tricks up her sleeve. Like colorful sparking fingertips and telekinesis and things he had only seen in movies.

Well, and the old witch at the circus. Suvi. Right then he would have given anything for the old crone to swoop in and take care of this girl for him.

He wasn't having much luck handling her on his own. Which mostly meant he was playing with her. Play with enemies long enough and they will misstep eventually.

"Are you ever going to actually hit me?" Jarron prodded, barely escaping her last attack. Luckily she didn't seem to notice how close that was.

She was fuming now. It didn't take much to get her riled up.

"I've had more difficult fights with my grandmother." Jarron gave her a wink and another string of fire, which she once against dodged.

Damn it. He was going to have to corral her somehow, get her against the wall and do her in. Normally that would be a job for his swoony eyes and perfect smile. He had a feeling that wouldn't work for her.

"Your grandmother must have been weak. Pathetic. Just like you." She attacked again, some kind of sparking light catching on the back of his ugly brown plaid shirt.

Light spread over it like some kind of fire, but unlike most fire, the ripples of heat tried to burn into Jarron's back, the heat like a branding iron against his spine.

Restraining the gasp of pain and fear, Jarron stripped off the shirt, casting it aside as he tried to turn, madly searching for any residue of whatever he had been hit with. And he thought the last time had been a close call.

Damn. This bitch had to go.

"Hardly." His dragon glared through his eyes, golden steam rippling over his bare chest. Frightening? Hot? The girl wasn't reacting either way.

"Why won't you die already. Pretty boys always die quick." The girl fixed her beady little eyes on him as she scowled. "And you are as pretty as they come."

"Pretty and weak are two different things. Ask me how I know," Jarron spat back, his words smothered by the screech of Elliot's Phoenix, the cave filling with the golden red of her flame as she transformed.

The powerful dragon in Jarron's heart gave a loud growl in return, the creature's head lifting in desire to turn, to see the perfect being that was his mate. To run, to protect her from the damn vampires that were still flowing through the door. Drake was taking care of that.

'Mine.' The growl almost overpowered him, turning him toward the golden feathered phoenix that was spewing a line of fire over the entire cave.

Jarron forced himself back to stare down the stringy-hair girl, who was still staring wide-eyed at the massive bird that had emerged in the middle of the Vampire murder-rave.

Jarron took his chance.

Fire ripped from him, pouring over tongue and teeth as his dragon reared up, pressing against every bone in an attempt to reach the masochistic little devil.

This time it hit his mark.

Glittering gold lava smashed into her side, sending her sideways and tumbling. Her screams of pain, or shock, blended with the Vampires screams of death.

Jarron stepped closer, ready to take her down, and instead, came face-to-face with the one person that could be worse than the dirty girl.

"Now, now, we can't have that. Murder will only piss off

her daddy, and trust me, we can't have that." Parris' ice-cold fingers wrapped around Jarron's wrist, the strangely long nails digging into the skin.

Jarron was sure the vampire was looking for a reaction, but he wasn't going to get one. Jarron leaned closer to him, pushing his arm closer to the chilled flesh of the man.

"Doesn't matter to me, I'll have to finish him off next. That one will be fun. I've already killed a demon, what's another little nasty to add to the list." Jarron's voice was a hiss, the sound seeping through the battle worn air in a hiss.

"A demon eh? Did you really?" Parris asked, countering Jarron's movement and stepping even closer, until all he could see was the vampire's head, and the wobbly form of the dirty girl as she pushed herself to stand a good twenty yards behind him.

Shit. His fire should have killed her. What was with him coming in contact with all these girls that were immune to his fire? Hundreds of years of inciting fear in thousands, and these two girls...

"How on earth did you kill a demon, Jarron? Not you, surely."

"It was easy, Parris. Just like killing you will be." Jarron snarled at the vamp, his focus darting to where Lilly was still crumpled up against the wall. The motion was slight, but Parris still noticed, turning to look at the girl that he had knocked out of the fight in minutes.

"Oh, I see. You *think* you killed a demon. How cute."

"No, I..." Shock dripped down Jarron's spine like ice, giving Parris the opening he needed for one well timed punch to the gut.

Jarron stumbled back, flame and scream trapped in his heart from the impact. There was no time to recover before the vampire was back, fist already rushing to intersect again.

This time with his heart. The one sure hit that would easily stop the organ.

And stop him.

Jarron threw himself away from the hit, stumbling foot over foot, he was barely able to catch himself. What he wouldn't give to blast the little man right through the window and send him tumbling.

"I would say when you turn someone into a bubbling mass, you have, in fact, killed them." Jarron's grumbled as he threw himself into the now laughing vampire. They both fell back, right into the line of fire of the stringy girl.

Luckily her lightning bolt like attack was blocked by the flame of another type.

"Need some help?" Ellie asked as she half-bounced, half-limped up to him. Her face was wound together in pain, no matter how hard she was trying to disguise it.

"Nah. I'm enjoying toying with the bitches before I take them down." He gave her a grin, fully aware that his worry for her was swallowing any gold he had left.

They needed to get through this and then he could help her. He could make everything all right.

"Perfect. I'll take the blood sucker. I'm kind of dying to see what this thing will do to a different kind of demon." She flipped a large silver knife through the air, the metal and ruby catching on fire.

The knife from Henry. This was going to be the perfect ending to the Vampire. If he could end the girl fast enough, maybe he could watch.

"Make her sparkle, baby." Jarron planted a kiss on her cheek, gave Ellie one last wink before he ran off, leaving her to Parris and him to the dirty girl, who was already sending an attack his way. An explosion of who knows what fired right overhead, sending rock and dust over him like snow.

"Well, games were fun pretty boy," She crooned as she took a step forward, the sparks dripping from her again. "But I think it's time we end thi--"

Her words were cut off by a ribbon of red flame that shot right into her head, throwing her across the cave and almost into the wall.

"The only thing we are ending is you, Fallon. Fucking bitch." Zoe ran up to them, another flame flying from her and right to the girl.

Oh, so bitch had a name.

"We have Callay." Zoe rushed up to him, her hand still raised and pouring both light and what he could only explain as wind toward the now cursing girl. "Drake is going to get her and Lilly out. We need to get this one out of the way."

"Trust me, I've been trying."

The two went back and forth the same dripping light and flame Jarron had seen flying from Fallon, fly from his sister. Except that whatever was streaming from Zoe didn't seem quite as drippy, not quite as dark.

This whole thing was officially a shit show, and Jarron couldn't tell which side was up anymore. Or if any of them were.

Zoe and Fallon were all wrapped up in their light battle, so Jarron took his chance, skirting around the edge of the cave to box the irritating girl in. They could end her together.

He only got about half way before the smell of something foul dripped through the air, pulling his focus toward where Ellie and Parris were both trying to be the first to kill. The smell couldn't have been Ellie, he could see her blood, but the smell was assaulting. Disorienting, and made even worse when Fallon turned and sent a blast of grey smoke right into him.

Everything burned with the impact, even his scream ripped with heat as it broke through his throat.

"Don't touch him," Zoe said, more of that same light cutting towards her.

It didn't even hit her.

Zoe jumped back moments before Fallon's attack hit, her own swirls of light and dark rushing toward the maniacally laughing girl. Jarron's fire joined in, two attacks rushing on either side.

"Let's end this!" He waited for her scream, for the end. Instead, golden streams of fire mixed with screams, yells, and all the profanity that you would expect to hear in a war.

"You are both fools," Fallon snapped, dodging every single attack they sent her way with ease. "You are only giving me exactly what I want."

She smiled, stepped in front of Jarron's next attack with a grin that sent Jarron's heart to his toes.

There was absolutely no way that this was going to end well.

Seconds before Jarron's fire was to impact with the girl, that Zoe was going to take her down, a pop broke over the screams of war, and Fallon disappeared.

"Killian!" Zoe shrieked, her shock and panic rattling right alongside Jarron's as they stared at the roof, at what had happened. "It's Fallon. The bird is fucking Fallon!"

8

ELLIOT

"Make her sparkle, baby."

Jarron's smile mutated into a rumbling growl as he bolted from my side, and right toward the maniacal crazy girl that was shooting fireworks from her fingertips.

A few days ago, I would have said 'fingerworks' were anything but normal. Now? Totally a completely real thing.

The scraggly girl's laugh twisted into a scream as she jumped out of the way, yelling something about pretty boys, right before Jarron and Zoe attacked her, sending her sideways and right into the wall.

Parris was clearly expecting to take advantage of the dragon's focus on the girl, his feet moving vampire fast in an attempt to bite Jarron, or maim Zoe, or do some kind of twisted tango. Or something. Instead, he slammed right into me.

Well, more like into my foot. Which was stretched out. Like a kickstand. Waiting for him.

Even a super fast vampire isn't immune to an old school tripping.

He went down with a screech, landing flat on his already

mangled face. It was a beautiful thing, seeing him spread eagle like some kind of roadkill. I did the only logical thing I could think of. I planted my bare foot right in the square of his back. I stood like a pirate, hilt of my knife pressed against my hip. Good thing I was covered in a heavy layer of ash, or this position would be really embarrassing.

"Not yet, old man, I think you and I have some business to take care of first."

"Yes, we do," Parris said, twisting his head from where he lay so he could look at me. His already pale skin was beginning to crack into dark grey lines like I had seen Stacia's do. I was sure he was trying to look ominous. Instead, he looked squished.

"I believe you have something that belongs to me." I had been so focused on the vampire's twisted face that I hadn't even noticed his hand wrapping around my ankle. He turned before I could break free of the awkward hold, super-vampire speed twisting us together like a pretzel as I went down on top of him.

The knife slid over the icy floor, spinning and glinting in the firelight as Parris and I wrestled in an attempt to stand.

Blazing heat rippled over my skin in waves of purple, fire and smoke twisting between us as we rolled. Me reaching for his face or arms with my super-heated skin. Him dodging and grunting in an attempt to escape.

I didn't want to think about what we looked like to everyone else.

Especially seeing as one of us was naked. Naked wrestling.

With a vampire.

O.M.G. No no no. This could not, and should no longer be a thing.

One vampire pancake coming up.

I twisted, curling myself into a ball of fire. A naked Phoenix fireball was dangerous enough on its own. But I was going for full Vampire destruction, not just a great ball of melty. For that, I needed the knife, and him away from it.

It only took one well-placed kick and Parris skidded across the stone, hands clutching a now bruised groin.

"What's wrong, Parris?" I taunted, grabbing the knife as I jumped to my feet. "Did I bruise your ego?"

"Not a bit," he gasped, words ground between a grimace that gave him away.

Why yes, I believe I did bruise his ego.

The smug smile I gave him was well deserved, the laugh sneaking out as he slowly pushed himself back to standing, grunting and groaning the whole way.

"Bruised something else, then?" I gave him a wink and flexed my free hand, sending a line of golden Phoenix fire right toward him. He barely recovered in time to dart away from it in a blur of marble lined skin and black leather.

I was so ready for him. I stepped out of his path, swinging both hand and flame and catching the back of his jacket on fire so that he looked like he had an ass rocket of his own.

The pale skinned bastard screamed as he danced around to extinguish the flames, cursing and scowling the whole time. He looked like a fussed up peacock the way he was dancing around.

Yes, it was funny. But not funny enough for the laugh I gave him.

The loud blasting sound was meant to irritate, and it worked.

"Aww, come on Parris. Don't you want to tango?"

"I would love to dance with my Phoenix, I have missed your body against mine, my queen." He smiled, although the look might have been a sneer. It was really hard to tell with the way his face was pulling down, the chalky flesh melty and bubbling thanks to our meeting at the fountain.

He looked like a melted waxwork. Gross, bubbling mass of flesh. Yep, I totally snickered.

The sound ignited his rage and he rushed me.

Well, tried to. He didn't get very far. The second the cold of his icy flesh hit me I lifted my knife, stabbing it into his abdomen. Well, I would have if he hadn't felt the point and stepped back, eyes wide as his skin paled.

"Nu-uh," I whispered, leaning into him, lifting the tip of my knife against his neck, the sharpened point at the ready.

"I don't know where you think you are going, Parris, but I need you here. I want to see if you can bleed," I whispered, pressing closer to him until the ice from his skin dampened my own burning heat.

"So, you remember everything, my beautiful daughter?"

"I am not your daughter." I pressed the knife harder, my heart stuttering in hope of blood.

"I helped you to become what you are. I helped to mold you into something useful. You are my child." The shake in his voice was music to my ears.

"No blood, no relation. I am going to make you pay for what you did to me," I was lying through my teeth, but I was totally going to go with it. If only because his fear meant that the knife would make him bleed.

Either that, or he was scared. Scared like Henry when I had moved in to end him. Scared like Parris when I had told him I was burning his factory to the grou--

Oh Shit! So, not scared at all.

The realization came a second before his smile did, too late to prepare for the hands that smacked against my rib cage and sent me back through the air.

The mural right beside me rattled as I slammed into it, a large crack that was running through the center snapping like a whip. I half expected the whole thing to shatter and crumble, but it held. The murderous scene still in place, the bushy eyebrowed man in the back still in one piece.

Although I could have sworn he was staring at me. Not that I could check.

I currently had a Vampire headed right for me, and seeing as my own blood was everywhere, it was no wonder the guy looked hungry.

The tall pale monster straightened his singed leather jacket as he walked through the dragon fire, his eyes glazing over mine, his tongue darting over his lips as he scanned my blood, before falling on the silver knife that had fallen to the stone between us.

Oh shit.

I guess losing hold of things when flying through the air was a real thing.

I moved the second I saw it, every bone screaming after my recent meet and greet with the solid stone wall. I may have been closer to it, but the vampire was faster, both our hands wrapping around it at the same time. Mine around the hilt. His around the blade.

A wicked smiled pulled at my cheeks as I gripped the handle with all that I had, and pulled.

Bright red blood sprayed over everything.

"Perfect."

The scarlet rain dripped over everything, the rancid fluid covering my face and dripping over my shoulders to swirl with the warm fluid that was pouring from the opened gash in my back.

My hips and legs were soaked in a red that was brighter

and thankfully not as foul as what was dripping from Parris' hand.

"You bitch." He balled his fist against his chest, staining the satin shirt he was wearing.

"How original," I snapped against the growing pain in my spine, plunging the knife forward with the full intent to slice his neck, and therefore his head, right off.

He wasn't quite as absorbed in his hand as I assumed and he side-stepped, causing the blade to hit his jaw instead. More specks of red showered over me, splattering over my face and bare chest like some macabre art exhibit. I flinched and stumbled back, the icy drops catching me off guard almost as much as the smell of the stuff.

Like death left too long in the sun.

It reminded me of some bootleg booze I had tried to make once, before Zoe found it. Probably with her super dragon sense of smell now that I think about it, the same sense of smell that was causing them all to turn to me, noses wrinkled, disgust painted on their brows before melting to the shock and confusion.

"Who's the bitch now? Because you seem to be mine." I flipped the dagger once more for effect and stepped closer to him. His curling lip twisted his melted face as he changed direction, stepping slowly around me and pulling me in a circle as we postured each other.

"I've never been your bitch, Elliana, although I would love to give you a ride someday."

Gag me with a fucking spoon.

Ew.

Just a spoon, no fucking allowed.

My blood was boiling disgust now. I swung the knife toward him, prompting him to flinch and jump to the side as

I turned my head and spit a line of flame right at the bastard.

Take that blood-sucker!

He tried to dodge the attack, but wasn't fast enough, the fire hitting him across the arm. I expected the flesh to melt, for him to scream, for his bloody arm to fall off and turn to dust.

Something.

Instead, I got a whole lot of nothing. Nothing but his damn smile and a chuckle as he wiped the still smoldering flecks of flame off his arm, just as Lilly had all those days ago in the cave.

'Lilly.'

I jerked and looked toward the girl, but she was still curled in on herself against the stone wall, silver blood trickling from her mouth. I didn't see any bite marks, but that didn't mean...

"I didn't bite her," his icy voice slithered over me and I took a quick step back from his advance, the knife foolishly slicing through the air.

"Then what did you do? Build another Phoenix to bleed all over you?"

"No. Why bite the offspring when I can drink from the source? That one has the Unicorn's soul in her, and it has been years since I have tasted her. I couldn't resist. Same as I cannot resist the taste of you. I will drink of the goddesses again. I helped create you into what you are, you should be mine to enjoy."

"Huh?" I may not be completely confused, but the flood of information was jumbled in my head now.

"I thought you said you knew everything, you little liar," he scoffed, stepping forward. I brandished the knife again, but this time he barely even flinched.

Okay, so that lie lasted way longer than I expected. Didn't mean that the knife still didn't work, didn't mean that all those fire rockets, and traveling, and a million other things that I could do were ineffective too.

One fire fart rocket coming up. May not burn him, but would still be hella fun.

"Not lying." Totally lying, albeit as confidently as I could. I brandished the knife again, and he still barely flinched. "But I think you are."

Smoke and flame dripped from my fingers, mostly for effect, the smoke curling over the blade of the knife I held it toward him, drifting up my arms and burrowing in my chest. My phoenix let out one pure note as the heat took over, the creature threatening to break free again. I could feel her press against me, feel my spine try to lengthen.

Try.

Whatever they had stabbed me with had seriously done a number on me. The piercing shriek of my phoenix may have scared the vamp, but once he realized I couldn't shift he was back to smiling and posturing.

"You are also an idiot," I smiled ignoring the fact that my ability to shift had broken and instead went into super combat mode. Holding the knife with my right hand, I swiped, shooting fire and smoke at him with my left.

"Are you sure about that?" He was right in front of me and gone before I could gasp, before I could take one swipe of the knife. "You may have the blade, but you don't know how to wield it. You don't know what it can do to you. What it *has* done to you."

He moved again, back and forth, darting in and out so fast that I must have looked like a fool swiping at the air.

"You don't know what you gave in exchange for that. What you ruined."

"Ruined?" So much for swiping the air, that froze me in place. It sounded like something out of a bad comic book, but the way he said it filled my veins with ice.

"Yes. You sold your throne for that, Elliana. Your choice destroyed the city of soot."

Like the idiot I was, I blinked in confusion and was instantly assaulted by a flash of a blackened city, of the same beautiful woman I had seen in the mirror, screaming at me.

Screaming at me not to do this.

The image vanished as fire erupted over the ceiling, red flames licking everything as Parris laughed, as Zoe yelled.

It took me a minute to realize that in my confusion, in the flash of memory, the vampire had ripped the knife from me.

"Killian!" Zoe shrieked; her voice hollow as it pulled through the deep weight of the air that was consuming me. "It's Fallon. The bird is fucking Fallon!"

I turned toward the shout like I was being pulled on a string, jerking toward the flash of white and black as smoke and magic collided in a bang that shook the cave, and sent me to my knees.

I couldn't stop him.

The blade embedded itself into my side. My blood poured over my flesh. Everything burned, and the room opened up with a scream as terrifying as the dark that took me.

I didn't even feel my head impact against the solid rock of the floor.

9

JARRON

JARRON HAD SEEN DEATH BEFORE.

So much death that he no longer thought of it as something frightening, but rather as something to be revered. Accomplished with flare and a grin and the awe of a crowd who damn near worshiped him.

Watching Elliot fall to the ground, however, the silver hilt of the dagger protruding from her side, was not a death he would ever revere. It was not something he ever wished to see, and even before her knees had hit the ground, Jarron's dragon was screaming in a sound he had only heard a few times before. A sound he would never want to hear again. He and Drake raced toward her, the Phoenix light gone from her eyes as she stared ahead, right into the Vampire that laughed and tittered like a school girl who had made their enemy cry.

Jarron almost changed his path to the Vampire, but Killian was already headed that way, black smoke mixing with Dragon fire as he rushed him.

Dragon screams rattled stone, glass, and bone, the heart wrenching sound blending with Parris and Fallon's laugh as the two darted around Zoe and Killian's attacks, making it clear they had been playing with them the whole time. Jarron couldn't even think beyond what he was seeing in order to care. Elliot's blood was everywhere, it dripped from the gash in her spine in rivers of gold tinted scarlet. It gushed from her side, pouring from the dark canker where the knife was lodged. It covered her flesh in a dark vermillion that he had never seen before. It was almost worse than the dark blood of the demon. You expect the ebony blood of the demon, but from Ellie...

"Ellie, Ellie!" Drake yelled, dropping to his knees as Jarron did, both of them catching her before she slammed into the hard stone floor.

"Oh my god, Ellie. Say something! Stay with me!" Drake was sobbing now, holding her close as his dragon growled and burned underneath his skin. Pressing. Pushing. The creature was desperate to emerge.

"Control it, Drake," Jarron pleaded, trying to move Ellie enough that he could see the silver hint of the dagger. The thing that was made to kill demons. Not her. "Hold her tight and focus on her. Don't shift."

"I won't," Drake's voice was shaking enough that the risk wasn't going anywhere. Jarron gave his brother a look, Drake giving a tear streaked nod before pulling Ellie into him, Jarron's hands pressed against her spine, against the inflamed skin around the blade. A slight whimper fell from her throat, although she didn't blink or shift from the weight of Jarron's hands against her.

She still wasn't looking at anything.

Oh god. This couldn't be the end. Not after demons and time travel and underground prisons. Fallon's laugh dug into the fear, coating him with ice even as his hands and side were soaked with the warmth of Elliot's blood.

"What are you going to do?" Drake's voice was shaking as much as his hands, the sensation made worse as the floor shook underneath a blast of white light that erupted from somewhere behind them.

"We need to remove the knife. It's cursed or something and it can't be good to leave there." Jarron wrapped his hands around the cold iron, his fingers flexing as he tried to get a good grip beneath the wet. The thing didn't even budge, a sure sign that the edge had driven itself into her ribs, lodged between the fragile bones.

Removing the dagger could very well be the wrong choice, but after seeing what the knife had done to a bloodless demon, leaving it in was worse. It needed to come out. If he moved fast, he could cauterize the wound before she lost much more blood. If they could stop the flow of blood then perhaps her Phoenix could begin to let her heal.

"Hold her." Jarron shifting his grip before he pulled. The knife vibrated as it ground against bone, and she began to scream.

Her scream turned to fire as a line of gold almost as vibrant as Jarron's shot from her mouth, rippling over the ceiling and pulling everyone's attention.

The whole world glowed in the sparkling the sun of her flames. It dripped from the sky and showered them in specks of glittering acid.

They were dragons. They were used to burns. Burns like this, however, were a true unknown. Every speck of Elliot's fire that hit him shot straight to the bone. It melted everything away, singeing clothes and skin in little black specks.

Jarron jerked and screeched away from the pain, but Drake did nothing more than grit his teeth, giving Jarron enough time to fuse her skin together with his fire. Working through the acidic pain, his dragon pressed against his heart, growling in ownership as he spit on the wound. The golden flame that killed so many, that could kill her, landed against her and slid right off.

"What the fuck?" Jarron asked, Drake was now no longer the only one struggling to control his dragon. The beast wanted to rip its way out and end this.

"There is no saving her," Parris taunted with a laugh, dodging another attack from Zoe as he swung through the room.

Zoe was the only one not distracted by Ellie's flame, by her screams, and was quickly gaining on Fallon and the Vampire, who had thrown the still unconscious Lilly over her shoulder.

"You can try," Parris continued, dodging another attack. "It will do no good. Even the power of light and dark can't save her, even if you could manage to join it together. Not from that blade. Only one thing can stop that blade when wielded correctly. And I can promise you, they won't help."

"What have you done?" Killian roared, rushing the vampire.

Vile Parris was only laughing now, the sound pounding violently against blood and pain. Fallon's laugh added to the agony, her beady eyes narrowed at Killian as the spindly talons of her fingers curling around Parris' shoulder.

Jarron wanted to rip them apart. He wanted to destroy them. But he couldn't leave Ellie, she was all that mattered now.

Jarron scooted closer to Ellie, he and Drake holding her between them as she bled. Her eyes were closed now, the flow of blood slowing to a trickle, Jarron's heart slowing right along with it.

"What have you done?" Killian roared on repeat from somewhere behind him, the sound garbled in his own tears.

"Ended this. And even if she does face her darkness, she will still return to me. To us. And she will drag you all behind her when she does." Parris' smile lined each word, his laugh pulling Jarron's focus as the room ignited in both Zoe and Killian attacks.

The lines of fire, light, and smoke streamed toward Parris, Lilly, and Fallon, her beady eyes closing with a pop as her feathers flew everywhere. Red and black flames mixed together in swirls of light and dark that smashed against the stone wall, sending everything rocking again. Nothing else was there to block their way.

They had gone. That damn bird had taken them away. Perhaps they should have given Killian more stock in his warning.

"Shit!" Zoe roared, the sound of her dragon ripping at the air.

The sound had once been terrifying to Jarron, mostly when he was a child. Now it was just another rumbling noise that coated the agonizing air.

Everything was in shambles, rock fallen, window cracked, even Callay lay tangled and forgotten on the stone floor. Nothing was as broken as what was right in front of him, however.

Elliot had begun to shake in his arms.

Drake's eyes were saucers as they met his own, the fear that Jarron had been feeling creep around the edges of his mind pounding on the door.

"Please no," Drake's sobs choked his words, Killian's own tears adding into them as he collapsed beside them all.

"Let me see her," Killian growled, his large hands

already pulling and prodding her away from Jarron. He was not willing to give her up that easily.

They could all be here. He could share, but he would not leave.

Elliot's shaking slowed as Killian wedged himself beside them, all of them trying to get as close as they could. Her hand flopped to the side, her fingers raking through the puddle of blood they all kneeled in, painting her fingers as red as her hair.

As red as the world that was devouring him. Devouring everything. The red grew darker as it consumed him, as she stopped shivering and gave one shudder of a breath.

And then there was nothing.

"NO!"

The world may as well have opened up and swallowed them all. The cave might as well have given in and collapsed, rock and stone and agony was everywhere and nowhere. Sucking all the air out.

Jarron had never felt pain like this, he had never known it was possible. Now that it was here, swallowing him from the inside, he wanted nothing more than to escape it.

Drake's shout came first, followed by Jarron's, then Killian, and then a childlike laugh that snapped through sobs and pain like a barbed wire whip. Jarron jerked up, his brothers following suit as they tried to pull her closer, to protect her from whatever was here. Not that he could see anything. A laugh, but no one attached to it. Even Zoe looked terrified from where she stood over them.

Killian rounded himself over her as another laugh bounced off the walls, Ellie's limp body slipping right of Jarron's grip, if only because Killian was the strongest amongst them.

"Look at the little princes, Sister, they cry. They cry." An

85

unfamiliar female mocked them as her and another walked toward them all, as though they had walked through the wall to join them.

"Such sad little princes."

The one who had spoken was tan and tawny, everything about her tall, nearly perfect frame the color of sun and wheat. Even her golden hair shimmered with each step, reflecting what was left of Ellie's fire like a halo.

The other was as tall, as slender, and perhaps even more perfect if that was possible. Her almond eyes, smooth skin and ebony hair nearly a polar opposite to the other.

They didn't look like siblings, let alone nationalities.

Jarron had never seen them before, they were not dragons, or anything else he had been around from what he could tell. Even their aroma was... wrong. The sweet heat that drifted from them was something more similar to what he had sensed in Elliot when he had first seen her in the steam room.

Spice and power and flame.

It was always Ellie.

And now it was these two.

He immediately shifted in front of where Killian cradled his mate, Drake moving to flank her other side. Although the look he was giving these women was less fear, and more recognition.

"Dragons are emotional beings, Sister, if you had spent the last four centuries living alongside them rather than underneath them you would know this," the darker haired of the two replied, something in her voice familiar. Something in her eyes even more so.

Like he had seen her before. Although, given his history, Jarron was sure he would remember someone of her.... caliber.

"You are the only one foolish enough to dabble in such monstrosities, Sister. Well, you and the Phoenix. Although, I do think that she did not mean it."

Pain was everywhere, Jarron's heart still ripped in two as it bled over hope and future. To hear these two talk about them all so callously was quickly turning all that pain into a rage. He may have lost his chance to make Parris pay. These two snide women seemed like a good substitute in the interim.

Jarron jerked forward, ready to do well... he didn't know.

Didn't matter either way, Drake was up and blocking his path, protecting Ellie as every exposed bit of his skin began to smoke.

"Goddesses. You stop there." Drake demanded, his back stretching dangerously as his Dragon fought to emerge.

Goddesses? Drake had been rambling about them before, but that was nonsense. This all was nonsense. Couldn't they leave them alone? Come back when everything didn't hurt quite so much.

"Now, now," the tawny female said, inspecting her fingers before turning her golden eyes onto them. "Is that any way to repay me for not eating you. I even gave you the easy riddle."

The woman pulled her lips into something that could be mistaken for a pout before she laughed.

The sound was as grating as how she had spoken about Ellie. But Jarron couldn't force himself to move that time. He couldn't even force a single word out, he was frozen, jaw sagging in shock.

"What the fuck?" Zoe clearly didn't have that problem. Her voice snarled as she tore around them all, wisps of white trailing behind her like some kind of heavy dragon smoke.

"You see it don't you?" Drake's voice shook, standing beside Zoe who had knotted her hands into fists.

Okay, make that two people who apparently knew what the fuck was going on. Shit. Make that three, Killian was looking at the women with as much understanding. Although, he didn't seem nearly as pissed.

Had he walked into an alternate universe?

"See what?" Jarron said in full voice, no one moved.

The tawny girl laughed harder, the tall Asian's lips pulling into a smirk. The look was as familiar as whatever light was hidden in her eyes.

"Be nice, you don't know what they've been through." The dark-haired woman stepped away from the other, leaving the girl to smirk and chuckle as the beautiful Asian approached. Her illustrious eyes focused on the fragile body of the girl in Killian's arms.

"We will be taking her now," she continued with a nod toward Ellie.

For a moment, Killian was ready to hand her over, the gorgeous woman's kind smile had done him in.

One move in the wrong direction, however, and Jarron was prepared to stop this nonsense.

"Please," Killian choked, "I can save her. I know I have the power."

"Nothing can save her..."

"Because she is a goddess," Drake cut over the woman, stepping between her and Killian like a sentinel.

Jarron was still trying to wrap his head around everything that was going on. It was all too similar to something that Lilly had said back at the cave. About Goddesses and power.

"I can still eat you, you know." The tawny woman

magically moved ten feet in less than a second, her teeth bared as she chomped at Drake like some rabid zombie.

"Stop!" Jarron pressed himself between the two of them, once again not thinking through the action. His already shattered heart sliced through him in its journey to his toes as he found himself face to face with sharp teeth and yellow eyes that for a minute did seem ready to consume him.

"What's going on. Who are you two? I need answers."

"Sure. But seeing as you are the only one who doesn't know, let's get this over with first." The tawny girl's smile didn't reach her eyes as she snapped, a spark of golden flame appearing on the tips of her claw-like nails. It popped to life in her fingers, as it did on Ellie's chest. Terrifying flame spread over her, burning the flesh above her heart and spreading fast.

"What the hell?" Killian nearly dropped her, all of them rushing to extinguish the flames, to stop whatever was happening.

The fire burned as much as the flame that had rushed from Elliot in her last breath, it burned his hands and heated the air. None of that mattered. Jarron couldn't let the fire devour her. He was near to throwing himself over her and let his Dragon extinguish the flames.

He never got the chance. In another snap and a maddening laugh, the fire spread, devouring her in a poof of smoke, leaving nothing but a pile of ash behind.

10

DRAKE

"Did you really have to be quite so dramatic?" The Unicorn said, swinging her sheet of black hair behind her with a flip of her hand.

A flip. Like it was nothing. Like it was all nothing.

Did they not realize that the world had stopped turning? When the same women from the large murals in the underground city had first appeared, Drake had hoped that they were here to save her. That with whatever super power they had that they could wave their hands and stop her blood from flowing. The Sphinx had said the Phoenix was lost, that they were trying to regain her, but it was the Sphinx that had set her on fire. That had ended her.

One flash of fire and she was gone. Nothing but piles of grey and heartbreak.

Drake's knees hit hard against the stone floor as he collapsed besides what once was his beautiful mate. Billows of ash swirled around him, covering him, glittering in the air in the last memory of her. Starlight and flame. They fell over him, coating him as he buried his hands in her ash. In the last bits of her.

"What have you done?" Jarron roared, ash shifting like snow drifts as his brother rushed the sisters. Drake couldn't pull himself away from the soft grey flecks, he clung to them, as if he could put them back together.

"Stop Jarron." That time it was Killian who roared, ash falling over Drake again as the two wrestled to a stop.

"They killed her, Killian! I'm not stopping anything." Their roars rattled everything, the growling dragons building to a scream, the frightening sound broken by a laugh.

If his heart wasn't so broken he might punch that laugh. He might still.

"Do you all really not know?" The Sphinx laughed, her hair shimmering as she shook her head.

Forget punching, his dragon might well bite off her head, Goddess or not, she would deserve it.

"Look at the fools, sister. They hover around her like bodyguards for hire. Did you really all have to be so foolish? Did you all forget that she's an eternal? A phoenix who can *never* die. Wait twenty minutes for her to figure out what she wants to come back as and you can all get back to your happy harem... or whatever it is you have going on here. Dragons are some of the most bizarre creatures I have ever encountered. Always thought so."

The Sphinx prattled on like she was talking to herself, Drake staring up at her from the ash, his fingers still clenched around the soft particles.

The woman laughed again, presumably because they were all giving her the same look of disbelief. If Drake hadn't seen them in the cathedral, he may not even think they were the same. This woman was so much worse than the Sphinx, and the sphinx was terrifying.

Heartless. Careless.

But also honest.

He had heard that before, about Ellie's inability to die. But from Fallon, a source he really wasn't on board with trusting right now. Not considering the girl had turned into a bird and then magicked Parris away somehow.

Seeing the smug look on these two, Goddess or not. He wasn't quite ready to jump into the all believing pool quite yet.

Neither was his Dragon. His powerful soul was fully growling now, pressing against his heart, against his bones. He didn't care if he shifted now, if Jarron's flames finished their long quest to devour him. It would be worth it. To die with her.

"God. I am never letting you lock yourself up for centuries again. I bet you did the whole massive feline, licking her chops, and talking like 13th-century royalty act on them didn't you?"

"I took my true form, if that's what you mean. Not like you can talk. When was the last time you stabbed someone with your horn, or didn't frolic around like some pre-teen with a complex?"

"Stop!" Both Killian and Jarron said together, the sound full of growls and anger that rippled through the air above him.

"You are saying she's not dead. How?" Jarron said the solid step of his shifter rattling the ash that was covering Drake.

"I just told you, and you still waste my time asking? No respect, these dragons."

"Answer the question, Sphinx." Anger pulsed through everything as Drake spun to stand, ash fanning off him as he faced the two women, his brothers still standing guard between them. The tawny girl smiled, slits in her eyes flashing yellow.

He had no question of who she was now.

"Why would…"

"That blade would have killed her if we had not burned her," The Unicorn interrupted, giving the other a look. "Killed even her immortality. We saved her."

"Saved her?" Drake could no longer restrain the growl in his voice. His fists were still clenched around the bits of her, holding the last specks as close as he could, letting them fuel his anger. "There is nothing left. You should have eaten me rather than force me to endure this pain."

"I've already said I don't like Dragon." The Sphinx ran her tongue over her lips, it appeared she thought otherwise.

"Too dumb and gritty. I mean, how many times do we have to say…"

"The blade is the only thing that can kill a god or a goddess." The Unicorn gave the Sphinx another disparaging look. Clearly this was a common dynamic between them. Not that Drake cared, he could feel his feet lengthening now, the gold twisting over his arms as the pain seeped through.

"Hilda burned her…" The Sphinx gave the Unicorn another look, that must be her name, and she really didn't like them knowing it. "The purifying flame of a Goddess is the only thing that would have removed the power of the blade. Elliana died a mortal in your arms. We turned her back into a god. We allowed her to die so she could be reborn."

"Well, I did," The Sphinx named Hilda said. "I saved her. Wait around and she will burst forth into flame in her usual over-dramatic way. Let's hope she chooses to remember you. She might not. She can be a bitch like that. Fucking Elliana.

She might still think she's in love with that fallen angel. God, if she's not over that I am going to stay here and keep killing her until she realizes how much of an idiot she is and we can fix this mess. The mess she made, mind you."

"Fallen angel? Do you mean Henry?" Jarron asked, causing both of the woman to stare at him. Okay, everyone to stare at him.

"Yes," The Unicorn smiled. "I assume, seeing as you are all here that Killian was successful in reaching you in time."

"I got there, but Ellie had already killed that demon thing," Killian provided. "I did manage to defeat Mattia, as you asked."

"As you asked?" Drake and Jarron turned in unison. What the fuck was going on here. Killian knew her?

"I was unable to defeat Fallon, however." Zoe said, pulling their focus the other way, like a ping pong. "I am sorry. She and the Vampire escaped."

"What in the fucking hell is going on here?" Jarron yelled, stepping away from everyone. Drake took one step along with him, not really wanting to be surrounded by liars and conspirators.

"You really have been busy," Hilda laughed again, her eyes back to cat slits again.

"We will deal with Parris and Fallon. What is important is that we have recovered what was needed. The girl, Lilly, where is she?"

"She's with the damn vampire!" Jarron was raging now, gold bleeding from his eyes as he stared down the two women. He was always very foolhardy, and this was possibly one of his less thought through decisions. Thank God Drake had chosen to stay on this side, although it was probably not a bad idea to pull Jarron back before he did something that would turn him to ash, too.

"What?" Great, now the Unicorn was pissed. "And what about the knife?"

"Probably with the Vamp as well seeing as he is the one who stabbed her." Jarron waved frantically toward where Parris had been, taking two quick steps toward the dark-haired goddess.

Everyone else took two steps away. Drake, however, was frozen. The ash in his hands was beginning to grow very warm, his dragon must be very close if he was starting to feel the heat of the beast.

"Now, how about you tell us all what the hell is going on?" Jarron towered over her, his fists tied into knots as smoke drifted from his nostrils.

"Where is Callay?" She asked, the response not what Jarron wanted. He let out a full dragon roar, the sound ripping over everything. Drake couldn't stop himself from jerking at the noise, a bit of ash seeping from his fist, sprinkling over his feet and mixing with the chilled vampire dust that was still there.

Except that what remained of Ellie was hot, almost too hot to hold now. But Drake held on tighter, trying to control his Dragon so as not to burn the last bits of her into nothing.

"There," Killian jerked his thumb behind him.

"Dead?"

"No."

"Will someone please explain for those who can't follow your one word nonsense?" Jarron was near to attacking, every rumbling consonant full of warning.

Didn't look like these two cared. The Sphinx was laughing as the Unicorn turned to him, her eyes flashing in a color that Drake could neither place or understand, even seeing it was splitting through him, his skull aching.

"Well, seeing as you asked nicely. Callay, Killian, Zoe,

they all work for me," The Unicorn said with a snap of her fingers, the same light from her eyes appearing over her nails. "So do you, even if you do not know it. I created all of this with the help of a little starving child, and a woman beat down by her power hungry brother for too long; a brother who Killian seems to think he destroyed."

"I did destroy him! I burned him along with the rest of the village." Killian interrupted, pulling the Unicorn away from Jarron who was now staring blankly ahead.

Brain overload. Drake had been there.

The guy was even clutching his chest and gasping, anger growing.

Oh shit. Now was not the time for Jarron to lose all rational thought. Drake pulled his brother back before he could lunge after the Unicorn, using his fists like weird appendages as he kept his fingers curled around the now smoking ash.

"I would suggest you don't do that," Drake hissed, Jarron's body weight collapsing against him as the bulkier brother gasped for breath. "They could snap and end you too."

"Worth it," Jarron said between breaths. "I don't trust them."

"Neither do I, but I also faced one of them and saw their images in windows in an underground ancient city…"

"What the hell are you on about?" Jarron interrupted, "has the world gone completely mad?"

Drake shook his head, "You are the one who defeated a demon. Not like you can talk."

"Did you pull out his heart, Jarron?" The Unicorn interrupted their hissed conversation.

"Excuse me?

"The demon, did you pull out its heart?" She was now

staring at where Callay was starting to moan and groan her way back into consciousness.

"No."

"Then you didn't kill him." The Unicorn sighed, pinching the bridge of her nose as the other continued to laugh. It would be nice if she would stop that, the weird grinding sound of her mocking was making the horrors of this whole thing so much worse.

"He was a bubbling mass of goo. We got him."

The Unicorn snapped her fingers again, the action causing Callay to jerk, the girl leaning forward and vomiting before she began to stand. "Humor me, then. Did Elliana stab herself before the demon?"

The woman turned on them, the same painful light in her eyes. Drake pulled himself behind his brother if only to stop whatever agony was beginning to pull through him. The question wasn't for him, anyway.

"No," Jarron said.

"Wonderful. So nothing has been done, and we let two powerful servants return to their master. Let's hope that Callay has good news for me, otherwise I may not have use for any of you." She turned from each of them, Hilda's laughing finally ending in lieu of an extended glare.

Okay fine, maybe he could make do with the laugh. Anything to not have to stare into those yellow cat eyes.

"If we are going to start killing, I call the big one," Hilda said, stepping toward Killian. He didn't even move, although that strange black smoke did begin to swirl around him. "I like the feisty ones."

"Don't even try it," Killian's eyes were completely black. Warning met.

Well, unless you're a goddess. She stepped closer.

"Feisty." She snapped her teeth together, cat eyes blazing. Drake and Zoe took one solid step back.

"Pull yourself together, Callay," The Unicorn snapped, ignoring whatever was unfolding behind her and leaned towards Callay. The girl looked up, groaned, and immediately collapsed against the wall again, pinching her eyes shut.

"Damn it, Xi, I hate it when you fucking do that. Oh, and you're an adult again. Great. I prefer the kid, she doesn't scare me as much." Callay snarled, sending a ripple of a gasp through everyone. All except Killian who joined the Sphinx in a laugh of his own.

"Xi?" Drake could barely get the word out past a gasp, luckily Zoe had snapped a profanity loud enough for all of them.

"Okay, I am really going to need some fucking answers." Jarron was demanding now, his dragon so close that even the air around him was glowing yellow.

"Oh shit," Callay hissed, backing herself into the stone wall when she caught sight of everyone else in the cave, although her focus was more on Jarron and Killian than anyone else. "Please tell me we didn't completely fail. I'm so sorry, Xi. That girl was friends with the vampire. And Dabria... oh god. Dabria. She's in my head. She's going to track..."

"Dabria is dead," Killian interrupted, waving behind him toward corpse number one, her limbs only partially visible in the midst of burned Vampires she was surrounded by. "Although that is of little consequence now. I believe I may be in agreement with my brothers, now. Had Callay been working for you this whole time? Exactly what is going on here?"

"Callay has been helping me to move you into position..."

"Into position? Is that why you were pretending to be a kid at the circus?" Drake really didn't want to think of this beautiful woman as the punk kid at the circus, but she did little more than turn and smile at him before he had his answer.

"Damn it!"

"How long, Callay?" Jarron continued his roar, stepping through the piles of ash to posture the Unicorn, or Xi, or whatever was going on.

His brother had no respect, the ash behind him shifting over stone and through air as he dragged his ugly ass shoes through what was left of the rest of her.

He would have yelled, except that the second his brown pleather shoes left the piles, the ash moved, snapping back together like it was being gathered by something, gentle hands smoothing it all back together.

"Wait your turn, Jarron," Xi's voice rumbled through the back of Drake's mind, Jarron's yelled response only mumbles as he stared at the now smoking ash, what was in his hands reaching a temperature that he could no longer cling to. But he stubbornly held on, well until a voice that was of a purr echoed in his ears.

"You have to let her go, Drake. She has to be altogether to regenerate. Her ash has to all be there for her to have a chance to return to her true self."

Drake jumped at the soft purr, one of his hands opening and dropping the handful of soft grey ash to the ground, the stuff instantly moving to join the rest, as though it had been called there.

"But what about all those experiments?" Drake asked, bits of burning ash pushing their way through his still closed fist. "How can she all be there if so much has already been taken away?"

"We cannot replace that," Xi said.

"All we can do is get her as close as we can," the Sphinx whispered in his ear, her fingers wrapping around his in an attempt to force open the still closed hand. He jerked away so fast he may have pulled a muscle.

He gave the girl a look, her cat eyes flashing in her smile as he stepped up to the ash. He had every intention of seeing Ellie again, but he could do it on his own, not with the help of a cat eyed goddess.

Goddess.

'*Let's hope she chooses to remember you.*'

A goddess reborn.

His dragon growled hungrily, but even the creature that dwelled in his soul was filled with a fear that he couldn't quite shake. If she didn't remember him, if their bond was broken, he might ask the smiling cat to eat him. Whether she liked Dragons or not, she was still licking her lips and staring at him.

Drake had hesitated, hand over the pile. Killian, however, had not, he stepped forward, pulling a folded square of fabric out of the pocket of his suit pants.

"What is that?" Hilda stepped forward, a hiss in her voice.

"I stole it from Mattia. It's her. It's you," he said with a nod toward Xi before he opened the fabric and let the contents fall to the ground.

Specks of the darkest black cut through the dimly lit cave, catching the absence of light as though they were diamonds. They stood in a circle, watching the specks fall. The heavy bits of ash falling against their much lighter colored counterparts, hitting against the ash like rocks.

Rocks that might as well have been bombs.

The second they hit, everything in the cave rocked, the cracked stone splitting below them as though the throne room would open up and send them soaring to the city below.

The sound of cracking stone blended with what he could have sworn was shattering glass. Not that he could see it anymore.

The dark cave had gone, replaced by a tornado of grey. Smoke swirled around them, dancing with lines of fire that he recognized at once. He had only seen them a few times before, but would never forget the beauty.

"Ellie."

On cue, the single glorious note of a Phoenix rang through the cave, cutting through him and pulling the answering roar of a dragon from him, the roar followed by four others.

"Drop it, Drake!" Xi screamed, ash and flame everywhere now, in his eyes in his nose.

He wanted to hold on, to keep this last part of the girl he knew, the girl he loved, against him. But as the air burned his skin, and the fire ate away his clothes, he had no other choice.

He opened his hand.

"I love you, Ellie."

11

PARRIS

Parris was in more trouble than he would ever admit.

He knew that his luck was on a thin line the second the Falcon had appeared in the rafters of the throne room back in Rydaim. She was made of little more than black smoke, a projection placed there by the dark magic of the woman who served the man he had spent the last hundred or so years avoiding.

One wisp of smoke and all of that was for naught. He couldn't kill her, enraging her master would have been worse. Still did not make his predicament any easier.

Plans of escape and battle whirled through his mind as he followed her, the filthy girl only a few steps ahead of him, the blonde child he had worked with Henry to create thrown over her shoulder. Fallon's spoils of war.

The child's silver hair swung through the dark, her sparkling magic dripping from each strand of hair and the limp fingers that hung below her, nearly dragged over the stone floor of the cave. If it wasn't for the drizzle magic he would think she was dead. His attack had been more of shock and reflex, throwing her back as he did with the full strength of his kind, but it turned out to be a good thing. He may not have seen the girl since her birth, but he knew what she was bred for. Considering he was the one to have sired her.

But she had spent the last eight years under Henry's delusions, and who knows what the demon had done. Having her unconscious was safer.

"Why is he dragging us through a fucking cave?" Fallon's question ripped through the dripping dark of the stone tunnel they had been wandering through for the past hour. The grumble was the same she had repeated incessantly after Mattia's magic had pulled us away from the battle and towards him. Which was where they were headed, and why Parris was fucked.

He hadn't seen his creator in centuries, not since Mattia had taught him to spread the dark curse he carried and they worked together to take down the city of soot. A successful end that could have led to a positive reunion. But that was nearly five hundred years ago. Parris had done far more unsavory things since then, including convincing the Phoenix to attempt to kill the Warlock. That little foray hadn't ended nearly as well as he had hoped.

"Probably because it's as dark as his heart." He had meant to say that low enough that Fallon couldn't hear. He foolishly had forgotten who he was speaking too.

"Says the broken creation with no heart whatsoever." She was sharp, angry, the same jealousy that always fueled her coming to the service. Parris was Mattia's first. She and her broke ass ability would always be Mattia's sloppy seconds.

"Oh, you know I have a heart, darling. You want it as much as all the others." Parris took two quick steps forward, brushing his shoulder against hers and basking in the feel of her radiant heat against the ice of his existence. Ice she had loved as little as a few hours before, before Mattia's spell had begun to cloud her again.

His breath drifted over her neck in one soft exhale and she shivered, the still unconscious child swaying dangerously from where she held her. Even without his heightened eyesight he could see her flesh prick up, hear her heart accelerate under the touch. He snickered, pressing himself against her until he could taste the magic that pumped in her blood, the sweet tang coating his mouth. His fangs were already protruding, his mouth filling with wet.

"You know you want to feel me, Fallon. Feel me everywhere." He moaned as low as he could, the remnants of his ancient accent bleeding through. She shivered beside him, her heart accelerating into an orchestra that only he could hear.

He knew he should be careful this close to the Warlock, but he couldn't help himself. He had always wanted to bite her. To taste her. But she was Mattia's, and to taste her was to die.

"Cold iron and stone. No one wants to feel that." She tried to hide it, but the shake in her voice perfectly matched the shudder in her heart.

"You weren't singing the same tune a few hours ago," His smile stretched as she turned to him, the look in her eyes burning with a fire that if he had a heart, he was sure it would increase to match hers. "You want me. Admit it."

"Once upon a time. Before your face looked like shit and you failed to kill any of the dragons that I practically spoon fed you. Then... maybe."

"We retrieved the girl."

"And lost the white light..." Her rebuttal was swallowed by a masculine laugh that sliced through the dark, pulling their focus to a sliver of yellow light ahead. Parris' lust evaporated as the thunder of her pulse picked up for another reason.

Shit.

"Mattia." She practically raced to the light, the kid bouncing on her back like a sheep for the slaughter. The imagery was more fitting now. Parris followed with a sigh, hand dragging through his hair as he checked the knife he had pilfered away from the traumatized dragons. The thing was tucked into the back of his jeans, the hilt hidden underneath the leather jacket and out of sight.

They had been so busy panicking over Elliana, they hadn't even noticed him grabbing it.

He wasn't even sure if Fallon knew he had the thing. Which was for the best. The value in the blade might be the only thing keeping him from facing punishment for centuries of treachery.

That or let him stab the man and give him a chance at escape.

The laugh came again, different this time. Fallon was still charging ahead, toward what he could now distinguish as a white marble kitchen. Parris, however, was frozen in place.

"Holy fuck." He knew that laugh as well as he knew the other one, but it couldn't be. Two steps ahead and a clear view of the two men and he would have given anything to melt into the dark. But it was too late, the two hovered around what looked like a murky bell jar in the middle of a wooden table, looking right at him.

Mattia and Henry. Laughing. Joking. He could have sworn they gave each other a fist bump, but he might be losing his sanity in his panic.

Parris had never expected to see the two men together. He had never wanted them to discover one another, if only because he knew what the combination of their power would do to his aspirations. He could never be more than a servant with those two in play. The crown he had spent so many years aligning himself with was already gone.

Walking into a room with them could easily be a death sentence, except that he was carrying the only weapon that could destroy them. It would either be a bargaining chip to ensure his survival or the tool to his escape.

Neurotically checking the knife again, he followed Fallon into the brightly lit room, and the refined living space that Parris hadn't expected in the middle of the dank cave. Surprising, given that most of his life, human and not, had been spent serving the Dragons that had mastered building their homes in the massive underground crevices.

"My Master," Fallon said with a vile giggle. She walked into the yellow light of the kitchen, the kid bumping against her spine as she sprinted to his side, lifting herself up on her toes to kiss him.

Mattia pulled his arms around her, pressing himself into her, tasting her the way that Parris could only dream. Lust bubbled through him, one of the only human emotions he possessed slamming against him and forcing him to take a step forward. The need to join in was something that he should probably disguise more. He was well aware he was openly staring.

"Why, hello Parris," Henry said, in that crisp accent that he had adopted only shortly after his fall from the bowels of heaven.

His voice was the only recognizable thing about him at the moment. Elliana had bragged that she had killed the demon, and while he had been certain that she had failed in her assumed attempt, she had been able to get closer than he had assumed. Henry hadn't quite been able to return to full human form after Elliana's attack. His limbs were too lengthened, his jaw sagging to his collarbone where a bit of golden drool was rolling off his cracked lower lip.

Even with the knife, he had no interest in facing the powerful demon.

"Henry." Parris gave him a nod. "I didn't think I would see you again after you stole the infant I created. My child."

Both men turned toward the still swaying blond locks of the girl, the child unknowingly trapped between what had become a full blown make out session. Henry smiled, the grin cracking his jaw back into place.

"Yes, well, it appears you have been reunited with her after all. So no harm, eh?" Henry's wicked glare bored into the Vampire as he stepped to the grinding pair, lifting the girl from Fallon who was far too willing to give her up.

"Thanks for bringing her back to me."

"I didn't bring her back to *you*," Parris said as Henry turned back, one monster glaring at the other as Henry laid the kid on the table beside the foul-smelling bell jar. Formaldehyde, no doubt. "I didn't expect to see you with the Warlock."

Henry froze, his hands still in the process of pushing hair away from the child's face. Even Mattia pulled away from a now giggling Fallon with the sound of a suction cup.

"You mean the magician who created you? The one you kept me away from for centuries? I'm disappointed in you, Parris. Imagine all of the amazing things we could have accomplished together. All that we could rule. Instead, you selfishly pilfered away our future." The demon made a sound like a disgusted parent and shook his head.

"You are not the only ones to have aspirations to a more successful future," Parris said, shifting his weight so that the knife dug into him enough that he knew it was still there.

With the way Mattia was stalking behind him, Fallon having transformed and perched on his shoulder, he needed to be ready. The two demonic men were now on either side of him. The cave might as well be closing in with how close he was coming.

"And you assume that your pathetic aspirations are enough to make you anything other than the silt you are?" Mattia chuckled at his statement, stepping around Parris to face him.

The Warlock wasn't behind him anymore, although having him inches away was less preferable.

The look in his eyes, the black smoke that was suddenly everywhere, it brought every single human fear back into him. All the strength and skill of the vampire he was sucked away, transforming him into the frail pathetic human he was before Mattia. Before he had kidnapped him and his sister when they were little more than children, a thousand years before. There was a reason he had avoided the man after he had 'paid his debt' and helped him destroy the city. He had been much more careful who he brought into service after that, and restricted himself to kidnapping humans for food purposes, and not for service.

"Silt. Fitting. Sediment that falls away with a single touch. Like dreams, hope, life." Henry sighed, Mattia smiling as he stepped around the table to stand beside the Demon. The two stood together, like some sigil to the end of the world, eyes gleaming before Henry bent over the sleeping child, placing a single finger in the middle of her forehead.

"Isn't that the way of the world?" The demon sighed, the flesh around his touch beginning to grow black as the color in the rest of her faded. As though his touch was pulling light out of her.

Parris had seen this trick before, and he stepped back, this was not something he wanted to be close to.

"Everyone wants to rule. Everyone thinks they are worthy to be revered as something more than they are." Henry was only looking at the girl now, his voice stretching as much as the dark over her skin, as much as his limbs until it was a hollow boom that echoed over them from where he had grown.

"Imagine the glory that would have come to all of us had you brought us together earlier, Parris. Imagine all that we would have showered you with. Glory. Wealth. Titles." Mattia's accent rolled, his dark eyes narrowing as Fallon gave a squawk that was more like a laugh, the bird ruffling her feathers.

He half-expected her to jump from her perch and return to the shape of a woman, but she remained on his shoulder, staring.

"Imagine the carnage that we could have left behind. Imagine the feast, for your kind, and for mine," Henry continued, his bones snapping together as his voice normalized. Henry sighed in delight of whatever he had stolen from the girl.

Whatever he had devoured from inside.

The girl was smothered in darkness now, the sparkle from before gone, her skin a rough ebony as she lay immobilized. He couldn't tell if she was dead, or if she had been filled with a bit of the demon's spirit, completely under his control. It was how this power normally worked, one touch and he sucked away their life, turning them into frightening little puppets.

The child wasn't moving however, she wasn't even breathing. He wasn't even sure if she was alive.

"You could have had everything, Parris. I created you, I

would have given you everything." There was no reason to believe this. He did place one hand on his hip, however, just in case.

They weren't there yet, but they were close.

What would it be? Murder or bargain.

The real question was, could he take all three at once.

"Instead you will have nothing," Mattia finished with a smile, both men leaning over the table in a clear warning.

The look in his eyes answered his question.

"We could still have everything," Parris forced as much strength as he could into his voice, playing the game he had played for centuries. Or, he would have, if these three didn't know him as well as they did. The bird was back to making her vile laughing sound again.

He gave her a glare and slid his hand under his jacket.

"I may not have brought you two together, but I have returned the child who may be the last attainable carrier of light," he gave a nod toward Henry, although the man didn't seem very grateful considering what he had done to steal and hide the child. "But I have more. I have the name of another light. I know her dark counterpart, as do you I believe," he gave a nod toward Mattia before quickly plowing on, "I also took away their only weapon."

With that, he unsheathed the knife, letting the light of the underground kitchen pull against the ruby, against the steel, and blind them all.

"I also bring you the blood of the Phoenix, still wet on the blade from where I stabbed her. From where I crippled all of them. The Phoenix has fallen, her magic is yours for the taking."

With a grin, he placed the knife on the table on the other side of the girl and closer to him, lest he need to take it up again. Thankfully, the two men smiled, Fallon giving a different kind of caw as she ruffled her feathers.

"It looks as though you are still of use to us," Mattia said, leaning over the table to grab the knife. "Now, I need you to do one more thing."

"Anything Master," Parris said with a bob of his head.

The word burned his tongue, but nothing but good would come from padding the man's ego. His lips were already spreading into a grin, his greedy eyes narrowing as he looked at the vampire.

"I need you to create me a new army. And I need it by tomorrow."

12

ELLIOT

DEATH IS easy when you are immortal.

Doesn't mean it doesn't hurt though.

Right in this moment, I could have sworn that every single bone was being splintered and pulled out of the back of my skull and stabbed through my spine while I was simultaneously being stabbed with burning knives and run through a wood chipper. It was a good thing I was dead and lacked the ability to scream, otherwise I might be haunted by my own blood curdling agony for the rest of eternity.

Immortal? Sure, I guess so. Death is brutal either way. As it had been each and every one of the four hundred and some odd deaths I had endured.

Four hundred and sixty two.

I had somehow managed to keep track through it all, even if I didn't take my memory with me. It was so much worse than I had thought. So much worse than fucking Henry had told me it was. Worse because I remembered everything.

All four hundred and sixty two lives. All four hundred and sixty two wood chipper encounters. Four hundred and sixty two broken hearts and four hundred and sixty two times I decided to run away from responsibility.

It was all there.

Releasing Henry from heaven, I did that. Tricking my sister into making the knife so I could kill the demon that I created, I did that too. Locking my sister away when I realized what I had done to her. The destruction of my city as I sat restrained by the demon I created. Watching Henry steal the ash I needed to be able to fully regenerate as he killed me over and over again. Feeling Mattia rip my wings from my body as I tried to protect Henry and Parris from what they had told me was a monster. Maybe he was. I had no way of knowing. But they were monsters too.

So was I.

A frightening narcissistic monster that looked back at me in every memory.

In every single life.

Every single heartbreak.

It was all there, and it was making my wood chipper death even worse.

'*Oh god, what have I done?*' The question floated somewhere between me and my Phoenix, the woodchipper agony starting to dissolve as something that I could only describe as an afterlife appeared.

Well, it damn well better be. I couldn't think of anything else that was white and swirling and one step away from breaking into a high-pitched choir.

White light drifted over everything, swirling through the air until it began to form into something from my memory. High ceilings, flying buttresses. Of course it was the cathedral. What better place to have my white smoke regeneration party than the church I used to be worshiped in. White drifts of dust and smoke formed into marble, specks of light twisting to become four tall glittering windows, the colored pieces twisting into people that I hadn't seen in so long that my heart twisted into another pain altogether.

Loss. Guilt. I would almost prefer to have my bones pulled through my skull again.

Xi. Hilda. Rana. Me. The same me that was standing, as naked as in the window, as naked as on the wardrobe, as naked as I always was. Although, window me was all fire and bush and bare as I stared serenely into the beautiful cathedral that I had been the one to destroy in the end.

Monster? I think I was worse than that.

I had been fighting the idea that I was a villain for weeks. Now there was no denying it. I was, and I had to face that head on.

Litral-fucking-ity. I mean, I was currently being stared at by the most judgey face I had ever seen in my life. Disappointment, anger, and frustration were glaring into me with intense beady eyes that before now had only lived inside my soul.

Now they were right in front of me.

My Phoenix had burst through the white light of my death in a flash of fire and was now hunched in the middle of the white smoke, gold and red feathered wings folded against her, sharp yellow beak snapping in frustration and disapproval. As they did every time.

Four hundred and sixty three times.

Every time I cried over my mistakes, as I tried to justify them, as I chose to run away from them, as I yelled at her, as I bargained my way out of taking responsibility. Like the teenager, or the child, that I decided to return as. Four hundred and sixty two times.

Hundreds of years of being unable to accept

responsibility. God, even at my core I was a punk ass teenager who needed a good slap upside the head.

'If you would like, I will be the one to give it to you. Wouldn't be the first time.' Okay, even with all my memories I could still be caught off guard.

I could hear my phoenix talk. Full sentences inside my head.

Although, I did stop my jaw from dropping, the bird still snickered with a sound that could only be explained as a laugh, golden smoke drifting from the corner of her beak.

Damn it. Not only was my soul more beautiful than in the stupid painting the demon had, she was as saucy and snarky as I was. No wonder she was mine.

"I don't think that is needed. Sitting in my own guilt is enough," I said, glad when my voice was more than a floating thought.

'It's my guilt, too.'

"I can't agree with that. I made all of those decisions. Not you." I said after a moment, looking between each window, each sister, and finally stopping on Rana. The tall slender goddess stood serenely in a landscape of mountains and clouds, her close shorn hair and smooth dark skin beaming as unearthly light filtered through the panes. We had been closest. She had trusted me. She still did, even though I had essentially cursed her to a life restricted behind glass. I didn't deserve any kind of trust.

'I chose Henry.' I couldn't even argue that. She had. I had fallen in love with his charisma, back when he was all golden and pure and peering through the waters from heaven to seduce me. But she had named him. She had brought him from the depths of heaven to be with her.

With us.

It was a bad mistake, a mistake that started everything. A

mistake that nearly shattered the world. But there had been a million other mistakes, a million other chances to fix it, but few attempts to actually make things correct. And for the first time in hundreds of years, I think I could stand before myself and not feel as much like a villain.

"You also chose Jarron, and Killian and Drake. *We* chose them, and we chose to fight alongside them. We could have run then you know. We have before, especially when that fighting took us right back to Henry, to Parris..." I almost said that we had killed them, that we had been successful in one thing. But Parris had been right, I didn't remember how to use the knife, and I hadn't killed either of them. He had almost killed me, though.

Damn it all! Of all the times for me to be stubborn and not let all the memories through. I could have stopped it all then... oh... who am I kidding! I would have run away.

Run away and not gotten myself stabbed, that's for sure.

I didn't know who had decided to burn me, but I would have to thank them later. Let's hope that someone was able to keep the knife away from Parris, the last thing we needed was him taking off with it. I had a feeling he was going to head right back to Henry, and with Fallon with them... that put Mattia in the mix.

Fucking shit. We were so fucking screwed.

I had accidentally pushed a thousand years of turmoil into a war. A war I was keenly aware that I couldn't run away from anymore.

Oh god. I couldn't linger here long. This whole thing was going to come to a head. And I was still a pile of ash in the real world, where who knows what was going on. For all I knew Mattia could have emerged and was systematically picking them off.

Holy fuck. Mattia. Killian. The black smoke I had seen

from him. I knew what it was now. Same with Zoe. And I only knew one person who loved to hand out little curses like that and cause havoc in the world.

"Fucking Xi." Unicorns were mischief, and I knew she had been putting her fingers in all sorts of pies for years. I never would have expected that she would have infused magic into two power hungry and slightly neurotic dragons. After what I had seen in the cave, they really didn't know how to control it either.

All of this was a mess. I wasn't sure if it was me or if it was Xi who had brought it to a head, but this war was about it come to an end.

'Are you quite done rambling?' My Phoenix snickered, tilting her head to the side as the white smoke sparkled and swirled, sending spots of color through the panes and over everything.

"Not rambling," I said with a scowl to her before turning back to images of my sisters. "Just coming to terms with my weird ass life."

'Well, do hurry up. I believe we have a few dragons waiting for us, and I would love to see them again.' She purred then, the sound low and filled with as much love and passion that I usually had for them.

Except right now, my mind was buzzing with something else.

My Dragons. The three men who had fought the same villains as I had, who had protected me when I could no longer protect myself.

Who had loved me when no one else could. Who had taught more than hundreds of years of mates and mistakes ever could.

Killian, who had faced his father and worked against him after years of fighting with him.

Jarron, who had killed so many, and then worked to save even more.

Drake, who didn't give up even after everything around him had been destroyed.

I knew what I needed to do.

We couldn't run anymore. I had to face my mistakes and actually fix them instead of continually trying to cover them with bandages and pretending that's good enough. All my sins were bleeding out like a bad Monday.

Ugh. This was going to hurt.

My Phoenix bristled, the coo of the bird sharp and frightened. I turned from the windows to face her, the dark of her eyes filled with fire now. The same fire burned against my bones, pressed against my skin and filled my soul, pulling me right back to her. Into her.

A part of her.

'It's time.' The sweet sound of her voice filled my mind. *'Have you decided what you will become. What your life will be in this cycle?'*

I swallowed as bits of black covered the white walls of the temple, the lines of the carvings darkening as familiar ash seeped over the walls, turning everything into the charred world I had cursed my home with so many life cycles ago. My very first life, when I destroyed this city. When I had died for the first time and I had sunk into ash.

This ash.

I hadn't seen the pure ash of my soul in generations, it sprinkled over my head like rain, igniting my soul and bringing back a part of me that I had been sure Henry had stolen forever.

"How did...?" My gasp melded into my Phoenix's song as the bits of death and life covered everything, the sparkling light of Xi's mischief coating the black until the temple glimmered in ebony.

"I stole it from Mattia. It's her. It's you," Killian's rumbling voice broke through the veil of my death, pushing against the temple and rattling everything, sending the ash back down to the ground. Back to me.

Bits of black clung to my feet, twisting around my naked body as it sunk into my skin, spiraling up my legs, over my hips. Pressing into me.

"Are you ready, my darling soul?" I said, stepping forward, the specks of my ash trailing behind me like some ethereal gown. My hair lifted in a halo, each strand sparkling until the deep red looked like a flame. I had seen the hint of the same before, with Callay, but this was more. This was a whisper of the power and magic inside of me.

The magic I was about to unleash. But not like the villain I spent so many years being. Well, unless it was a villain who was going to kick ass and fix all my shit.

Pulling the massive head of my bird against me, I cuddled the creature as her fire moved into me, as the powerful soul of the creature meshed with the goddess that I was, the goddess I was ready to be once more.

"It's time to save them all. It's time to fix this."

'It is our time, Elliana.'

"Drop it, Drake!" Hilda screamed through the ash, pulling us back to a life that was very nearly shattered.

'Who will you be?' My Phoenix's voice was drifting into song now, the ash from the walls swirling around us as we were reborn.

"I will be me. I will be a goddess again. I will stand by my sisters and heal the world."

13

ELLIOT

FIRE LICKED through the sky as my skin pressed into the heat, everything opening up as my massive avian soul melded herself inside my heart once more. Flesh pricked and bristled with magic and energy, the power so familiar, so comfortable I could have wrapped myself up in it. Heat struck through my fingertips, hair rising into a true flame that sparked around me in both heat and light.

Everything was fire, energy, and power as the ash continued to swirl, the heavy stuff coating my skin before it fell away, revealing every inch of my nakedness to the Dragons that surrounded me, two of my sisters smiling with the all-knowing ego they always had.

Little bastards. They seemed to think they had something to do with my choice to return to my true self. I wasn't about to give them the satisfaction. My hair burned in a flame as I hovered in the twist of my magic as I so often did before, always longing to fly, never truly ready to cement myself to the ground.

"So, you've decided to return to us," Hilda said, folding

her arms one over the other, tapping her toe as the cat inside her always did.

"It has come to my attention there is something I need to fix," I had forgotten how echoey my voice was, the heavy sound always traveling on the back of a wind that didn't exist.

"About time," Xi snapped. "Because I would say there is more than a *something* here. You left us with quite the disaster. Well, me. You left me with quite the disaster. It's not like anyone else helped to solve the problem."

"A *problem* which you made even worse with your mischief, Sister," I said with a rumble that shifted some of the stone beneath my feet. "You offset the balance of power more than I ever could have. Cursing Dragons who already bare too much weight? Casting an urchin with light to give yourself a servant for your shenanigans."

"Hey! I would like to think I was more than some dumb servant" Callay said from where she was propped up against the stone wall. She tried to push herself up, swore loudly, and went back to scowling at everyone.

"Nice to see that you are no longer interested in trying to kill me." I gave her a smile and she rolled her eyes. She had spent too much time with the powerful Unicorn.

"Xi, my sister, you hold as much blame as I." Fire ripped up my skin in a flash of anger, the golden flame traveling over my arms to blend with the flame of hair that was so much a part of me.

Me.

I was myself. It had been a while. It felt damn good to have all the parts of me returned together again, even more so with my powerful mates surrounding me.

Turning toward those amazing Dragons, however, was not the awe-inspiring reunion I had expected. Instead, they stared back at me with a wide array of fear, shock, and pain. Not that I should be surprised. I had essentially swallowed the girl that they had been bonded to. They couldn't understand what had happened. What I was. Not yet.

"I spent decades following your dumb ass around and making sure you didn't cause too much trouble," Xi snapped, exhaling with the sound of the horse she was. "Don't fault this, Sister."

"Yes, you did. I need to thank you, as well as the old witch for concealing me. Also, the future Queen for giving humanity to a child who could have been nothing more than a destructive villain. It was those acts that may have allowed me to return. That brought forth the end, as well as a beginning. It was the acts that all of you gave me." I turned toward Zoe and the boys, giving them a smile that I had hoped would calm them, but their shock only deepened, Drake going as far as to take a step back.

Perhaps appearing in my true form was too much for them.

"Hmmm," I murmured, Hilda laughing behind me. Perhaps she had seen the frightening awe drip from their eyes.

"You live a thousand lives forgetting everything about yourself and you still manage to scare the crap out of Dragons. I'm impressed," Hilda's chuckle melted into a low purr that held as much mockery as her human counterpart.

She better watch it. It may have been a few hundred years since we had worked together, but I wasn't above shooting a fireball into her mane. I did enjoy watching her mew in panic as her hair singed.

"It was only a few more than four hundred." I gave her a look of warning, it missed its mark. The purr melted back into a laugh, Xi rolled her eyes at both of us.

"Oh, oh. Am I supposed to be impressed? Because I've lived one life, Elliana. One. I am pretty sure you are only supposed to live one life. Just because you can die a million times doesn't mean you should. Your memory is proof enough of that."

"If you have only lived one life, then you haven't truly lived, Sister. You've hidden. I however have loved, and lost, and grown. I took a journey and found where I belonged." My Phoenix sang with each word, her feathers bristling under my skin as the heat pulled back into my heart. The flame that I let burn through me pulled away from my hair as I finally lowered myself to the ground, bare feet pressing against cold stone as the last bit of Phoenix flame swirled around me in a different way, twisting into long feathers of red and gold that pulled through skin as the beast that was inside blended with the magic that was truly mine. In the last flash of flame, I was left with a dress that matched my insides as much as I did out, long feathers pressing against my skin, glittering with a hidden flame.

"I found where I belong, and who I belong with." I smiled at each of the men in turn, my Phoenix song growing as their eyes blazed in the fire of their dragons.

Lost, partially confused dragons.

"Don't worry, it's her," Hilda said from somewhere behind me, she wasn't laughing anymore. Her feline could sense danger better than most, even I could hear the low growl of the dragon's permeating the air.

But this time she was wrong.

"Come," I said, holding my hands out to the four of them, pulling all of them right to me. Even Zoe, who even though she might not know it, who even though she may not be bonded to me in the same way, was still a part of this equation.

Part of me.

"Come," I said again.

The four of them surrounded me, pulled so tightly together that even with their bulk there wasn't much room for me to move around. Which was fine by me. I liked this, being surrounded in their heat. Surrounded in them.

Soon I would need more.

I was already longing for it, the feathers of my dress falling away in desperation to hold them against me. Well damn it all, I was a bit of a voyeur.

I think I liked it.

"You are still mine," I whispered, letting my Phoenix, and my magic bleed through each word. "And I am still yours."

I tugged at them, wrapping my fingers through theirs as I locked them in place until everything was a twist of fingers and palms, Zoe sandwiched somewhere in the middle. My eyes burned into hers, the single sharp note of my phoenix pulling through everything and igniting her fire. Pulling her dragon right into me.

"You all are," I continued, before bending over our hands, kissing each finger, pressing heat and magic and everything else into them. With each touch of lips and heat, one of their dragons responded with a growl. The sounds of their souls had been powerful before, now it was a blend with my own. It was music that rang from my soul.

Each of their shifters pulled toward me, the sound of their growl familiar and understandable. Before, I had only heard Jarron, heard the low moan of ownership. Now, I heard each of them.

I knew them.

"Mate."

"My lovely."

"My only."

"Mine."

I was sure now was the time they expected me to crack some wise ass joke, but I couldn't make anything come right now. This was far too important for some joke about ass rockets and orgies.

Although now that the thought was in my head, my insides were swimming, the feathers on my dress beginning to smoke and fade away.

"I am still yours, and I will protect you, as you protect me. Love you, as you love me. And I can promise that we will all be together after this. As one. In any way that you wish." I was amazed my voice didn't break there, to be honest.

"Is it you?" Drake began, that subtle line of insecurities that always carried with him bleeding through. His eyes shaking with as much fear as his voice. "You are still you?"

"Yes," I said, stepping closer to him, although I did not release the others from my grip. They shifted closer to me as I did to Drake, bringing our circle in even tighter. "I am still me. There is just centuries of me now. But I need this. I needed to be brave and return to the form that I was created in. You were the ones to give me that strength. All of you. I could never have done it without you. I can do anything with you."

I looked at Drake with those last words, leaning into him as I pulled him back into me, as I pressed my lips against his, letting my tongue press its way into him. To taste him. To taste the flame of his dragon, the sweet flavor growing as the powerful creature that was bursting inside of him in its own effort to meld against me.

"I am full of pride with you," I said as I pulled away from Drake, turning to Killian and pulling him into me, just the same. He welcomed me against him, his lips and tongue moving in a tango of fire and smoke as drops of his fire filled me. Hot and spicy. I craved more.

But that would have to wait.

"I will conquer mountains with you," I whispered to Killian before I turned to Jarron, the beautiful man already ready to take his place. He was as eager as Killian, although perhaps not as forceful. His touch was soft, his fire like sunlight against my tongue. Bright. Beautiful. I think I could have lost myself forever in that kiss.

In his heat.

But not yet.

Soon.

But not yet.

"I will forever be brave with you." My voice was soft, the rolling purr of my Phoenix pressing against Jarron before I pulled Zoe into me. Even as I stepped closer, the heat of her brothers raging through my veins, pressing against my back. Heat was everywhere, but it was hers that I wanted.

She tasted like sugar and maple, her smoke a liquid lust that filled my lungs as she kissed my back. Her free hand twisted around my waist, ready to pull me into her. To taste more of me.

To taste more of her. I moaned in want as the lips I had left behind pressed against my shoulders. My neck. My back.

They were everywhere, and I wanted all of them.

Everywhere.

"Together we are strong."

Kisses littered my skin, more and more of the feathers falling to ash on the floor.

"Do I really need to be witness to some kind of goddess orgy? I can watch porn on my own time thank you very much," Callay said loudly from behind me, her accusation pulling Drake and Zoe away. Killian and Jarron, however, took a step closer, hands winding over me.

Interesting.

I would have to see how deep that would go later. Jarron must have caught the devious look in my eye. The guy was grinning ear to ear. I unwittingly stepped closer, letting my hand trail up the side of his thigh. He shivered. This was neither the time or the place for this, but I wasn't about to stop myself either. It was hard to control myself when he stood there, bare chested and beautiful. It was just those pants. The ugly as sin brown corduroy had to go. And I needed to control myself.

"Besides," Callay continued, pulling herself to standing, like she was going to barge her way into battle right then and there. "I only see two bodies here and I am pretty sure there are four baddies, shouldn't we be sending in the cavalry. Or throwing Ceres body through the window or something?"

"I like that plan," Jarron chuckled, his voice strained underneath my touch. I was sure he wasn't talking about the plan of throwing his father through the window.

He stepped closer to me, his heat radiating through the dress I had made for myself, mixing with my own until everything was fire. I leaned against him enough that I doubt anyone would notice.

I was already failing, the look in Xi's eyes was something close to murder.

I laughed and stepped away. I would have to finish that little escapade later. Too bad I was leaving the poor guy in quite the situation. Corduroy was already too tight and uncomfortable to begin with.

"I'll do that," Jarron said with a laugh, turning toward Ceres and away from us with too much gusto.

"Stop," I said, holding up my hand and careful to keep the same magic I had used to pull them into me locked away. "The window must stay intact. The window cannot be broken. Not yet."

"I have been wanting to break that thing for years," Jarron protested, his back still to us.

"You're not the only one," Killian and Drake said in unison.

"It will be broken. But not yet. Not until we need to call him. It is not just Parris who got away. Fallon was here. Fallon is always here for a reason."

"Yes," Xi said, flipping her hair back in the oil slick shimmer of her Unicorn. "She will take the Vampire back to the monster I created."

"And the girl...?" I really didn't want to know the answer.

"She and the knife are gone," Hilda had too much sass in her voice, and I about caught her on fire right then and there.

"I am going to be really fucking pissed if something happens to my daughter," Callay snapped, from where she had finally pushed herself to standing. "She was right here, and you all lost let that damn vampire take her."

Shit. All of my fears were a horrible reality, of course I pick right now to return to my former glory. I had a whole pile of shit that I needed to clean up. It was my shit, but still. Damn it all!

"And I didn't kill the demon." Flames flashed as my feet tried to pick themselves up off the ground again. Not yet, I was going to need my energy. "Which means that Lilly will pull him right to her. And if Fallon took them to Mattia..."

"We already got that far," Xi said with a sigh. "What we need is you to fix your mess so we can fight what's coming."

"What was that you said about Xi making mischief?

Seems you made well enough on your own." Hilda asked, her yellow eyes dancing against the red and gold of the fire that was rippling over me.

"Unicorns make mischief. Phoenixes make explosions." I turned toward the mural, and to the figure of the man that had confused me before. The same one I hadn't understood back in Henry's cave.

Now I did, and it was like a stab in my heart. If only I could go back and return the knife to the mirror for safe keeping. Stop all of this from happening. Hell, perhaps I could steal Rana's power for longer and go back to where this all began. Put it right from the start. But time doesn't work that way, my sister had taught me that. It was the last thing she said before I stole her power. Before I had hidden her away.

"We cannot defeat these demons with only three, Elliana, you know this." Xi stepped right beside me, staring at the window as I was. "It's time."

"I know," I said, stepping to the window, right to the old man with the flyaway eyebrows. Old man, young woman. It didn't matter when the young woman disguised as an old man was staring right at you. "Rana, we need you."

The figure of the man blinked once, the glass shimmering as he gave one solemn nod and I lifted my fingers, pressing them into the glass, the surface cool and hot, as it had been in the mirror back in Henry's dungeon of a bedroom.

And just like then my fingers moved through the glass, into the world beyond, into the world of death, destruction, and pain.

"It's time," I whispered again. The bushy-browed man pinched his eyes shut before her hand wrapped around mine, everything heating and sparking with the contact. My

Phoenix was screaming, her bird was rejoicing and with a gentle tug, I pulled her through. A blast rattled the cave, a million cracks breaking through the glass, shattering it in a spider web around the man, and breaking him out of the prison. The mask I had placed on her fell away as she lithely stepped through the pane, leaving behind a shattered past. As cracked as it was, it was amazing the thing was still holding together.

The bushy haired man had gone, leaving a girl standing in the middle of the dank cave, staring furiously at me through golden eyes.

"This will not end well," she hissed, the hair that she normally kept close shaved having grown out into kinky locks as flyaway as the feathers of her gryphon. No wonder the man's eyebrows had grown so much bushier over the years. "You have released me, Elliana. He will know. He will come for me."

"He will come for me too, child. And don't worry, I have fought them long enough that I know the tricks. I'm ready," A scratchy voice hissed near the door, everyone turning as one to the newcomer. Who, for the first time I didn't feel quite so much like a scolded child to see.

"Suvi."

"I came as you asked," the old woman said with a nod to Xi, and a smile toward me. "I think it's time to finish this. And there is no better way to summon a demon and a Warlock than with a bit of bait."

14

KILLIAN

THE MOMENT XI, the real Xi and not the snickering child, stepped into the massive throne room, dark magic zipped through Killian's veins. As it had on the mind-beach that had almost killed him.

The volatility of his magic increased with each step the goddess took, each word sending it flaring as though she was calling for it. It was hard enough controlling his power with both his sister and his creator standing side by side.

So, why not add to that?

Suvi walked into the blood-soaked hall like it was a Denny's, her old lady strut setting off a nuclear bomb inside of him. She pulled at his magic the same way. Pulled at the murderous blood lust.

Saliva built in his mouth, his dragon's claws pressing against his fingernails in need to escape. Something made worse by the magical pressure that was now trying to press through every pore.

"Suvi!" Zoe's screeched exclamation pounded against his temples as she ran past him, knocking her shoulder into his in an attempt to reach the old woman. The two of them embraced while his brothers stared, dumbfounded.

How had they not seen this one coming? Seeing as the Unicorn was also the smug kid from the circus, maybe it was just overload.

He could understand that.

"I didn't think I would ever see you again," Zoe said with a gush, the air around them shimmering with a white light that created a halo around both of them.

No wonder the violent need had gotten so much worse. Suvi was the same. The same light that lived in Zoe lived in Suvi. That wasn't the magic of a witch he had seen in her before. It was light. The polar opposite of him.

He wanted to kill her. Kill them both. This uncontrollable magic was burning the flame of his dragon right against his tongue. Attempting to take control.

The Unicorn was right. This power was a curse. There was nothing good of something that brought this much death.

If this was even a quarter of what that demonic Mattia had been fueled by...

Killian bit his tongue and stepped away from the others. He really didn't want to be the one to admit that such dark things were waiting. Both in him and in others.

"You have light in you, I see?" Suvi said, the cracks in her voice not as prominent as they had been back at the circus, in fact, she didn't appear quite so old. Quite so fragile. Shame. Would have made it easier to snap her in two.

God damn it!

He shouldn't be thinking like this! It had to stop. He had to make it stop. He took another step back, closer to the cracked front of the mural.

"Yes, I was blessed with this gift."

"Blessed? Oh, child. Even the best of gifts can be a curse. Even the powers with the most light can bare the most dark. I would not call it a gift as you would, child. You must beware of your alternate for their power..." That was all he could take.

Killian turned to where Ellie and the woman she had pulled out of the glass were standing.

Somehow a woman that emerged from a mural seemed the more normal scene than what was unfolding behind him.

His chest heaved as black smoke swirled around his feet, dark clouds pulling themselves up from hell to smother him. Ready for what was to come next.

What came next, however, was a worried mate, and Rana. It was clear by the way her dark eyes were downcast that she was not an instigator. The dark-skinned beauty was a peacemaker, not like the smirking redhead that was taking a step toward him, his dragon purring and pulling towards her with each step.

"Oh, my dragon," Ellie smiled, her hand pressing against his suit, right over his heart.

With the heat that was radiating from her touch, she might as well be burning a hole through it.

"You are so strong to walk away from that. To walk from that power. I believe Xi was wrong about you, about your soul. I love your soul, Killian, as I love you."

It was the same girl, she sounded the same. She looked the same.

But oh, so different.

An ache pulled through his chest with how different she was. How strong. Powerful. It was beautiful, and their connection was stronger than ever. He still missed the spunky girl that swore like a sailor and was apt to make things accidentally explode.

Then, as if she could sense his longing, and maybe she could, her face broke into a wide grin, the tip of her tongue poking out from between her teeth.

"I..." he stalled, his heart twisting. Her smile didn't even falter.

"I know," she said, her hand sliding down his arm to grasp his hand, leaving a trail of heat behind. He could have sworn he felt the scales of his dragon prick through his skin at the heat, as though she was calling his beast to attention.

"Let us destroy the monster that wishes to destroy us all, and then perhaps we can find a bit of normality."

"If normality is with you, then I am all over that."

Killian had been so focused on Elliot, that he hadn't noticed his brothers encroaching on his personal space like a bad dye job. Drake was right beside him, his Dragon growling through his chest so loud that even Killian jumped. Drake's Dragon had never made that sound before.

"Woah, excited some, baby brother? I'm loving this new improved Ellie, but it looks like I might have some competition," Jarron said with a chuckle, flashing his golden eyes at Ellie with a wink.

Killian about punched him. Looks like he might have more than just Drake as competition.

They were both growling now. Killian wasn't going to be able to keep his own dragon locked away if that kept up. Ellie's intoxicating touch was already adding to the dangerous cocktail that was brewing inside of him. His little brother's injured dragon's attempt to make some kind of play was turning that cocktail into a Molotov.

It was blatantly obvious to everyone around him, too.

"Woah, Kills. Are you okay?" Jarron stepped right in front of him, hands spread out protectively.

Whatever evil was staring out of him must have been bad if Jarron wasn't trusting him.

"I just... it's too much..." The statement bit against his pride. Nothing had ever been too much for him.

"It's his alternate," Ellie said as she pushed her way around Jarron.

"What do you mean?" Yep, his voice was all dragon.

"When Xi passes on the power of her kind to another she divides it. Not because she must, but because she is a sardonic being...."

"Mischief," Rana cut in, stepping into the group, although she made eye contact with none of them. "Unicorns are creatures of mischief. She splits the power to create what she calls equality. Everything in balance, but only until those that hold each piece seek out the other and wreak havoc on their world."

"The halves must return to a whole," Ellie interrupted, the fire in her eyes trained right on Killian. "There is only one way for that to happen..."

Killian knew the answer to this one. "I have to kill Zoe."

"Kill Zoe?" Drake screamed in shock, cutting through any conversation on the other side of the hall and pulling the women's focus right to them.

"She holds the other half of my power. Power that was split and must be reunited."

"There will be no peace between the magic you hold until that happens." The goddess shook her head sadly, her tightly wound curls bouncing in opposition to the pain on her face.

Zoe was looking right at him now, Suvi on her heels as they practically sprinted over them.

"How did that happen? How did Zoe end up with the other half of your... the...? What did you do Killian?" Drake's eyes darted between his quickly approaching sister and their beautiful mate, as though deciding which one to protect.

It would be great if his baby brother would choose neither. He had no interest in hurting him. No matter how much he had infuriated him in the past.

"I gave the Unicorn a name of the person who I thought to be the most good. The most pure."

"And I suppose she didn't tell you what you were doing?" Ellie asked, Zoe practically to him now, thankfully the white light in her eyes wasn't beaming at him yet.

"She said it was my first act of villainy."

"I did warn you." The dark snap of the woman bit through Killian's quickly growing anger, the black smoke that billowed around him swallowing everything as he turned to the Unicorn, her eyes sparking as she shifted her hair behind her.

"You did not warn me of this, you siren." Every word growled from his throat, the tawny Hilda sliding back into a giggle as she looked between them. "You did not tell me that I would seek to destroy my own sister. That whatever *gift* this is would destroy us both!"

The Unicorn smiled, everything about her glittering in that prism of magic he had seen at the beach.

"I warned you of your villainy, Killian. As I did to Zoe." She gave the girl a nod, pulling Killian's focus, which might have been a dangerous action had his sister not been as mad as he.

"You warned me of the dangers of power, child." Zoe snapped, Xi flinched, her smile sliding off her face. Killian would have given her a high five if he wasn't so sure skin contact would have created some kind of explosion.

"You lied to us both. You must fix this."

Xi smiled, the tips of her hair beginning to change color, shifting into a rainbow of facets the same as the light that drifted over her. The beginnings of her shift. Killian nearly stepped back in fear and awe, but her next words stopped him in place.

"I will fix nothing, I have done nothing wrong, and when all plays out it will be for the better of our world, and the one above."

"How can you not take responsibility for this? You have cursed us to commit murder!" Each word grew in volume as the Unicorn's smug smile stretched in malice.

It was not a good look for her.

Hatred-filled murderous rage poured through him. Instead of flowing to Zoe, his sister now so close he could feel her warmth, everything was directed to the Unicorn. The damn beast that had tricked him.

That had cursed both him and his sister.

Mattia's hatred toward the beast made sense.

His own hatred toward the beast made sense.

He was still determined to fight it. He would not kill the Unicorn as Mattia was obsessed with.

He would not play into her games.

He would not kill his sister. He would not fight her. It may have been his first act of villainy, but it would also be his last.

He could only hope that Zoe felt the same.

"She has done nothing, Killian." Zoe snapped, lunging toward him before Suvi held him back. "You were the one to give her my name. You have your own fault in this."

Okay, so Zoe did not feel the same way.

It was going to be really hard to not kill her if she kept acting like this.

Killian's brow pulled into a scowl, his fist clenched against his suit as he took a step back. Both Dragon and magic were winding back up as everything around him unraveled. Time to derail this before the twist in his spine became even worse.

"Can we get back to throwing Ceres out of that damned mural?" Ellie said with her familiar moan.

Thank god. It was enough to pull him off the ledge.

"Agreed. I have no plans for murder and I am ready to show all of those bastards down there what we have done," Killian had waited for years to watch the shell of the man tumble through the air, turning into nothing but a puddle far below. A red carpet, if you will, signaling the end of his reign, and the beginning of another.

Killian straightened his jacket subconsciously. Not that it mattered. When he made his appearance as their new King, it would be as his dragon, as was custom.

"Not yet," Xi said with that same tone he had heard when she had given him his magic. Once was enough for him to know not to double cross the goddess. "We need to be ready to present the Queen to those below, first. And we are not ready for that yet."

"Wait. Queen?" The eager growl of his dragon turned volatile, hitting against every nerve ending and pulling him to attention.

"Do not be dismayed, Darling. All will be well in the end," Ellie answered, the feathers of her dress swaying away as she stepped closer to him. Even the exotic sway of her hips wasn't enough to drown his bubbling anger.

It was swirling at him from all directions. He hadn't expected it from Ellie.

"It will only be well when I am King," he snapped, rounding on his mate. "I have done everything to save my people, to gain the crown and take my place as the Alpha of the dragons! She has not retained the right to take on that role."

Killian turned to his sister, his growl shaking the fragmented glass with the sound like a bell.

"You have got to be kidding me," Zoe said, the tinkling laugh turning into a mocking guffaw as her eyes narrowed toward him. The opaline shimmer sucked all the color away from her, and all of his control from his soul.

"No, Zoe. No, I'm not." His smoke swirled around them, mixing with her white light in a show that was becoming too frequent for his liking. "I spent years fighting behind the scenes. Fighting our father, seeking to undermine him. Doing it all, while working to save our people from vampires, and I guess demons."

"And I spent hundreds of years before you. You don't really want to get into a dick measuring contest with me, Killian, because I will win every time." She took one large step closer to him, her eyes all white. The lightning of her magic was everywhere.

It was a terrifying sight, the way their emotions blended together and battled against each other.

Their magic swirling, dragons growling.

Killian needed to move away. But his sister's Dragon was pulling him forward. The crown and the role that he had fought for for years was locking him in place.

"I don't even have a dick, Killian, and I will still out measure yours every time," she continued inches away from him now. Her teeth were clenched and bared, the sharpened points of her dragons' beginning to present themselves.

She snapped them once, white magic mixing with her fire as smoke dripped between her teeth. Don't kill her.

Please, don't kill her.

"This is why you don't play with fire, Xi," that Hilda girl said with what was quickly becoming the most irritating laugh he had ever heard. "She was already in line to take her role, and you had to go fuck things up."

"She will still take her place," Xi said, the smooth voice of the beautiful goddess breaking yet another one of her flimsy promises.

She had never meant to lift him into a higher role as she had said. She had never intended to tell him *everything* and watch him take his crown as she had said. She had played him to get what she wanted.

Fine. He would play.

He snapped, once twice, three times. Each pinch of his fingers against nails produced a picket, the little demonic sprites leaping from his hand and straight to Zoe's face. The tiny things clawed and pulled when he swung his hands behind him, fingers flexing as he lifted the former king from the ground. With one swing, he released him from his magic and sent the fallen King soaring.

"No!" Ellie screamed, her hands flying forward to stop the flesh and limbs of the king from continuing their journey, but the Unicorn laughed, a flash of light filling the room as the dead man continued on his way.

He impacted against the glass with the final blow the frightening mural needed, sending pieces shattering over everything, and the king hurling through the hundreds of feet of air to the already disrupted square down below.

It only took seconds before the screams reached them.

"Shall we measure now?" Killian said with a wink, his

low chuckle breaking the stunned silence of every face around him.

"Well, damn it!" Ellie screeched from somewhere behind their standoff, the girl sounding as close to Ellie as she had for the last few minutes. "You guys had to go and fuck everything up, didn't you?"

15

DRAKE

He was gone.

Well, he was gone from the moment Drake had killed him, but now the old man who had terrorized so many was really gone. Thrown out the window and turned into nothing more than a red smudge.

"Shame. I wanted to do that," Jarron said, a smile pulling at the corner of his mouth.

He nudged his brother as though the two of them were sharing some great joke, nodding toward the ledge that they were both standing by. Drake had no sympathy for what had happened to his father, but he could find no humor in this. Not with the screaming and laughing and snaps of magic that was going on behind him.

"Be glad you didn't. I don't think you would have survived that," Drake said, nodding back to Zoe and Killian.

The two were reaching a level of shouting that was more dragon than man. Everything was shaking under the weight of their Dragons' growls, even the shards of glass around his feet were jumping with every rebuttal the two threw at each other. They may not have shifted yet, but Zoe's arms were completely covered with scales, and Killian's eyes were pure black. Although that might have been from whatever was possessing him.

There was no way this was going to end well.

Drake would have moved further away from the two, but unless he wanted to take the same tumble his father did, he was glued to the spot. One misstep would have been it for him. His dragon was too injured to fly, let alone try to make a play for the throne.

Which could easily be what Jarron was planning, given the way his eyes narrowed at the ant sized people gathering around his father's carcass. They were already gazing up to the two shapes that were peering over at them, waiting for one of them to shift and declare themselves King.

One shift. It was all it would take.

"They are kittens compared to what we went through," Jarron said, cracking his knuckles and taking a step, the toes of his ugly loafers hanging over the edge. "If they don't tire themselves out soon, they are going to find that crown claimed."

Guess Drake should have placed a bet on that one.

"You thinking of making a play, Jarron?" Normally Drake would give him a nudge, but the guy had moved even closer and was now so far over the edge that even a tap would send him tumbling down.

Maybe that's what he wanted.

"Naw. I mean. I'm not scared of them, and I can take Killian. The guy's a push over. But Zoe...," he paused, looking back as Callay and Suvi tried to pry the two apart, Xi and Ellie arguing right beside. And that damn Sphinx was still laughing.

Drake was hating her more and more.

The two witches, or whatever they were, weren't able to

pry his siblings more than a few feet apart before they snapped back together, everything around them glowing and shimmering. "Killian has a death wish to even attempt that." Jarron sighed, taking a large step away from the ledge before taking a small step back from it. Drake wondered what would be more deadly, stepping between two arguing dragons, or stealing the crown from them.

"You ran away and hid, Zoe. I stayed!" Killian busted free of Callay who was still trying to hold him back. Batting her away when she tried to regain her grip.

"You stayed because you had killed thousands of Fae, Killian. You stayed because you stood by him! Because you were like him!"

Drake flinched as Zoe's outburst turned into a scream and a flash of white light that ran through the room in a blast of air, or whatever it was those two could do now. Didn't matter, it still slammed against him, sending him stumbling back.

Right out the window.

Or it would have if Ellie wasn't to him in a minute, her hand wrapping around his waist and pulling him against her. Good lord, she was so small against him. But those circus muscles, or goddess muscles, or whatever they were, were so tense and tight. She was so powerful, even if her tiny frame was quivering against him, as though she was the one who had almost fallen to her death.

With his weak dragon he wasn't sure that even he could survive the fall.

"Let's not test those wings quite yet," Ellie whispered in his ear, the heat of her breath sending him into a matching shudder.

"Trust me, I'm not testing anything." Even his voice was

shaking, although that might have been more from the near fatal plunge.

"Not yet," she whispered, her fingers running down his arms and sending yet another shiver through his spine as her fingers rubbed against the grit of her own ash.

"What are you talking...?" His question was drowned by a screech, a spiral of black and Zoe's fist impacting against Killian's jaw.

"Damn it," Jarron said, racing away from the open mural, spitting a line of golden fire between the mess of fists and hair and magic.

"Why don't I be the one to break up this show, then? Never mind all the goddesses that are standing around, I'll be the one to solve this mess," Jarron said with more of a snap than usual.

The guy walked between the two battling parties as he always did, hands outstretched as though he alone was going to stop them from shooting black smoke and magic and fire and whatever else was involved in their duel.

Probably would have, until he realized as everyone else had that he might have gotten himself in over his head.

"This can't be good," Drake said, Ellie pulling him after her as she sprinted into the middle of the fray, right next to Jarron.

"Get out of the way, Jarron," Killian snarled, more of those little fiery demon things dripping from his fingers to gnash and flame on the stone floor beside his feet.

"Not going to happen, bro. I know you well enough to know how dumb you are being. Like full-on idiot level. You don't want this, Kills." Jarron stared right into Killian, leaving Zoe fuming and *glowing* behind him.

She was freaking glowing.

Too many impossible things were happening for Drake

to be surprised anymore. Except that this wasn't so much impossible as it was dangerous.

And Jarron had thrown himself right in the middle of it.

"You know him because you fought with him, you killed thousands right beside him. But you do not know me, Jarron. The vile *golden prince*. Perhaps I will end you first. Make you pay for what you have done." The colorless light around Zoe sparkled underneath each growled word, her hand lifting in what was going to be an attack.

No. What the fuck had happened to her? Whatever was inside of her was making it so she wasn't thinking straight.

"Jarron may not know you, but I do." Drake had always been a bystander, always been the last to speak up, and perhaps the first to run. But he couldn't stand back and watch his sister become a monster.

Stepping away from the warmth in Ellie's touch, he threw himself between the burning attack that was growing on Zoe's fingertips, his back pressed against Jarron's. This close, he could feel both growl and heart of his brother.

Even he was scared, and he could shift and spit fire on them all. Drake was seriously regretting this decision.

Too late to go back now.

"This is not you, Zoe." Drake continued, thankful when his voice did not shake. "You fought for hundreds of years for life. Yours. Everyone around you. Killian..."

"Took it all away. He killed them all. He tried to kill me," she interrupted, the power still dripping from her, the light growing. "I think it's time I repaid the favor."

"You want to kill me, Zo. You want all of this for yourself." Killian's howl roared over the cave, the sound of his dragon blending with the giggle of the Sphinx, the girl joining the Unicorn as they stood between them and Ellie, her and the woman she had pulled from the mirror fighting their own battle to get past them.

Fucking Unicorn. They said she created mischief, looked more like she bathed in it.

"I deserve it all to myself, Kills. And after what you did to me, to all of them, you deserve nothing but death."

The black smoke that was drifting around Killian was frightening, but the sparks of power that sprang around his sister were downright terrifying. He didn't see how they could survive the blast from whatever Zoe was brewing.

He and Jarron stepped back against each other, the two of them plastered and shaking together. Surrounded by fighting goddesses, and confused circus owners, and a former slave that looked as confused. And through it all, that blasted Unicorn was watching everything with a look of joy in her eyes.

"That may be true, but not all of my actions have been in death. I worked to save so many."

"Too little, too late, Kills. All you wanted was the crown. You are going to have to fight me for it." It was as though Zoe didn't even see them. She sent an attack right for Killian, a ball of what appeared to be lightning crackling through the air.

Drake was barely able to get out of the way, dragging Jarron down with him, the blonde prince so focused on their older brother that he didn't even see it coming.

"Thanks..." Jarron groaned as Killian lifted his hand, a spike of black smoke shredding the attack and sending the scattered bits over them like stars.

Painful burning stars that dug themselves through clothes and flesh until he felt as if he had been stabbed a million times.

"I do not want to fight you," Killian roared, even though

he countered with a bit of smoke and few more of those fire demon things.

Shit. Trapped on the floor under a demonic magic fight was not the best idea.

"Then you shouldn't have started this!" She yelled, another attack traveling on the word. That one deflected as easy as the first, the sparks of painful fire sending both Drake and Jarron scuttling away from the battle.

There was no way they could stop this. One of them would die. Well, unless the super powered goddesses or witches or whatever stepped in, but that damn Unicorn was hell bent on stopping that from happening.

"She said that giving her a name would be my first act of villainy. But she was wrong. It wasn't mine. It was yours." Killian shook his head, the last of his curls falling away from what used to be a braid as he turned to Ellie. "I love you baby, but I can't be here anymore."

That was the last thing he said before he turned and stormed out of the door, everyone left standing staring dumbfounded at the door.

That was not the ending anyone had expected.

Zoe, however, recovered first turning toward the open maw of the cave where the window used to be.

And laughed.

Laughed with a sound that echoed and grew, mutating into something that was very much not his sister.

Drake turned, meeting Jarron and Ellie's eyes as they looked at the blood-stained door that stood closed behind them.

"What the fuck just happened?" It was the only thing Drake could think to say. It was like they were stuck in a bad 70s sci-fi and his brother and sister had switched heads.

He knew neither of them.

"Badness happened," Ellie said with a sigh, still looking at the door before she turned to them. "Don't let Zoe out of your sight, and don't let Xi do... don't let her do anything. Rana will help."

She nodded to the beautiful goddess from the window and pressed her lips into a tight line, taking off after Killian as Zoe let her dragon scream in a full howl, the sound of the beast rattling over everything and sending the shocked cries of below into screams. She didn't even need to shift. Every dragon knew the screech of her roar, they knew exactly who was taking control.

"Shit." That one was from Rana.

16

ELLIOT

"KILLIAN, WAIT!" My plea echoed off the stone walls, blending with screams that were echoing from somewhere both far behind, and far below.

Damn it, Zoe didn't take long to wreak havoc on everything. Everyone else would have to handle it, I had more important things right in front of me.

"Will you please slow down?" Yes, I could catch up to him, but between the dark smoke of hell and the low growl of his dragon, I wasn't about to.

I knew him well enough to know that this needed to be on his terms.

"Please?" That time he gave me a glance back, his eyes pure black and terrifying. If I hadn't seen that level of evil peer back at me before I might have turned and high-tailed it back to relative safety.

Almost did anyway.

The sheen in his eyes was darker than the monster I had both created and slept next to for hundreds of years. Darker than all of the holders of dark magic that Xi prided herself in creating. Dark, frightening, glistening with a hint of a tear. There might have been a bit of humanity staring at me from behind those ebony depths.

I could rejoice that she hadn't ruined him completely, but it didn't matter. This time Xi had gone too far.

"I can't stay back there, Elliot. It's not safe." Pain dripped from his voice and stabbed against my heart as he turned away from me, picking up his pace.

"I know, Killian. But you don't need to go off and brood on your own, either." I sped up, although still not enough to catch up to him. Just enough not to lose him in the serpentine of tunnels that made up this place.

"I don't want you to get hurt." He could make a million excuses; I was still going to bat away each one.

"Honey, I reemerged from a pile of ash after being stabbed by a blade made from brimstone me and Rana stole on an excursion to hell in which the devil fell in love with her and I had to hide her in a mirror to keep her safe."

That got him to stop, the burly man turning toward me with a look of pure confusion. I smiled, fully aware I was being a tiny bit smug.

"Nothing is gonna touch this." I ran my hands down the feathers of my dress. Twisting my lips deeper into that smug grin. The look felt familiar and recent, which is probably why the corner of Killian's mouth twitched.

"Unless you want to." Seductive, alluring, this felt familiar. Although not as recent. And definitely not as welcome. Killian's smile fell, the incoming scowl the exact opposite of what I had expected.

"While I like this side of you, baby. I have bigger problems than figuring out how to reveal those curves of yours. In case you forgot what you told me a second ago, I am doomed to kill my sister..."

"I remember." I interrupted in an attempt to comfort

him. Instead his eyes narrowed, twirls of black smoke dancing behind him like some kind of demonic wings. An extension of both his soul and the infection that lived inside of him.

I stepped back. I had pushed it too hard, too fast.

"Then leave me alone so I can figure out how to fix it." As dark as his soul had become, humanity bled from each word and I threw caution to the wind, taking a step toward him.

"Which is why I need to come with you. You can't possibly think that I am taking my sister's side in this. She made a mistake, Killian, and I have every intention of fixing it. Of helping you. Let me help you."

He gave one huff, nostrils flaring with twists of smoke before he turned on his heels, expensive rubber soles squeaking as he sprinted further down the tunnel.

I was so going to take that as an invitation.

Keeping my magic and power restrained inside of me, I took off after him, running down the tunnels in order to keep pace. I would have given anything to lift my feet off the ground and soar after him, let my fire protect him, wrap both soul and power around him.

But again... slow.

No, I didn't think Killian was some kind of wounded animal that was going to attack and slit my throat at any moment. But given the out of control nature of his magic, it was a risk. He didn't know what he was doing, and if he did and had meant to summon those demons... Well, we might have a whole other issue.

I raced around the last corner that he escaped down, not wanting to lose sight of him, and instead slammed right into the mighty width of his back, his muscles rebounding against me like I was on some kind of springboard.

"Ooof!" I stumbled back, ready to slam into stone before he caught me, his arm twisting around awkwardly to catch and press me against him.

"Quiet, baby. Someone's there," he said, his voice rumbling against where my cheek was pressed against his back, the low growl of his dragon following behind.

'My mate.' His dragon's low call of ownership was like a lightning bolt to my already flaring need of him.

Oh lord, the feathers were fluttering again. The troublesome bird inside of me was getting too needy.

I mean, I wasn't opposed to being naked in any sense, but this really wasn't the time.

"Did you hear that? It sounded just like her," some unfamiliar dragon said from around the corner from where we were hiding. I pressed myself into Killian more, the growl of his dragon having changed.

I sure as shit wasn't trying to hide, but if Killian lost control and went after whoever was there, I needed to be ready to stop him and take out the others before they got hurt.

Easy.

"I don't believe it." A second voice said, sending Killian's beast into an even deeper growl. Dangerous seeing as the two were growing closer. "I saw her die. Besides, did you see who was standing behind the mural? It looked like..."

"Don't say it. He's dead."

"So is Ceres now. We need to hurry and get out of here before the whole city falls apart."

Footsteps drowned out the last of Killian's low growl, grumbles blending together and fading away until we were left in silence.

"I fought for years, Ellie,' Killian said after a moment, his arm still wound around me awkwardly, holding me against his back. "I wanted the crown. I wanted to fix everything."

My heart turned into a rock in my chest, tense and tight and slamming into my ribcage with every beat.

"Do you believe Zoe will do the same thing?" Let the thunderous pounding commence, the question was sitting on treacherous ground, and with the way Killian was holding me against him, I damn well couldn't avoid it.

"I know she will. Or she would. I don't know if what I see in her eyes is a danger in her, or the danger of the two of us together. I don't know what to think anymore." His voice was dark, the air around us growing black. He was really going to have to learn how to control this before he killed someone, other than Zoe.

Damn it.

I hadn't realized how much my Phoenix had bonded to her before, but that one thought sent her into protector mode, against Killian. Who I was also trying to protect.

Talk about being pulled in opposite directions.

I pushed the stubborn bird away. Zoe wasn't here to protect and I needed to get a hold of myself.

I needed to focus on Killian.

"Say it's just the connection between you two, and the good is still in her, do you think she will?"

Killian exhaled, his arms loosening as he pulled me around to face him, the green in his eyes finally making a return.

The emerald color shimmered, even in the dim light of the cave it drew me closer to him. My fingers were already winding through the dirty and tattered hem of his jacket.

"I don't think the crown is the problem anymore." Killian stepped back, weaving his fingers through mine as he pulled me into what I thought was another tunnel. It could have easily passed for that with the amount of stone and rubble that consumed every inch of the massive place.

Between the ruins and the now shattered eye that had hovered above the city, Rydaim was unrecognizable. I had only been here once before, but I doubt repeat trips would have helped me to flesh out the remains of the buildings as something more than a dystopian playground.

It wasn't until Killian had pulled me into one of the tilting houses, and into what vaguely looked like a white marble kitchen that I knew where we were.

I was amazed Killian had found his way at all.

"Damn Dragons," he muttered, kicking some marble and what may have once been a cabinet door to the side.

"Damn Phoenix's, you mean," I gave him a wink as he pulled me past the kitchen and toward a hall that looked like something you would find in a funhouse, the planks all folded in on itself.

"You didn't do this, Elliot."

"Actually, I did, when I saved your ass, remember. I was all explosions and fiery and shit. It's actually sad I didn't have memory of all my powers. I would have loved to see how much more of Parris' face I could melt off."

That time I got a snicker. A tiny little snort of a sound that escaped before the darkness took over again. I took a step closer to him, over the wooden sea of a floor and towards the green glowing room that was our target.

"Well, instead, maybe you could melt off that Unicorn's face."

"I'm not going to do that," I grunted as I nearly lost my footing, slipping on wood and falling against the wall that was as splintered as the floor.

"Why not?" Killian's voice was strained as he pushed a heavy slab of what looked like mahogany out of the way, letting the green light flood out of the room and over everything. The hallway looked so much worse, so much more horrifying with that green tint over everything. "Afraid you can't take her."

"Ha ha!" My sarcastic laugh was rewarded with a smile and an extended hand as he pulled me into the room. "I can take her. I'm not dumb enough to start another war between sisters when I haven't fixed all the problems I made with the last epic battle that I also happened to start."

"So you can't take her." He deserved the icy look I gave him.

"You don't want to see the full breadth of my power, Killian. Of any of us. It puts all your black smoke to shame."

He flinched again, but instead of the tiny movements I had seen so many times before, he looked as though he had been punched in the gut, all color draining from his face.

"Does that mean you can take this away?" He waved his hand to the side, black smoke and demonic sparks falling from his fingertips. Hope was shining so brightly in his eyes, that the black smoke had faded away.

"It doesn't work that way. Only the Unicorn can remove the power she has given, and even then, it has been so long since she has done so that I am not even sure she remembers how."

His shoulders sagged, his sunken shape frozen in the middle of a room as broken as the rest of the house. An old billiards table was absolutely shattered behind him, bits of that same mahogany wood covering everything like splintered twigs.

"It doesn't matter, even if she won't fix this. I'm not going to kill Zoe. No matter what that damn Unicorn wants. Zoe can rule for all I care. The crown she wants isn't even the one I was fighting for. I was so blinded by whatever hatred is between us that I didn't notice."

"As she wanted." Maybe I would rethink that whole not starting another sister war. Even if I could stop it. I was getting to the point that I didn't think I could.

My sister was a bitch.

A royal bitch.

The look in his eyes was absolutely tearing me apart. I was to him in a second, my arms wiggling underneath his suit jacket in an effort to get as close to him as possible. Thank god he didn't shy away. He pulled me against him, his muscles holding me in place as his fingers trailed up and down my spine.

I hadn't realized how low my make-shift dress fell until the heat from Killian's fingers drifted over the ridges of my spine, tickling against the dimples and the round curves of my bottom.

It was my Phoenix that gave me away, the renegade bird chittering like an excited teenager. The feathers of the dress rippled, turning to smoke and leaving me bare, and his fingers to wander.

Instead of traveling lower, however, they traced their way back up, over spine and shoulders and over the soft tissue of my neck to gently lift my chin.

I only caught a glimpse of the gleaming emeralds in his eyes before his lips pressed against mine and my eyes fluttered closed. A moan echoed straight from my soul, and I leaned into him.

Killian's hold on me tightened, my feet lifting off the ground as the golden scarlet of my flames rippled over my skin, filling the air with the smell of burning wool.

I guess I wasn't the only one destined to be naked in this situation.

Fingers curling around his powerful shoulders, I clung to him, dragging my tongue across his lower lip. Nipping at it as I let the smoke of my phoenix mix with the heady aroma of his dragon. With his smoke. With his taste.

My head spun, my insides danced - that was all it took for me to lose control.

I snapped my fingers, what remained of his suit vanishing in the tiniest bit of flame, leaving him as bare as me. As bare, excited, and beautiful as me. Every inch of him pressed against me, making everything warm and wet and wonderful.

"I want you, Killian. I know the eve of war is not the most romantic of times but..."

"Beg." Holy fucking crap. His eyes were twinkling with a playful spark of fire, his dragon peering through him as the two of them took control, and turned me to nothing more than jelly.

"I want you..."

"No," he said with a shake of his head, long curls bouncing down his back. "Beg."

"Please..." I hadn't planned that moan to coat my voice, but it did anyway. "Please take me."

"Where?" The growl alone would have been enough to do me in. Everything was fire and pressure and wet and exploding.

I moaned with a sound that was coated with lust and fire. Killian smiled, his hand trailing over my arms as he guided me backwards, the darkness of his power dimming the haunting green light.

"Take me everywhere." Another moan, the hard points of his fingers against my hips trailing down my ass, pressing against me.

"Where?"

He was going to make me say it. Oh god. I audibly swallowed and tried to move back, but he wasn't about to let me go anywhere.

"Say it Elliot, because I don't want to wait anymore." He lifted me against him, fingers tracing the underside of my breasts as I wrapped my legs around him, desperate to bring him closer.

"Tell me where you want me. Tell me what you want me to do."

"Take me."

His chest rumbled with a low moan, chuckling as he spun, setting me on the edge of the now repaired billiard table. Guess he had more control over his power than I thought. A lot more control. Even the table was raised, right at the perfect height. Warmth pooled over my abdomen, down my hips, and between my legs in a swell of a different kind of fire as he placed himself perfectly against me.

So close.

Not quite.

Oh god, I couldn't breathe.

"You're mine tonight, Elliot." It was his dragon that said that, the words mixing with his own as he hovered over me.

I didn't know if it was day, night, or somewhere between. But I didn't care. I was his. Forever. "I'm yours. Take me."

His hands supported me, cupping my ass as he pulled me into him, his hands rough, his fingers pressing into me. Holding me into place. I wasn't going anywhere.

Thank god.

He pressed into me, every inch of him pressing into me.

"Holy fucking hell." I gasped, back arched, the words the only I could manage.

"No, baby. Hell is not fucking you. I'm fucking you."

Damn.

17

JARRON

"Well, now that demon number two is gone. Let's get down to business," Zoe turned from the window to face them, a smile on her face as the startled screams and shouts from the dragon's below drifted up to the throne room. The echoing call of her dragon was still ringing in Jarron's ears, lingering over everything as the powerful creature declared her place as Queen.

Ellie was right, an "Oh shit" was definitely needed here.

If she wasn't looking right at him, Jarron would have been the one to give it.

They had all officially gone from defeating a king, to losing a vampire, to getting stuck in a sibling fueled murder-race, to having a new Queen. Zoe looked downright smug about the whole situation.

Which seemed fitting, because all of the goddesses and the old Witch who stood beside her looked pissed as hell. The only one who didn't seem to care was Callay, but she had tucked herself against the stone wall in what Jarron could only assume she thought was "safe viewing distance".

Suvi looked ready to do some real damage to the *future*

queen. Her brow was pulled into a pinched scowl, her eyes a sky blue as they sparked with the same light Zoe's had. It was a look he had seen a few times on the old woman, but now that he knew more of what it was, it was a tad more frightening.

"What business is that, you fool?" Suvi spat, stepping around Hilda to step toe to toe with Zoe. Zoe didn't even flinch. "Because we were all set to summon a demon and end a war, but you seem to have something more selfish in mind."

"Selfish?" Zoe's light lifted to match Suvi's, the two sparking and glowing with what Jarron could only assume was magic. Seeing as the Unicorn was smiling like a loon in the background, it would have to be.

They said she liked to create mischief, as of right now, it was starting to feel like mayhem. Nothing good ever came of mayhem, Jarron had seen that enough. He wasn't really interested in watching that repeat itself with these two.

Jarron clenched his fists, mouth filling with golden fire, in case. Drake shifted his feet from where he stood beside him, lightly colored smoke drifting between the tight line in his lips as their eyes met.

First their siblings, and now this. Great, because they sure as shit didn't have bigger problems heading their way. They clearly had time to engage in some kind of cat fight.

Once upon a time, Jarron might have enjoyed this. Right now, he would rather throw himself out of the window, declare himself as Alpha and stop all this nonsense.

"I have killed the King, Suvi." Zoe continued, her voice grating in a shrill tone that only pulled his dragon closer to the surface. "After hundreds of years of fighting him, I have succeeded in my only real goal. I was born to rule, and now the crown is mine!"

Talk about a crazed bitch. Jarron had always thought his sister to be level headed if not a little power hungry. But damn, we were taking this to a whole other level.

"Excuse me," Drake said with a snap, taking one quick step toward the powerful women, who turned to him in unison. "I killed the King, Zoe. And Killian threw him out the window."

"Are you challenging me?" Zoe asked, Drake didn't take so much as a step back.

Jarron had to hand it to his baby brother. Zoe didn't look anything like herself. It was as though whatever white light that was inside of her had consumed her. It peered through her eyes and shimmered over her skin until even the tanned flesh of her dragon was looking like polished marble.

Drake may not take a step back, but Jarron was. Chances are high that his fire wouldn't do a damn thing to her anyway, and standing beside the beautiful woman that Ellie had pulled from the glass was the much wiser choice.

"Give me a break, Zo," Drake said with a wave of his hand, bits of smoke and ash falling from his fingers. "You know I wouldn't do that. Besides, if I wanted the crown. It wouldn't take much to *ask* you to give it to me."

Well, shit. If he hadn't meant to piss her off before, he sure as hell did it that time. The white in her eyes mixed with the bright red of her dragon's flame until she looked like a demon possessed, the sound that was rattling through her chest making the imagery even worse.

It wouldn't take much for Jarron to turn around and disappear through the door that Ellie and Killian had rushed through a few minutes ago. He needed to go check on his hoard anyway. Seeing as their house had been destroyed, he wasn't holding out much hope that anything was left. But it was an excuse as good as any.

"You wouldn't dare." Zoe took a step forward, and Jarron took a step back, closer to the door. He was half tempted to drag Drake with him. Let the goddesses take care of this. Callay looked to be a tad bit more interested now.

"I would. Especially if you keep acting like the bullheaded ass hat that you are currently playing as. I don't know about anyone else. But I am done with it. *Knock it off.* " Drake didn't even try to disguise his dragon in his voice, the rattle of command stronger than Jarron had heard in years.

Powerful. Strong. Even Jarron felt himself bend to it. His feet froze under him, locking him in place as the fourth goddess wrapped her hand around his forearm, pulling him back.

"You wish to be queen. *So, act like it. There will be no more killing here.* " Drake's dragon was even louder, his words knocking Zoe back a step, even as Hilda giggled again.

"*And you can stop that,* " Drake said, turning on her. "*It's driving everyone crazy.* "

"Holy shit..." Rana gasped as Hilda's hand flew to her throat, her eyes flashing with surprise before throwing daggers back at Drake.

The Sphinx stood silenced, Zoe stood restrained, and the Unicorn laughed, the light whinny of a sound echoing over the stone. She moved to the broken opening of the mural, staring down at the Dragon's whose faint screams and shouts for answers could still be heard drifting through air and against stone.

"Did you know your brother was touched?" The goddess asked in barely more than a whisper, her hand clenching around Jarron's bicep.

"Huh?" Jarron sputtered, shaking his head in confusion, an act that only caused Rana's eyes to widen more. She looked like a cartoon character.

"What are you talking about?" Jarron asked in full voice, but the goddess only shook her head, dropped her hand and stepped away.

Good god, or rather good goddess. These ladies were starting to drive him mad. It was like being stuck in a Rubik's cube. Except the cube was made of people and secrets and all together sucked. Which, now that he was thinking about it, was exactly like a Rubik's cube.

"You have created quite the problem, Zoe." Xi turned to face them as she took a step back, closer to the gaping hole where the mural used to be.

Zoe looked ready to both explode and rush after the woman, as if Xi was going to soar down and take her place. Even though she jerked, Zoe didn't move, she was still locked in place by the power of Drake's dragon. She was fighting against it with what Jarron would have to assume was her full strength. Not that he could tell. She didn't move, just looked constipated.

"The crown is up for grabs," Xi continued, ignoring Zoe's fight. "The first to get the allegiance of the people will be the new Alpha. The new king. I would assume any spies that Parris had in Rydaim have now reported the King's fall to their master. Which, if we are correct, is with both a demon and the man who has absorbed every bit of black magic I have created. All of them ready to come right to us."

Now would have been the perfect time for Jarron to turn around and high tail it out of there. But, that fucking Unicorn decided now would be a great time to start monologuing and giving answers.

"What does it matter?" Zoe spat, finally forcing herself to move one step closer. She still looked constipated, however. "They were always coming. Just let me fly down there. They are my people now. They will fight with us."

"Geeze, can I have some of her positivity Kool-Aid," Callay said stepping away from the wall. "I'd like to go into this disaster with that much hope."

"You are confusing tyranny with devotion," Xi said with a chuckle that was nearly as grating as her sister's. "Do you really think that those below will follow you blindly once you swoop down and declare your father's crown your own."

"It is the way of our kind."

So much for leaving, Jarron was laughing.

She rounded on him, that same terrifying light covering her. Good thing she was still mostly bound under Drake's dragon. She couldn't manage more than a step.

"You have been gone too long, sister," Jarron said in answer to her scowl, her eyes narrowing even more.

"It has only been twenty years, Jarron. You speak as if I don't know my people."

"You don't know them," Jarron said with a shake of his head. "You haven't been a part of them since before you attempted to overthrow their king, and that war began nearly a hundred years ago. You were raised in a Rydaim that was based in culture and strength and community. Now, they know only lust and tyranny. Brutality and dominance. And they certainly don't know you."

"Are you trying to take my crown, too?"

"I will if you don't get your head out of your ass," Jarron said with as much snarl as he could force into his voice, it was as though Zoe had lost all reason, as though whatever had consumed her had eaten her. Left nothing but a shell of greed that he didn't know.

"How dare you!" She screamed, her dragon growled, but she was still locked in place.

Drake's dragon gave a throaty chuckle, the guy turning to give Jarron a glance that said one thing. *Mayhem.*

Yes, that's exactly what this is.

"No one will take your crown," Xi said with an exasperated sigh, pinching her nose between her fingers. "That will be yours if you can conquer the demon who is on his way to retrieve it for himself. Or the Vampire that spent years grooming himself for the role, or the monster of my own creation who will take any form of power for himself."

"Then let me take the crown before that battle begins. Let me rule my people, and together we will fight! All of us. Together."

Ice dripped over Jarron's skin, his dragon's fire extinguished for half a breath before it came back, drenched in a panic he did not expect.

"Do you think it will be that easy? We already lost round one." Jarron said under his breath, this was all starting to feel like a suicide mission.

Adding the dragons into that fight would spell death for them.

"We will fight, Zoe. As Goddesses." Xi paused and nodded to her sister. "As holders of light magic," she nodded to Suvi and Callay who were standing together, both looking as though they had been slapped. "And as the Forgotten holders of magic who dwell below. My sisters and I will return their power to them, and they will stand by us and we have stood by them. But the dragons are not our allies..."

"They are my people." Was she even standing in the same room as them? Her stubbornness was easily going to get them all killed.

"They don't know you, Zoe." He began, taking a few very large steps toward her. So much for getting the hell out of there. "Wait until they do. Show them who you are, who you really are. I have seen the demon. We know of Parris. Danger is coming, the crown can wait. We need to get our act together for that battle. Hell, win it, and they will come to you."

"I will face them all, I am strong enough to face them all."

This time it was Callay's snort that pulled her attention, the Fae not even trying to hide the laugh. Damn it all, with the look in Zoe's eyes he was going to have to play human shield again. Except that the light in Callay's eyes was as white and terrifying. God, was he the only one that wasn't blessed by whatever assery the Unicorn was handing out? Well, him and Drake. Except Drake was touched, whatever that means.

And he was back to formulating an escape plan. He was always to throw himself in as peacemaker, but he was in over his head in this situation.

"Are you sure you pegged her for the right team, Xi," Callay said, her hair beginning to lift as she faced Zoe. The same thing happening to his sister.

Why was he not out of that damn door already? He was trapped like a deer in headlights.

"No offense, Zoe," she continued, folding her arms over her chest now. "I mean, I spent a century helping to keep you safe. But if this power has gone to her head this bad, imagine what a fake crown would do."

"Fake?" Zoe shrieked as Callay rolled her eyes with all the skill of a thirteen-year-old. Thank God, Suvi was already stepping in front of her, Drake's hold appeared to be slipping.

"You might be correct, Callay. I am beginning to think that I misjudged your souls. I looked at your lives, and assigned the power by the hope in your hearts. But I was wrong. You are not worthy to hold the magic of light."

"Perhaps you do not know what light is," Zoe took three

slow steps toward the Unicorn, each one labored as she finally broke through Drake's binding.

He opened his mouth to stop her, but it only took her one quick swipe to send him tumbling back, slamming into the stone wall with a hollow thud that sounded more like bone than stone.

"Holy shit," Jarron gasped as he ran toward his brother, Callay breaking past where she had been hovering behind Suvi and the others.

"Enough of this bullshit," Callay hissed as they helped Drake back to sitting, her hair still lifting in the invisible wind of her power. "You've got to stop her, Jarron. Xi and the others won't do anything. They don't operate that way. Fucking narcissists. You have to do this."

"Are you crazy?"

"No, just not quite ready to face that," Callay smiled with a nod to Zoe who was now racing toward the window, arms raised like she was a lord.

Damn it. Callay was right. What he wouldn't give to have the gall to say no, just once, and save his own skin.

"Perhaps you do not know what power is," Zoe continued, her voice booming as Jarron raced after her, ready to tackle her to the ground if needed.

"How about you show us later," He only got a few steps before she tried the same thing as before, her hand flexing as a white wind raced toward him, ready to take him out. He only barely dodged it, the power clipping him in the shoulder. It didn't throw him back, but it did send him stumbling to the side, back into Drake. And Callay.

With all their talk about how she shouldn't declare herself as queen, none of the Goddesses made a move to help. Xi stood before them, arms folded, smiling with all the mayhem that lived inside of her.

"Don't, Zoe!" Drake screamed above her laugh, spreading her arms and falling backwards, sending herself through the air. It wasn't even a second before her beast broke free, its roar rattling everything.

"This will not end well, sister," the darkest of the goddesses said, her voice mellow and so afraid that the emotion could have been plucked from the air.

"I don't know what you mean by not ending well," Jarron said untangling himself from Drake and Callay and pulling himself to his feet. "This is going to be a shit show."

18

ZOE

Long talons the color of rubies wrapped around the remains of the roof that used to top the massive hall in the center of Rydaim. The red sheen of the mural may have been gone, but the color remained. In my scales. In the long swathes of my wings that stretched over everything. In the blood of my father, as he lay in the drying pool of his own blood, his body mangled and crushed from the fall.

He was nearly unrecognizable. But enough of his face, and the clothes, and cloaks that he had always worn remained that you could make him out. It was clear what had happened, and what I was claiming.

The throne.

I had never wanted it so badly. I could scarcely think beyond ruling. Beyond power. Something inside me was recklessly driving me there, and I let it.

I chose my landing spot carefully, swooping over the city with wide wings and a screech that pulled every one of my subjects focus to the sky. To me. To their new ruler. To their new queen, the benevolent Queen that all my people deserved. Fae, Forgotten, and Dragons alike.

'This is my fate.'

Fear, awe, and shock lined their brows, their dragons knew what had happened even if they did not. Their primal instincts were already bringing them to me, bowing to me. Jarron, Xi, even Drake didn't know what they were talking about.

This was right. Even the powerful magic inside of me knew that it was right.

Stretching my wings, I extended my neck toward the ceiling, my dragon in full control as she released a roar that ripped over everything. Hundreds of my people jerked at the rumbling boom, covering their heads and shielding themselves from the sound and the rubble that fell from the already derelict buildings.

There had been so much more once. There would be more again.

I roared again, heart pounding against scales and human bones as another long line of my fire broke from my maw, stretching toward the ceiling and the shattered remains of the mural. The seven figures clearly outlined in the shadows. Watching me.

'Stare all you want. I will show you how wrong you are.

I roared again, ready for the answering roar of my new subjects. Waiting for the sound that would herald me as their ruler, as their Queen.

Instead, I was met with screams, shouts, and profanity from all sides. Rocks soared from the crowd, rubble turning into javelins as it hit my sides. Smacking against scales and wings as the crowds screams mutated into laughter. Had they grown stupid in the last few years? Rocks weren't enough to do more than irritate my dragon. Which they were doing quite nicely.

Well, shit, I knew what that meant.

I needed to take control of the situation, show them who they were dealing with, because they had obviously forgotten.

I released another roar, another line of fire ripping toward the ceiling and catching against the bits of black charcoal, like in the City of Soot. None of them noticed, the rocks were still coming, a few potatoes and tomatoes being added to the mix now.

Great. A waste of a perfectly good salad.

I was done with this insolence, my magic was done with the disrespect. Power buzzed with a need to explode and stop them all. That magic, however, was trapped inside of me. Trapped inside the very human part of me.

Well, shit. It would figure that I couldn't be both a dragon and a super-powered white mage... or whatever it was. Even Suvi hadn't given the power a name. Letting out another howl, I forced my dragon back into my heart, bones snapping into place, wings folding against my spine. Every bit of me was gripped with agony as the shift I had dreaded so much as a child ripped me apart.

I didn't let out so much as a peep. I never thought I would agree with my father, but standing here above them, there was one thing I did: Never let your subjects see your weakness.

Smoke swathed around me, the last of my fire dissipating at my dragon did, leaving me standing in the ripped and stained jeans and vampire dust covered hoodie that I had come into this place wearing. Too bad there hadn't been time to change into something more worthy of a Queen. Good thing they didn't seem to care. They were all staring up at me, the anger melting into awe.

"Zoe? Is that the king's daughter?"

"The first born of the king? How can it be?"

"I thought she was dead."

"I saw her die."

"This must be some kind of miracle!"

"That, or a cruel joke."

"Does it matter? Zoe has killed the king."

One last pebble hit against my shoulder, the tiny thing falling to the ground with a clink that echoed through the hush. Only awe and shock remained, all of their wide eyes and slack jaws hanging open. I turned, giving one last glare towards the figures in the open eye of the throne room, but only two were left. I could tell exactly who they were if only from the broadness in their shoulders.

Drake and Jarron.

"See, boys, I knew they would welcome me," I whispered to them.

The light I held inside pressed against my skin, gooseflesh pricking up as white sparked from my fingers. The tips of my hair lifted, heat and power blazing everywhere. Gasps rippled through the crowd, a few at the back turning and running into the allies, probably to get some of the stranglers.

They saw me for what I was. They saw the power. If they hadn't accepted me before, they would have no choice now.

"Dragons of Rydaim!" I yelled with the full strength of both voice and beast, the sound of my soul carrying over the whole city of Rydaim. "As you have seen, your king has fallen. The king who brought tyranny, and slavery, and hatred to a Kingdom that was once full of anything but. For years you have been guided by a monster who had been seduced by a vampire, his mind addled by one of our own. He brought the undead among you, to feed from you. To use you! He drew a line between us and those who used to be our companions. He ripped apart our kind, and our culture. I will put an end to that. I have killed the Tyrant!"

My magic was boiling, ready for its moment, for the power and crown to fall to me. Instead, their eyes shifted from one to another, more hushed whispers scratching together like a broken record.

"I don't believe..."

"...we can't let her..."

"This is abhorrent..."

My stomach fell, the darn thing twisting into knots of concern. What was going on? I was the new alpha. They should be welcoming me with open arms, not murmuring about the lies they had been spoon-fed for so long.

Blinding white energy heated everything, it straightened my spine, whispering the truth that I already knew in my ear. I don't know how I couldn't see it before. They had been blinded, their logic and dragons clouded so as not to see their true Queen.

I jumped down from the outcropping of the roof, hair streaming behind me as my human body soared the twenty or so feet to the mangled body of my father. His limbs shook as I landed with a crash, a piece of skull falling away and sending a wave of gasps over the crowd.

"I am the first-born daughter of the King who has deceived you for so long. I have defeated the monster, and the monsters who had controlled him. I bring you his blood, and his head." I gave them a smile, white sparks of power surrounding me as I dug my soiled tennis shoe into my father's chest, the already fractured bones giving way underneath me. I pressed harder, bending down and wrapping my hand around the hair of the bits of skull that was still attached.

With little more than a tug the whole head gave way, bones snapping, flesh tearing, blood still dripping as I lifted it to them. The jaw sagged open with the motion, the wide-open eyes staring, blankly into nothing.

Now, even the dragon inside him was gone.

Now, they slowly began to bow.

Finally. That should never have taken so long.

"My people!" I yelled, raising hands and head into the air as I addressed them, heart beating faster as more and more of them kneeled. "My Dragons! My--"

"Lies!" Someone near the edge of the crowd cut me off, their haggard scream turning every single head toward the woman with mousy brown hair, black beady eyes staring into me.

Fallon.

Shit.

Which only meant one thing. The demons that everyone had been talking about were here. The world-ending battle they had all been rambling about was going to start with me.

No worries. Without Killian and his ugly dark magic to distract me, I could finish her and the others off no problem. I let the lightning spark around me again, lest she had forgotten.

She didn't even flinch.

"Lies!" She spat again, her voice scratching in her scream. "The only tyrant you killed was yourself when you sold your soul for the pathetic power that is sparking from your fingers. You sold your life to a demon for power. You sold your soul and your dragon to a monster. All for a crown. You are the one whose head should be waved through the air. You are the only monster here."

I knew I should have sliced that sneaky little bastard when I had the chance.

"The only one who is lying here is you, Fallon." My dragon pierced my voice, my father's head falling to my side, fingers still weaved through the last of his hair. "You were created by a devil in sheep's clothing."

"That's only what they told you. You know nothing of my creator, or of the Vampires, or anything of this world beyond your own selfish desires. That is all you are, Zoe, first born of Ceres condemned to die for treason to the crown. You all saw her death." Fallon's voice lifted into something more like a squawk as she turned toward the crowd, dozens beginning to stand as she continued her rant. "You know of her fall. How can you kneel before her? How can you believe her, when she betrayed all of you? She does not deserve to rule."

She spoke the last words to me, more and more of the dragon's pulling to their feet as she stepped closer, those beady little eyes digging right into me.

"Let someone stronger than her rise up to challenge her for the crown. You all deserve an alpha with power, with strength, and with the confidence to do what is right the first time. Even if it means ending the life of the other."

Oh great, here we go.

Fallon was steps from the razed remains of the building I stood on. Every dragon behind her was on their feet now, every single one looking from me, to her, to their neighbor, waiting for someone to make the first move.

"Let us kill her for good this time," Fallon snarled as the bit of scalp I held on to gave way, my father's head falling to the stone with a sound like vomit and madness.

"You can try," I prodded, hurling the bit of hair and flesh

I held at the girl. "But the power that is within me, is stronger than the power within you. All of you."

I turned to the murmuring crowd, the horde pressing themselves closer to stare at me with both dragon fire and murder in their eyes. "You do not have the strength to defeat me. You do not have the wits."

"If it's only wits that matter than I believe this will be an easy fight to win." I jumped at the smooth voice, turning to the shorter man with bits of grey in his hair, his lined face smiling with a look that should have been friendly.

Could have been if his grey eyes weren't full of death. If they weren't staring into me with the same black magic my brother had. Except, instead of the grey smoke that I could sense in my brother's soul; this man's was ebony. His sucked all the light away.

I could feel it already attempt to devour mine.

I didn't need to ask who this was. I already knew.

Mattia.

Without a word, I swung my hand up, flinging what I thought was an attack his way, ready for him to tumble back and into one of the still standing buildings behind him. The light slammed against him, but he barely moved. He fucking blinked and all the power I had sent toward him vanished. It moved into him, like fog melting in the sun.

"Now, now, Zoe. I had expected more from you, but that was pathetic." Mattia took a step closer, that same pull tugging at both power and dragon, sending the creature growling. "You thought I would be so easy. You have no idea how to control that power you sold your soul for..."

"I sold nothing," I said with a growl, stepping closer and slamming my hand toward him, each finger sparking with lightning. Just waiting to seep into him and end him. "I will prove it to you. Darkness will never win out."

"Is that truly what you think? That those beautiful women are not evil? That they gave you a gift? That you can defeat me?" He snapped a finger before I could even touch him, black smoke so much darker than Killian's flooding the platform, wrapping around my wrists and forcing them behind my back.

Smoke, black as pitch, held me in place. Screams, gasps, and the renegade cheer broke from the crowd as Mattia snapped again, and either smoke or power forced me to my knees. I wasn't sure how he was controlling this, but it's not like it mattered. I couldn't fight it even if I did. I was trapped, and the crowd was erupting.

"You may think she is not a demon now, Zoe." His voice was like silk as he leaned over me, the closer he moved the more the lightning that ran through my veins was numbed. "But I know better. I have seen hundreds of years of her games. Only a true demon would curse you as she did. But no matter, I can take the power from you, as easily as she gave it. I have killed hundreds like you, and I will kill you as easily. Light can never stand up to dark. It can never rule out. I will never let it. And then I will take the crown from you, and I will rule the dragons in ways you would never dream!"

The crowd exploded in cheers of exhilaration, chants and pleas for my murder ripping through the crowd as Mattia stepped closer, my body sagging over itself. Oh god, he was right. They all were. It was a curse. With the power numbed, with all the confidence, and stubbornness drained from my mind, even I could see how much it was controlling me.

How much of a fool I had been.

And now, with a monster I could have never hoped to defeat hovering over me, I had to face that. I would die with it unless my brothers dropped from the eye, but I couldn't even turn to see if they were still there. They had abandoned me...

"I was a fool," I gasped, my limbs beginning to feel like jelly as more and more strength was sucked out me. As my dragon moaned in pain, as my fire began to extinguish.

"Yes, yes, you were."

19

ELLIOT

"Killian! Ellie!"

I'm not sure I had ever jumped to attention so fast. I probably would have jumped straight to the ceiling of Killian's billiard parlor and glued myself there. Except that one attempt to jump away from him sent Killian chuckling. His long muscular arms wrapped around me. holding me against him. Naked body against naked body, his fingers trailing up and down my spine as he continued to chuckle with that low rumble that had done me in over and over again.

My abdomen was already squirming with the sound.

"Ellie! Where are you!" Well, until that. Now it was squirm of a different sort. The voice belonged to Drake, and was growing closer. Given the angle of both voice and me he would be walking in to a great view of my ass and his brothers chest, the latter emblazoned with Phoenix tattoo.

Yeah, that couldn't happen. I tried to shimmy away from Killian again, but he was not having it.

"I will zap you away from me if I have to." I already had my super powers ready to go. He had one chance.

"Sure you will, Ellie girl. You are too kind hearted and love me too--" Chance exhausted.

I placed my hand against his bare ass, and let fire fly right into him. He was up and howling as he danced before me in all of his spectacular glory. I could watch that all day. Drake however...

"Put that ridiculous thing away!" Drake snapped from right behind us, his voice shaking with what I hoped was amusement at his brother swinging away in front of him. I however, was frozen. Well, locked in place. I wasn't frozen because every part of me had turned up to a million degrees as lust, desire, and confusion and twisted into an emotion that would better be left nameless.

"What in fuck's sake is going on here?" Drake continued, his nervous warble smothered by his dragon's growl.

"Fucking," Killian answered, his lips pulled into a broad grin as he placed his hands on his hips and puffed out his chest.

Oh god. Kill me now. This could not get any worse.

"Are you fucking kidding me?" Drake was shrieking. Okay, so it could get worse. Poor guy.

"No, just regular fucking." Killian cut Drake off, but the younger dragon plowed on.

"We are headed into some war that sounds like it's going to kill everyone and you guys are..."

"Fucking." Killian was still smiling. More sputtering occurred from Drake and I finally had the courage to sit up and face him with something other than my bare ass. Unfortunately for him, there were two other bare things that instantly put a color in his cheeks, and too much pressure in his pants. Not that I really noticed that part, I was completely swallowed by his eyes, the honey brown color pulling me in. The light ember of his dragon's fire like a beacon.

I couldn't stop myself. I stood, slowly walking toward him as Killian continued his tirade from behind.

"To be fair, little bro. This tends to be what people do when faced with the end of the world."

I barely heard him. Drake barely heard him with the way we were staring at each other. With the way our shifters were consumed with each other. I wanted him. Oh god, I wanted him more than I had ever had. But not in the same way I had wanted Killian, or Jarron. With Drake I wanted to be one with him. Be part of him.

I was faintly aware of Killian ruffling with what I was sure was a wall, not that it mattered. I was too wrapped up in Drake's eyes, in the low groan of his Dragon as it ruffled all my feathers. Damn. I was horny after a rebirth.

I grabbed the grubby front of Drake's sweater, pulling him into me and crashing our lips together in beautiful heat, tongues and hands everywhere.

And then, everything froze, my Phoenix going crazy as another dragon roar broke through the air. This one wasn't the same as it was before, when stubborn ass Zoe had laid her claim to the throne. This one was afraid. weak, like a final plea for help.

"Do you hear that?" I asked, my hands still tight against Drake's sweater as I pulled away and he gave an audible groan of loss.

"Hear what?" Killian said, peeking around the edge of the wall, and the secret room that he had pulled himself into.

The sound came again, low, mournful and pulling at every bit of my heart until it was about to crack in two.

"That." Given that they were looking at each other with

the 'Ellie has lost her mother fucking mind' face, I was clearly the only person to hear it.

The roar came again, the sound stabbing me even deeper before it was replaced by cheers, jeers, and a laugh I knew all too well.

"Mattia." Killian and I gasped in unison.

I jumped into the air before anyone could stop me, the same purple light that had made no sense before surrounding me as I bolted through the destruction of Rydaim like a torpedo, right to the same square I had fought the vampire in. The place was full of rubble, not one of the buildings standing as they once were. Other than that, it was the same. The same hordes of people surrounding what was leading up to a public execution.

Mattia stood over Zoe, the girl so surrounded by smoke that if my heart and Phoenix wasn't pulling me right to her I don't think I would have recognized her. But there she was, my mate, and I need only blink to travel right beside her. One flash of light and I stood, uncoiling to face the monster that I hadn't seen in decades, his face already twisted into a crude smile.

"Why, Elliana. I hadn't expected you to be here so soon. Or quite so natural. You certainly dressed for my arrival," He crooned, the black smoke zapping back into him, leaving Zoe heaving behind me.

I didn't know how much of her strength was left, hopefully enough to heal herself. If she could heal herself, whatever magic Mattia had stolen could regenerate. The fact that she was breathing was a good sign.

"Or perhaps you were dressing for someone else." His smile stretched, the little man leaning into what he thought was some guilt-ridden barb.

Bastard.

I slapped him hard enough that he not only spun, but was pushed to the ground like the sack of rotten potatoes he was. And yes, I totally pushed some of my magic into it, which is probably why I could hear Hilda's giggle from a few hundred feet above me.

"Shut up you weak little man. I think it's time we end this, don't you?" I kept my voice light, low and just for him. The crowd was fully vested in what was going on on this makeshift stage, but this wasn't a show I was interested in.

Mattia however... The man jumped up, swinging his head back like a movie star to plaster some of the hair that had come loose back into the oil slick that was atop his head. His grey eyes were growing darker as he turned to me, speaking in full voice as he pulled the crowd's attention right back to him.

"You wish to battle me for the crown? You? You are nothing more than a naked female. And we all know what naked females are good for." He narrowed his gaze, dragging those darkening eyes over my body with all the brazen lust that I had seen from Henry hundreds of times before. Even the way his lips were puckering was the same, the same narrow stare...

Oh god, Henry.

A demon with a million different abilities; and a power that I wasn't dumb enough to see through. Idiot had just given himself away. Too bad I didn't have my knife of I would end him right here. Now, the only question was, where is the real Mattia. If I had to guess, he was a hundred or so feet above me.

Seeing as Hilda's laughter had stopped... I needed to take care of this demon quickly, get to the other one before Xi and the others fell for whatever he was doing up there.

"Would you like me to show you what naked females are

good for." His voice was dripping with lust, poisoning the air. I stepped away from it, right into a large, broad, and thankfully suit covered chest.

"I don't think you will be showing anyone what Ellie is good for unless it is handing your ass to you on a platter." The crowd instantly broke into cheers, the rambunctious shouts draining all the exhilarated color from Henry-Mattia's face. God that guy loved to the center of attention, and he wasn't going to give it up that easily.

"I doubt the little naked female could even lift a finger against me." His lip twitched as he tried to command the crowds whose affections he had a second before.

It was cute to watch him try, and I totally gave him a tight-lipped sympathy smile for the attempt. He might have had a chance too, if Killian had been only one to show up.

"I'm sure the naked female could take you with just a finger," Jarron said, stepping beside me and throwing his arm over my shoulder as he always did, his massive frame and warm weight begging to be wrapped up in.

But not here, not in front of a crowd that was starting to act like a hoard of rowdy teenagers at a rock concert. The amount of screaming and jumping was really making me question exactly what kind of culture the dragons had turned into. These were nothing like the beautiful stoic creatures of centuries before. These were hormonal teenagers, and I needed a spray bottle or something to calm them all down.

Maybe Jarron too, considering he was now waving at a few of them.

I didn't have time to control the jealousy in both human and beast that was now rocking through me. I was facing a demon disguising himself as a monster. It was time to get down to business.

"Do I really need to remind you how much ass kicking I can hand to you," I said with a smile, pulling myself away from Jarron. "Or can I just tell you and get it all over with."

"Or I could tell him." Drake's voice was strong, it boomed through everything and silenced the crowd as though they had been doused with a wave of ketamine. Although, that may be more form his sudden appearance. Well, and the fact that they had celebrated his supposed death only a few weeks before.

Oh, and the fact that he was supporting a very alive and quickly healing Zoe on his shoulder. Thank god for that.

The shock of seeing all the King's children, surrounding his dead body, with two strangers who were in a pissing contest for power, one of which was naked, was too much for all of them. They were officially stunned into silence.

As was the faux demon before me.

The guy was now sputtering, the Mattia mask he was wearing slipping away.

"Why don't you come out and play, darling?" I taunted, giving him an exaggerated swing of my hips as I took a step forward. "Why don't you let me look you in the eye when I kill you?"

"You will never kill me!" He roared, the mask slipping even more as he slammed his hand forward. Black demon smoke slammed against my chest, sending me soaring through the air. I tumbled end over end before my back hit against a carved slab of wood, feet up, head down, like some kind of dead bug on a plastic spatula.

I gave a tiny grunt and slid to the ground like melted butter, watching from an upside-down world as each of my dragons roared, four unique sounds blending in the air. All of them aimed at the Mattia wanna-be who was now scooting back in retreat. Fallon, who I had totally missed in the front row, was trying to disappear among the transfixed, and equally horrifying, dragons in the crowd.

The roars increased as I scuttled myself to standing, ready to barge through my mates and rip Henry's head off his shoulder. Any path I had been hoping to take was quickly blocked, as one by one they began to transform.

Jarron, massive in his golden scales, each one shone both gold and white. The ivory color that was sketched around his wings, in his talons, and in his eyes making him look like a masterpiece of molten gold.

Killian, dark and oppressive, with scales the color of night. Each one shimmered with green, as though they had been dipped in oil. The color perfectly matched the emerald in his eyes, both human and dragon.

Zoe, covered in vermillion and scarlet, the deep ebony hue that shimmered through the tones of her scales making the blood-soaked image of her that much more frightening.

And Drake, the biggest of them all, the color of burnt honey and sugar, warm and electric. Each of his scales shimmering in the light of the cave, in the light of his fire as he screamed toward the sky.

But not in pain. Not in the mournful agony I had heard before.

The roar was powerful, awe inspiring, and perfectly matched the mighty creature as he extended his wings, neck pushed forward as his body was fully displayed.

Perfect. Flawless. Not a bit of the massacre I had seen on him present.

Drake was completely healed.

20

JARRON

'*THAT'S NOT POSSIBLE.*'

It was hard to tell in dragon form, but Zoe and Killian appeared as shocked and confused as he was. All of the fire that had been slowly eating away his brother's dragon. All of the fire that Jarron had cursed Drake with was gone.

'*How in the hell...*' Jarron couldn't wrap his head around it. It wasn't possible. It couldn't be possible without some kind of magic. Magic that they were surrounded by.

Drake was as strong and powerful as he had been before the coup. Before he had been sentenced to torturous fire and cast out. Bigger than all of them, full of brute strength, and probably as shocked.

His dragon took one look at his perfect scales before screaming to the ceiling again, sending a line of fire up toward the eye where he had left the goddesses with Suvi and Callay. They had commanded him to fetch Ellie, to have her intercede, and they would step in when the time was right. Guess the time wasn't right because they were nowhere to be seen.

The rest of the crowd, however, looked like they were

about ready to wet their pants. It had been years since the Kings four children had been side by side in their true forms, and it was clear by the dragon fire that was now beaming through each of them that they thought they were witnessing some kind of holy rights. A few had even fallen to the ground in the tradition prostate bow of obedience.

'*Wonder which one of us they are bowing too?*' Jarron snickered, looking from his siblings to the little man who was still trying to make a play for the crown, even with four full sized dragons surrounding him.

Mattia stepped closer, his hand lifting toward Ellie in something that might have been perceived as a loving gesture. You know, if the guy wasn't a psychotic killer infused with dark magic from an equally psychotic Unicorn. And that was if Jarron had been following correctly, and to be honest, he wasn't one hundred percent sure.

Killian and Zoe let out warning growls as his long spindly fingers reached for her face, Drake landing on his front legs with a force of impact that shook the partially collapsed building they were on. Mattia jumped back, hand retreating to his side as he tried to balance himself on shifting stone. Ellie didn't even flinch. She stood there, hand lifting to Jarron's jaw as he lowered toward her, placing himself within spitting distance of the idiot who was trying to straighten his clothes.

His fire may not do anything to Henry, but he had a feeling that this guy might not be as lucky. Even if he didn't burn, he could still coat him in a thick layer of his golden flame. Warning clear in his eyes, Jarron pulled his head forward, giving the man a low growl to keep him away.

He *really* didn't know when to give up.

"Do you really want to face four dragons? Are you that

much of a fool?" Ellie asked, her voice soft as her fingers ran over Jarron's glittering gold scales.

"I will face whatever I need to in order to take my place as their true king."

War had found them, and he needed to keep his wits about him, but her touch was making that impossible. His eyes drifted closed by the smallest degree, a rumble that was somewhere between a purr and a growl rumbling through his throat, pulling all the fire in his heart right to the surface. Ellie leaned into him, pressing her forehead against his and filling his dragon with her voice.

"*Find Mattia.*"

He nearly swung toward her, knocking her into the bit of wall behind them in his confusion, but Mattia pulled his focus, the man shifting as he moved closer.

One slow step after another.

Hands twisting. Eyes darting.

He had been so focused on Drake, on protecting Ellie, that he hadn't seen.

No one had fingers that long.

"These people need to be led by someone who will not run away from a crown and forsake their people." Even his voice had too much of an accent to it. Like he was trying to be Italian but wasn't quite sure how. "And if I am not mistaken, every one of you have done so. Including you." He looked at Ellie and Jarron felt his stomach twist, his fire building in his throat into something dangerous.

This conversation... it had happened before.

"I hold no notions about my past. I know what I have done. We all have sins." Ellie's hand dropped from Jarron's face as she stepped closer to him, putting herself right in the line of fire.

God! Could she not be so fool hearty just this once? He

needed to stay here, to stay between these two and protect her. You know, like the super powered goddess needed protecting. He was being ridiculous and his dragon snickered at him. At least the creature was able to find his own humor in the situation.

Thank god Drake had immediately moved to take his place beside her, Killian and Zoe leaning in even more. It still hurt to pull himself away from her, but it appeared he had bigger demons to find.

"None more than you, Elliana," The demon who had disguised himself as Mattia continued as Jarron took a few steps back, his claws scraping loudly against the stone and pulling a few of the crowd into a greater cower, revealing the mousy haired girl towards the back.

Running away.

Back to her master.

Jarron had spent most of the last few hours in a state of confusion. But between Killian's incessant ramble about a bird, and Xi's warning about Mattia, that much had stuck.

He took off into the air with a growl, unfurling his wings as he circled the city, sharp eyes scouring for anything out of place. Anything that spelled 'Warning, mega demon hiding here.' With all of the rubble of the city however, it was hard to see anything. And although his dragon could still smell the pungent aroma of the girl, he had lost sight of her.

Unless he was going to find a neon sign pointing him in the right direction, this wasn't going to work. Besides, he had a sinking sensation that they were going to see him coming, shimmering gold dragon and all. His fire may be super powerful, but he may have to give it up for a little bit more camouflage.

Never thought he'd say that.

Jarron pulled in to land as the yelling behind him picked

up a notch. The cave rattled underneath the roar of a dozen dragons, the sound growing as an explosion rocked through the still air of the cave. The dank stone walls went white in the blinding blast, sparks of black mixed through everything as the shadows of buildings and what he could have sworn were people cast over the high outer walls of Rydaim.

Buildings shook, groaned, and what had been left standing collapsed, one of the last tall structures before him giving way and tilting the side, giving him a perfect view of Fallon, standing next to the exact replica of the man he had just left.

Mattia. The real Mattia. He was primed, and ready to swoop in from behind and end them all given the knife that he was twisting between his fingers.

Wasn't Jarron lucky, talk about a two-for-one.

His dragon bristled at seeing him there, at seeing the knife and knowing exactly what was about to happen. Fire burning in his belly, he opened his mouth, letting out a roar that would have alerted his siblings to his discovery, if they weren't already locked in roars and screams that could only signify battle.

He would have to take care of this one of his own. Time to see if this monster was as immune as the last.

A stream of dripping gold lava spewed from his mouth, ripping through the air and right to Fallon and her master. The two of them turned at his roar, facing the massive golden dragon and the river of death he was sending their way.

Fear and panic that normally came with the deathly stream of his power were met by nothing but a smile.

The mother fucker smiled.

'*Oh shit,*' Mattia's smile was the last thing he saw before the golden fire obstructed his vision, building after building falling and making it impossible for his dragon to get any closer.

The golden fire of his attack cleared away as the smoke from the collapse did, revealing the same man, a bird on his shoulder. He held a hand above his head, like he was going to shoot a grappling hook at his dragon.

Instead, he sent a bolt of black lightning into the roof of the cave. Black magic hit against stone with a blast as dark as the one behind him had been bright. Everything shook, everything screamed, and what little bit of sanity that was around them reverted into nothing but chaos.

The cave was coming down.

The air was rent with screams from both dragon and human, the roars of the creatures mixing with his own as he tried to dodge out of the way of the large blocks of stone that were thundering from the sky. Grey, cracked stone was falling from the ceiling, smashing into the ground that was beginning to crack like china.

His dragon screamed in horror, fire flying uselessly forward as building and rubble sank into the floor, the cracks opening up to a giant black abyss that was swallowing everything, the giant maw of the opening spreading out like a wave in a pond. A wave that was swallowing everything into oblivion.

He had never been so grateful to fly. As long as he could dodge the thousands of pounds of stone that was coming down on top of him, he should be fine. The ceiling was shedding stone like an old man with dandruff, everything falling everywhere

He didn't have much time. He needed to get to Elliot. They would have to track down Mattia later. Wings arching, he dodged the hail storm, plunging his way toward the battle that was exploding behind him. Dragons had taken to the sky, fighting against his siblings, while others fought alongside. Fire was everywhere, and Ellie and Mattia were fighting in the middle of it all. If it was the real Mattia or not, Jarron had no idea, but he had to get there, to warn her that demon number two had the knife. Which meant that Parris was here somewhere too, as they had thought.

Now would be a great time for the Goddesses and those two magical women to get in here. Rush in and save the day or whatever they were planning, but unless they could turn to dragons too (which he wasn't going to rule out just yet) they hadn't plunged down from on high to save their asses.

Jarron let his dragon roar with a dangerous rumble, the sound pulling Ellie's focus as she had thrown the possible Mattia away. Before he could give her any sort of warning, a tiny bird was making a beeline for him.

Fallon.

She was heading right toward him, as though she was going to take him on was. He was sure he could inhale her if he tried real hard, in fact maybe that is exactly what he would do. One chomp and then they would be down a villain and piss a few people off enough that they would misstep.

Deal.

Jarron shifted his flight path a tiny bit, making it look as though he was avoiding her, watching her out of one eye as she followed every movement. Another dragon roar buzzed through the air, a string of crimson fire cutting right above him, startling the bird and sending her tumbling through the air.

Perfect.

Chomp. Chomp.

Folding his wings, Jarron darted to the tiny sprawling thing, spreading his mouth in preparation to swallow her and cook her on her way down. She was going to taste delicious. The poor thing was sprawling through the air so bad that she couldn't stop it.

Jarron sparked his flame, snapping his jaws around the bird and swallowing, ready for the single bite chicken feast. There was nothing.

Nothing but a squawk of the bird in his ear. The high-pitched squeal echoed through his head as she appeared to his left, black beady eyes digging into his, pointy beak heading right for him. He couldn't even deviate before pain shot through his head, the image of Fallon's falcon turning red and painful as her beak punctured his eye.

He roared, thrashing through the air as the pain overtook him, his dragon screaming. His wings flapped in a panic, barely keeping him airborne as he fought against the agony that was spreading to the other side. Without warning, the tiny bit of vision he had turned scarlet as her screech added to his agony.

As her beak plucked out his other eye, and all vision left.

Normally he would already feel the warm heat of his dragon as it tried to heal him, but the only warmth he felt was the blood as it seeped down his face, dripping over his golden scales in haunting tears. Pain was everywhere. Jarron couldn't control his flight, he couldn't control his massive body as he thrashed, as his fire exploded with each scream. It dipped over everything, not that he could tell. His entire world had turned a vermillion shade of agony.

Jarron screamed again, wings folding against his back as he continued to fall, tumbling into who knows where. It was only screams as he slammed against stone, massive boulders falling over him and smashing against head and back in snaps that he was sure broke more than a few bones.

Broke him.

He needed to get back to Ellie. His legs shook underneath him as he tried to push himself to stand, push himself toward the scream that he was sure was echoing in his head. Echoing through stone.

But he couldn't move. He could do little more than cry tears of blood as he stared into the darkness. His dragon pushed against the stone, the beast trying to press its way back into him, into a body that felt a little too human.

He couldn't tell if he was dragon, or man, but that little mattered now. Little mattered when one was faced with the end. Except one thing, one person. She mattered.

"Ellie... help..."

21

ELLIOT

HENRY WAS PLAYING a mighty good fiddle, I would give him that. But the fact that he hadn't caught on that I was seeing right through him was pretty damn hilarious.

"These people need to be led by someone who will not run away from a crown and forsake their people." Especially considering that he couldn't even keep his accent straight. That statement was so British it might have spilled tea all over the place. "And if I am not mistaken, every one of you have done so." He paused, stepping closer, his eyes darting from me to the dragon as though he might think better of it. "Including you."

Henry-Mattia narrowed his eyes into mine, the dark slits of black dilating as his facade continued to slip. I let my hand drop from the warm scales of Jarron's face and took one big step forward, away from the dragon that I hoped had heard my hint about the imposter. If this wasn't Mattia, but Fallon was here, the guy had to be somewhere.

Along with the knife and the Vampire.

We were still trapped in a shit show, hopefully we could make it less smelly if we found the main honcho before he did anything. Thankfully, Jarron was backing away, wings extending as he prepared to take off and search for the greater of two evils. I was going to consider that a win.

"I hold no notions about my past. I know what I have done. We all have sins," I said, giving one glance up to where my sisters were, trying to give them the same hint, but the former window was bare, my gaze obstructed by an eager Killian who already battling Zoe to replace Jarron's guard.

"None more than you, Elliana," fake Mattia sneered in an accent that could have been anything and took another step closer, ignoring the dragons and placing himself within a few inches of me.

He smelled like death. Death and blood and the vile ash that usually covered him after he had devoured the souls of my mates. My eyes widened, his smile stretching as I stared at him, watching the light in his eyes sparking.

Sparking.

Like white magic.

Magic that he very recently devoured. Zoe might be fine, her power regenerating, but that didn't negate what he had sucked away. Shit.

We might as well have been swimming in it.

"The sins that cover you and your Phoenix are as dark as the soul you pretend to cart around," Mattia-Henry smiled, stepped closer. So close that he could no longer see the flex of my fingers, the tips igniting like some kind of weird flashlight.

"Pretend?" I scoffed, flaring my fingers and letting the energy migrate to my palm. "I don't know about that. I didn't fall from heaven and destroy an entire civilization. Helped, sure. But I didn't take the first shot." I smiled as his face fell, shock lingering as his smile returned. The darkness in his eyes consumed everything as his mask fell away.

"There's no fooling you, Elliana," His words twisted as his face did, my dragon's growling as the crowd I had almost forgotten was there gasped and shuffled back.

Even if they didn't know what a demon was, watching him stretch into his true form, the black smoke wings of his kind stretching from his spine was still terrifying. I needed to act, he was going to return to himself for the first time in centuries, and fighting that would be impossible, especially without the knife.

"There's no winning either," I hissed, his eyes widening as he took a step back. Too late, my attack slammed right into him.

White exploded everywhere, magic ripping out of me with the full brunt of my power. Good, I needed to incapacitate him so I could remove his head with little effort. The ground shook with the force of the blast, the last of the buildings giving way and sending me staggering to the side. So much for removing his head.

Power throbbed through me as I watched him hurdle through the air. Right towards the far wall of the city where a massive crack had begun to form.

Demon splat against stone was going to be wonderful. Just like the King we had thrown out a window, or better yet a bug carcass against a windshield.

He barely made it halfway before the black smoke wings that had begun to form took their true shape, spreading out from his spine and snapping into place. And stopping the impact that I had hoped would kill him.

Instead, he hovered in midair, wings flapping, limbs extending, dark eyes boring into me.

"Fuck," I snarled.

The dragons who had been watching their own personal

soap opera screamed, many of them shifting as they all raced toward the exits.

"Get them out of here," I said, pointing to the panicked crowd, only to be met with narrowed eyes from Killian and Drake.

Stubborn ass dragons.

Zoe, however, took flight with a roar, her neck stretched down as she tried to herd a few dragons toward the exits, only to come in contact with a giant yellow beast hell bent on challenging her for the crown. The yellow guy was half the size of her. That would be an interesting fight.

She would have to give me the cliffs notes later.

Jumping into the air, my phoenix snapped into place, a line of fire shooting from my mouth before the transformation had even taken full form. I was a half-formed Phoenix, ready to kick ass, and the guy was already rushing me, demon eyes glaring as he sent his own power my way. While Killian's power, and even Mattia's power for that matter, was full of darkness, shadow, and all the evil doing you could muster. It was a completely different beast compared to Henry's.

Killian and Mattia drew from hell, but Henry had fallen from heaven and given up the power of light. When you take away light, all that is left is dark. All that is left is the demonic energy that Mattia hoped to hold.

Mix that with whatever light he had devoured from Zoe and I was in for it.

Screaming as he rushed me, Killian and Drake flanked me in what they thought was protection.

To anyone else it might be. Right now, they would just get hurt.

Stubborn ass dragons. I knew they wouldn't listen.

Another fire javelin to the quickly approaching demon

and I shot myself forward wings folding against me as I bee-lined toward the monster that was countering me like a bad boyfriend who had one too many to drink. His face extended as his jaw lengthened, his mouth opening as though he thought we going to swallow me of some shit.

Idiot.

You can't swallow a Phoenix and you certainly couldn't swallow a human.

A sped up, letting my magic rumble through veins, even though I couldn't access it in this form, watching his jaw stretch. I sent another fire javelin towards him, watching the violet string of flame eat up the space between us, watched him predictably move to dodge it, and immediately reversed my shift.

My human form snapped back into place like an old transformer, one stream of magic shooting from my hand before I changed back, wings extending to catch my fall and send me soaring gracefully away, watching as my magic intersected with the fire javelin that turned it into a bomb.

Sparks went everywhere, the blast rattling the already fractured cave. Everything groaned, the entire thing shifting as stone shifted and fell all around us. Okay, so I might have gone too far. There was a silver lining: the demon was tumbling to the ground. Killian and Drake were already making a bee-line for him, although who knew what they were planning. Their fire would do nothing, and swallowing him... or god, Drake was already opening his mouth, his fire nowhere to be seen.

What was it with these guys and swallowing things? Is it like the dragon equivalent of pissing on your property? I licked it, it's mine.

Fucking, no. I really didn't need that imagery. I needed to get there first before something went dangerously bad. I knew how to get rid of this guy. Swallowing him was only going to give Drake an ulcer, and he had only just been healed. I wasn't about to regenerate again and let him take another 'ash of my super-hot girlfriend shower'. Oh god, we've gone from male marking to ash showers. This all sounded like the worse fetish fantasy ever.

Better get my butt in gear and stop this. I shot a warning fire toward my dragons, hoping it was enough to get them to back down and darted my way back to the demon who was still flailing through the air, although his wings were beginning to form. Hurray, damn it!

Bee-lining for the monster, I got there seconds before he regained his flight, wrapping my claws around his shoulders and taking special care to dig my talons nice and deep into his demon flesh.

I felt the warmth of his skin opening up, but no flood of blood, no smell of iron and death. Damn it. I needed the knife for that. Good thing there was more than one way to kill a demon. Well, basically one other way. Ripping his head off.

This was going to be fun.

I let out another scream, the sound mixing with a dozen dragon roars as I lifted him high into the air before I slammed him down, sending him beside the other crumpled body of a former tyrant. The way his back was bent in two made him look nearly as broken as his counterpart. But while Ceres was twisted and covered with glistening bits of crimson, bones protruding from who knows where, Henry unwound himself as easy as if he was a piece of origami.

"What the fuck?" Killian reemerged beside me in a flash of black, his own power swirling through everything as the ground shifted, although that was probably from Drake's massive dragon landing behind me.

"How is he not dead yet?"

"Demon," I answered, sending a line of fire and magic twisting toward the quickly recovering demon, running as fast as I could to finish the job.

The attack hit its mark, sending him stumbling as I took to the air, ready to frog jump on his shoulders and rip his head off like some badass action star.

Instead, I was hit with something that felt too solid to be either magic or fire and was sent back into the shattered rock of the building, heaving while someone in the crowd screamed with something that sounded too much like panic. Hadn't they all moved on from this shit show yet?

Never expect a demon to fight fair. Why attack with magic when you can hurl a mother fucking boulder at your enemy?

"Bitch." I tried to shake my head and push myself to stand, Drake was already wrapping his arms around me in support.

"Yes, yes, swear at me to kill me, Elliana," Henry drawled, his wobbly shape beginning to come into focus as he took a few slow steps in my direction, Killian quickly blocking his way.

"I can't believe you thought that would work," Henry continued, still looking at me as he approached, so close to Killian now that I was actually concerned for his safety. I tried to yell at him to move, but all that came out was a squeak and a gasp. My lungs had not quite recovered from the impact of the massive boulder against my goddess body.

I guess even I had my limitations.

"And now you hide behind pathetic excuses for mates? I have seen you pick more powerful mortals that these two. I am ashamed that your Phoenix would want these pathetic, useless, ridiculous..."

His words were cut apart by a massive golden boulder that slammed into the side of him, sending dragon, demon, and what looked like a wall of blood into the building beside us. Stonework crashed over them, more boulders from the ceiling collapsing on top as Jarron's dragon roared, the scream of the creature pulling at my soul so abruptly that my heart might as well have been torn from my chest.

"Ellie... Help...'

That blood, it wasn't some twisted side show. It was pooling from him. It was his.

"Stop him!" I hollered at no one in particular, the shout covered up by what sounded like the scrape of stone against the edge of my skull. Every rattled, bones shaking as my Phoenix screamed. My feet could not get me to Jarron fast enough, I was stumbling over every piece of rubble in my way, Drake and Jarron quickly overtaking me as they tried to grab their brother.

"Ellie!" Zoe called as she ran up to me, horror lined on her face. Oh god, had she seen what happened to Jarron? I needed to get there, heal him and stop this or whatever was needed.

But she was right in front of me, hands tight around my ash-covered forearms as she held me in place. Fire blazed from her eyes, her dragon as scared as she was and any fire from my soul turned into nothing but smoke.

"I should have never sent him after Mattia alone."

Zoe looked confused for only a second before the panic drowned the emotion and she shook her head.

"We have bigger problems than hindsight, Ellie. The cave is collapsing. The city has begun to open up. We need to get out of here."

The screams from the crowd increased as the icy layer of my panic melted away, dread swallowing everything until the world was covered in iron and salt.

"The cave..."

"It's coming down," Zoe finished as Jarron extended the long golden sinews of his neck through the layers of rock that were smothering him, the scream of his dragon piercing everything as I turned to him, to the bleeding cankers in his scales, rivers of red flowing from where his eyes used to be.

22

ELLIOT

"You have to get everyone out of here, Zoe," I commanded, ready to bolt toward Jarron and heal whatever had happened to him. I had no clue if I could, not without dying and we really didn't have time for that magic trick right now.

I would figure something out. I had to. I needed to save him.

"Wait!" Zoe stopped me before I had been able to take more than a step, her hand tightening against me and holding me in place. "What about the Forgotten. They are trapped down there."

"I'll take care of it." Didn't know how, but I would figure that part out when I was thinking straight. I pulled against her as Jarron howled again, this one more human as he began to revert. "Get the rubbernecking Dragons out of here!"

I yelled the last bit as I ran away from her, towards the now human Jarron who was howling and writhing where he kneeled on the rubble strewn ground, hands against his skull as blood continued to pour from his eyes.

"Jarron! Jarron I'm here let me fix it." It was probably a

lie, but I wasn't going to give up that easy. I slid before him, hands wrapping around his shoulders, then around his wrists as I tried to see what was going on. Tried to calm him down. His sobs and screams, however, did not abate. They grew as he thrashed away from the agony that was crippling him, ripping himself out of my grip.

His blood lined my palms, making everything slick as I tried to hold him, tried to calm him enough to help, but he just screamed, and sobbed, and thrashed until Killian was able to wrap himself around Jarron, holding him as still as he could.

"Jarron, breathe. It'll be okay." The words sliced me in two, my heart thundering in my chest as I moved closer. My hand slipped against the cold damp of both blood and mucus that was dripping from him, but I dug my fingers against him, attempting to push what I had hoped was some kind of healing power into him.

Hundreds of years of killing things and I had no clue how to do the opposite. Great. Where was the Gryphon when I needed her, she could heal anything as easily as she could take it away. Which was another reason I had hid her after she had made the knife. Conceal the only person who could heal a pinch from the razors edge of that knife and I had a chance of being successful. A selfish decision.

"What happened, Jarron," I asked when his wails died down to a strangled sob, the two of us kneeling side by side as his back bowed, little bits of words bleeding through.

"I saw him... the bird... her beak." I tensed, not really wanting to hear what came next. "The blade."

The ground gave another great heave, more rocks falling from walls and ceiling in something that was more like an avalanche. Luckily, it all seemed to be contained to the other side of the cave, not like that was any consolation. We were either going to be crushed or trapped at this rate. Hopefully, thanks to Jarron, Henry had already met that fate. I didn't hear any more sounds from the rubble, but I didn't want to stick around to check.

We needed to get out of here, get the Forgotten and find an escape, and not lose Jarron in the process. There were only two things that could heal this, and one of them was still conspicuously missing. Shit. Could my sisters show the fuck up already?

"Neither of you would have happened to save any of my ash, would you?" I asked when it became very clear that whatever magical healing I was trying to attempt was not working.

The two looked between them, Killian patting his pockets, Drake running his hands over his sweater that was covered with the ash from his shift and perhaps a little of mine with the way it sparked.

"Wait." He gasped, shifting his weight and removing that damn sandal he had been wearing with socks this whole time, revealing lines of Phoenix ash where the contours of his feet had been. same with the other one.

Glittering foot ash. I wasn't asking questions. It was enough to stop the flow of blood before I could find Rana and have her heal him completely.

Scooping up the warm ash, I pooled it in the center of my palm, watching it glitter and giving silent thanks that it didn't smell too much like feet.

"Jarron," I sobbed, Killian still kneeling behind his brother, trying to hold him still as he flailed against the pain. "Jarron, I need you to move your hands."

Killian gave me a look that was pure horror, his grip on his brother tightening as Drake moved between us, wrestling against both of them to pry Jarron's hands away from his head, away from the seeping wounds.

Jarron wasn't going to give up that easy, he just sobbed and clung on, as if the pressure was the only thing that was saving him.

"Please, Jarron," I whispered, trying to move closer. I wasn't willing to risk losing the precious bit of ash we had to help.

"Move your hands," Drake's low growl, however, solved the problem.

Jarron gave one last sob before his hands fell to his lap, his body complying to Drake's powerful Dragon and revealing two gaping crevices in his head, right where his eyes had been. I had hoped that this would have been enough to heal him, but I had also hoped his eyes had just been injured. Not removed.

"Holy shit," Killian said as my stomach flipped. I nearly lost my nerve.

I blew the precious fragments of my ash right at him. Right into the bleeding spaces that he immediately went back to covering, although this time it didn't seem to be as much for pain. Jarron curled into himself, moaning and rocking as the three of us surrounded him.

"Jarron," I whispered, my hand against his back as I once again tried to push some sort of healing magic into him. I wasn't doing more than providing him a hot water bottle of a hand. "Are you okay?"

His blood-stained face was somehow more terrifying with the golden eyes that had spawned into place, the slits of gold and black were from his dragon. I wasn't sure how my ash had healed him by rebuilding dragon eyes in his skull. But I would have to ask questions later,

"Thank you, darling," he gasped, his voice choked and broken by the last of his sobs. "Thank you."

He wrapped his hand around mine, pulling me into him as he crushed me against him, thanking me over and over until the moment was shattered by a dark laugh that I had only heard once before.

Killian however, was already growling, his dragon rushing right to the surface. His skin imprinting with the dark lines of his scales, as he shot a line of fire toward the man that was slowing walking through the rubble toward us, Fallon right behind him. Jarron jerked, but I was ready to go into a full on rampage at seeing her there.

Fucking bitch was going to pay for what she did.

"Stop right there," Drake said, rising to stand beside Killian. I guess I wasn't the only one with revenge on the mind, his dragon's full growl lined each word.

The pair to stop in their tracks. Perfect. I knew Drake hated his power, but it was going to make this whole thing that much easier.

"Really?" Mattia said with a voice so deep, and a laugh so rich I was appalled I had fallen for Henry's projection of him so easily. "Do you really think a long forgotten, and poorly wielded gift will be enough to defeat me."

Mattia's smile stretched, Fallon laughing in a trill as irritating as her smile as together they took a step forward, and then another and then another.

Okay, so that wasn't going to work. Drake and Killian immediately counter-stepped, hands spreading as they prepared to shift, or protect me, or whatever it was that Dragon mates did. I wouldn't give them the opportunity.

"Can you fight?" I whispered to Jarron, holding him close as I stood, hoisting him along with me. He wasn't even able to hold his own weight before he began to wobble. I didn't need the quick shake of his head to answer that question.

"Can you walk?" He tried to stand again, this time with better success. It would have to do. "I'm going to send you with Drake. He will need the help, and it will be safer there."

"Safer? Where?" Jarron asked.

Drake turned with a look that said 'like hell if you think I am going to leave your side.' Poor guy didn't have a choice.

He would have to forgive me later.

"Everything is coming down. I need you guys to go down and get The Forgotten out." I spoke quickly, keeping my eyes on Mattia who was still walking this way, perfect timing for the rock that had begun to shift behind us. I guess we hadn't killed the demon that easy after all.

"I'm not leaving you," Drake said, even though he didn't fight me as I transferred Jarron's weight to him. "Not against this guy. we can't leave you."

He had clearly been hoping for Jarron to back him up, and while the guy was now holding his weight better, he wasn't in fighting condition. He knew that. The look he gave Drake knew that.

"You don't have a choice. We've got to get them out, and you are the only ones who they might still have a sliver of trust for." I pulled my focus away from the now laughing Mattia, ignoring the shifting stone to look at them. "You have to do this Drake. Trust that I will be okay. I'm a mother fucking goddess. I so got this."

That got a smile, the tiny twitch barely visible before he pulled me into him, planting a kiss against my lips in a desperate goodbye. Jarron's hand wrapped around mine, pulling me into him the moment my lips had disconnected from Drake's. Even with the weakness that was flowing through him, the kiss was desperate, longing, and panged through me as a tear dragged down my cheek.

"I love you, Elliot," he whispered, his voice as weak as he was.

"Be safe. But go." I couldn't repeat the words. They felt too much like goodbye. They felt too much like an end. He understood that, they both did. Pain and regret smothered them, but they didn't fight me, they slipped away as the last rock fell and Henry emerged with a laugh as loud as Mattia's.

We were officially surrounded.

Not going to lie, now would be a great time for Zoe to finish up getting the Dragons out of Rydaim and get her back down here. Especially since it was clear that my sisters weren't going to show up. Bastards. This must be their idea of cruel irony. Justice.

'Clean up your own messes.' If I had a mom, I'm sure she would have said just that.

"Well, I can think of a few worse ways to start a war," Killian mumbled as I took my place beside him, his black magic obscuring my vision as it flooded from him.

"You mean, like already dead?" I tried to force a laugh, but it fell flat against the slime that was dripping from the men that were now circling around us, Fallon adding herself in.

We were surrounded.

"Look how cute. They think they can take us," Mattia crooned, his eyes flashing from me to Killian. "You should know better, Killian. You can't take me. You should have stayed with me, I could have created you into something more. Something better."

"I've seen your creations, they are as pathetic as you are. It won't take long to crush her." He gave a nod to Fallon and

I could have punched him. Of all the people for him to choose to prod...

"Oh, her?" Mattia said, giving her a glance, but she only smiled, keeping her steps equal to the tiny man. "Maybe, but she is not my only creation. She is not the one you have to be afraid of."

More rock rumbled, and for a second I expected Henry to go in for the attack, but the guy was still standing behind us like some kind of reverse guard. Blocking the exit Jarron and Drake had slipped away in a moment before. The only exit that we could theoretically escape through, escape from the hundreds of pale faced creatures that were breaking their way through the rubble, Parris in the lead.

"Now, these," Mattia continued with a smile, even as my heart lodged itself in my throat. "These I do not think you will be able to destroy so easily. Not when they have all feasted on the blood of the child you so graciously let fall my way. Such beautiful blood. I doubt they would burn even under your flame."

Lilly.

He wanted to enrage me, maybe throw me off my game. Instead, all he was going to get was ragey Phoenix.

"Now, who would like to fire the first shot?" Henry asked, his fingers tugging at the tips of my hair, forcing me away from the Vampire's to face him. Damn it, I really hoped they didn't unveil a horde of rabid goats trained in Kung Fu. We were boxed in, and while not impossible, with just me and Killian this was going to take more strategic planning.

That we had to do silently.

Double damn it. Why didn't I get telepathic mating abilities? I really could use those right about now.

"Or would you rather we do you in right here?" Henry gave me a wink and I resisted the urge to punch him in the jaw. That would start the battle rolling. And I needed some kind of a plan before that happened.

"Really?" Xi's voice echoing over the groan of the cave as still more buildings fell, her and her posse moving into this mess like it was some fancy Sunday dinner. They had all changed their clothes. Callay included.

Between that and Killian's suit I was underdressed. Underdressed for the war to end a thousand-year war. Because that made sense. Who were these people?

Going to war like they are going to the opera. Too bad Rana wasn't among them. I doubt she would have dressed up. Her and I could have frumped it together. But it really wasn't safe for her to be before two demons spawned from a special corner in hell.

"Hello brother. It's been a while," Suvi said, so much of her age having fallen away that I barely recognized her from the old witch who had raised me. Mattia, however, was having no issue. His smiled nearly swallowed his face, the malice and greed overtaking his features as he took one large step forward. Looking between Suvi, to Xi, to Hilda...

He knew exactly what was before him. What was waiting for him.

"Finally, we can finish this. Henry, why don't you round up the rest of the dragons. Find the goddesses, I would rather do this in one shot. End you all so that true power can take your place."

Now the clothes made sense. If we were going to tango with this guy, we might as well do it in style.

23

DRAKE

DRAGGING Jarron's deadweight through the labyrinth of caves in search of The Forgotten was equal to being trapped in a game of whack-a-mole, and Drake hated that damn game. Everything was dark, confusing and if they stuck their heads out of the wrong hole it could spell disaster.

Thankfully, Jarron was mostly walking now, his glowing dragon's eyes cutting through the dark as they tried to follow the echoes of screams that were filtering from somewhere ahead.

Or was it below?

"How in the world are we supposed to get all of the Forgotten out of a tunnel system that we can't even navigate enough to reach them?" Drake's patience was on a thread.

"I think we need to go that way," Jarron said, his voice strained as he took a few steps away from where Drake had been helping him, only to collapse again.

"Do your new eyes have some kind of x-ray vision?" Drake snickered darkly, throwing Jarron's arm over his neck as he dragged him deeper into the cave, and closer to the screams that were growing with each step.

They had to be close, not that Drake was surprised. Every suggestion that Jarron had given him had turned out to be good so far, leading them closer and closer to what they had hoped would be an epic rescue plan.

But with the screams... God, please don't let them be too late.

"That way," Jarron heaved with a nod to the left. Drake followed the direction without question, tightening his grip and helping his brother farther down the tunnel.

Frightful screams were everywhere now, echoing over the stone and pounding in his ears so that it was making it hard to focus. He didn't want to think about what they were going to walk in on. They had only taken a few steps when the black stone that had been shaking underfoot vanished.

"Woah, woah!" Jarron yelled as rocks shifted underneath them, his hands rough against Drake as he forced him back. The two fell back into the stone cave, trying to regain their feet and not tumble into the ebony abscess in the middle of the mountain. Everything around them was so dark that they hadn't even seen the dark abyss ready to swallow them whole.

Two steps from disaster. Well, for them. Others had already been swallowed by the collapsing caves, their screams echoing from the pit.

They had found them. It wasn't the blood bath and carnage that Drake had expected. But it wasn't much better.

"Help!"

"God, someone save us!"

"Stop them! They are coming!"

Sobs and screams cut against him, the stone digging into his knees and he crawled over his brother to peer over the edge of the cliff, and down into the hollow canker. There was nothing there but black. Black and some hard-edged ebony that if he wasn't completely losing it, Drake would have sworn he had seen before.

No, he *had* seen before.

"Shit," he said under his breath, pushing himself away from the edge. "Of all the places for them to end up."

"What's going on?" Jarron crawled after him, peering over the edge with those glowing yellow eyes of his. They were like little haunted spotlights.

"What do you see Jarron?" Even with his immortal eyes, Drake couldn't see more than the few dark lines of the old soot covered buildings. Hopefully Jarron's x-ray vision had a few more tricks up its sleeve.

"The Forgotten... in a city? I've never... Is that the city you and Zoe were rambling about?"

Drake pressed his lips together in a hard line, his dragon shivering as he gave a nod.

"So, it's real?"

"Clearly," Drake said from behind clenched teeth. "They shouldn't be in danger down there... Unless..."

He was already feeling uncomfortable about having to go down there again. The Sphinx was no longer a danger.... But those statues, and probably the vampire or two that had followed the scent of blood.

He shivered again. Even he could smell the blood. Who knew how many had died, or were close to dying. He had to act.

"Stay here," Drake said, pulling himself to standing and peering over the edge as much as he dared. He would be able to see better in his dragon.

"I'm not staying here, Drake." Jarron heaved, trying to get himself to stand alongside his brother and not having much luck. "Not only am I dragon-meat-in-a-tube up here, but I am sure you are going to need more than your silver tongue to get them to follow you."

"I wasn't planning on..."

"I wouldn't use it anyway," Jarron cut in, his voice struggling as he was finally able to lean himself against the stone. Drake rolled his eyes. "No one likes being forced to do something. It's why you never use that gift of yours, and why you know they never really trusted you."

"Yes, I know all this. Remember, I'm the one who befriended them years ago." The absurdity of his statement snapped through Drake's words, but Jarron didn't even flinch, he smiled that beaming smile of his. The grin looked a hundred percent more frightening thanks to the glowing yellow eyes of his dragon peering through where his mortal eyes should be.

"Yes, but I have spent the last twenty years working to save them from slavery, and bringing them food, and regaling them with stories to pass the time."

"Regaling them? Are your stories magic or something? You and Killian sure have been up to a lot..."

"Plus, Ellie wanted us to save them." Jarron cut in, his smile spreading. "Leaving me here would be against her wishes."

Drake couldn't help but laugh. The low sound echoing through the stone as it rattled, the stone groaning from the battle they had left behind. They really needed to hurry, and Jarron was right, he was, how did he put it, dragon meat in a tube.

"Fine. Come smile at them and I'll convince them to leave." Drake threw himself out of the narrow opening in the cliff face before Jarron could respond, letting himself hurdle through the icy air before he let his dragon take control. Scales, claws, and wings broke through his bones, shredding his skin as he turned into his beautiful soul. The process was agonizing and one he had never fully mastered in keeping himself quiet during, but he really didn't care about that anymore.

He would scream if he wanted, he would laugh. He would bask in this gift, even if it was tearing his body apart.

A line of fire exploded from his jaw, the red and brown flame illuminating the abyss of the cave and silencing everyone below him. Circling through the air, he let out another line of fire. Dripping flames ignited against the glittering ebony along the side of the cave, igniting the same way that Zoe's fire had done to the city of soot before.

Looks like the charcoal was a never-ending source of light in this place. At least it would calm the Forgotten below, give him enough time to spin around and collect his brother before descending on all of them, Jarron sitting in the nape of his neck.

The few screams of those who didn't recognize his dragon broke over the loud flap of his wings. Until the caught sight of Jarron, who judging by their shadow against the soot covered buildings was waving at the crowd like Drake was nothing more than a parade float.

Drake may love his brother, but he sure drove him crazy, which was probably why he landed rougher than usual, and sending his brother flailing on his back.

So much for a graceful 'Golden Prince'.

"Thanks brother, nice to know you have my back," Jarron grumbled as he slowly slid down Drake's neck, kicking against his scales harder than usual.

Snorting, Drake shifted, sending Jarron to slide the rest of the way, and fall in a heap. The tall golden boy wobbled as he stood, as waves of Forgotten rushed them, their tear stained faces looking haunted in the dim light that was rippling through the ceiling high above.

"Always," Drake responded as he pulled back into his human form. "I'm always here to give you a new story in case you need to regale them in tales of your adventure."

Jarron gave him one dark look, dragon eyes narrowing before he turned toward what was quickly becoming a crowd. Well a mob if the scowls on the faces of those closest to them were any indication.

"People of the Fae!" Jarron yelled, his voice echoing over the buildings with the growl of his dragon behind it. "Myself, and my brother Drake have come to help you! We have looked after you for so long, and we will continue to do so. But this mountain is coming down. We need to get you out of here before more collapses!"

The crowd immediately broke out into a weird combination of screams, whispers, and side glances. The eyes of the few that still stared into us were looking darker by the second. Maybe having the golden prince down here wasn't going to be the saving grace Jarron had touted it as. Drake was actually surprised he hadn't referred to himself by the ridiculous nickname. Given the anger that was rippling over all of them, it was probably better that he didn't.

"Now?" A voice called from the back of the crowd, the single snap pulling everyone's focus. "You are going to help us now? Decades of begging Zoe and that brat to let us out of this damn cave, and nothing. Years of begging you, and nothing. You always claimed the king's spell has locked us here, that you could not break it. But now you can? How do we know you won't round us up and feed us to your pals the vampires like you did with the others?"

"I never did such a thing!"

"How do we know this isn't a trap of the spoiled infants silver tongue?"

Drake flinched. It had been years since he had heard the Forgotten refer to him as such, this man could hold a grudge.

"I would never use that against you!" Drake bellowed, his dragon's frustrations pounding in his veins so furiously that it was taking quite a bit of work to keep the creature controlled. "Not unless it was an emergency."

"Like now, when you claim that the cave is collapsing?" Another Forgotten, this one a woman with a bruised and bloodied child clinging to her pant leg yelled over the returned mumblings.

"Like now when you need our help!" Jarron snapped, smoke clinging to each word as he turned to Drake. They were both losing their patience. "God, you think that considering they were down here screaming for help that they would, you know--"

"Want help?" Drake had never seen the Forgotten like this, and yes, he knew Fallon had done some sort of number on them, but they were trapped underground and screaming mutiny. This was beginning to feel like a fool's errand.

"Stay here if you wish, but to those who want our help, it's time to get out of here." Jarron's eyes must have been flashing murder or something, because every single Forgotten took one collective step back, staring at him as though he had turned into a monster.

"Do you really think they need help?" A quiet voice pulled above them, the soft tones as loud as a lion's roar and pulling Drake and Jarron toward her.

Drake almost turned right back. The Sphinx had been enough for him, but this was almost more frightening. It had not, in fact, been Jarron that they Forgotten had been staring at.

Eagle talons curved over the edge of the building the massive creature had perched on, the dark eagle eye staring down at them, the tail of the lion that made up its body swishing lazily over the edge of the old stone facade.

Good god. A lion with the head of a woman was one thing, a head of an eagle was even worse.

"You are sons of the king. You will always see yourselves as the ones to save the others. But that is not your place. Your place is support, and these people do not need your help." The Gryphon spoke slow, every word controlled with a calm that followed her as she leapt from the edge of the building to land between them, Drake barely able to get out of the way of her massive claws.

"These people were stripped of a power that I gave them. stripped of their potential and their futures by a tyrant, but you do not need to help them. They can do that themselves." The mumbling confusion of the crowd had turned to an awed shock, most of the forgotten stepping back in a panic, content to take their chances in the dark of an unknown city than with the creature who was extending her feathered wings before them, sitting upon her haunches as though she was ready to lunge.

It was a miracle that more of them were not running.

"How can they do that themselves? As you said, their power was stripped from them. They have no ability to fight." Drake asked, struggling to keep his ground as she turned toward him, the sharp point of her beak only inches from his face.

His dragon did not like that, the creature growling loud enough that everyone could hear, including the bird that he could have sworn was smiling. Rest assured that a bird smiling was as frightening as a sphynx smiling.

Yep, he totally took a step back, much to his dragon's frustration.

"They can fight," she said, getting closer before she turned away. "You fought the vampires when they came to you caves, even though all you had was your bare hands. Would you fight for your lives?"

The statement lingered over all of them, the mumbles and hushed awe passing between them as she waited, her tail hitting him in the head with every flick of the appendage. Drake moved out of the way, but the tail only twisted with him. Clearly the goddess liked to mess with him.

Thankfully, this time, she wasn't giggling.

"What do you think we have been doing?" A man yelled, breaking his way through the crowd to face her. "We have been fighting for centuries. Every war. Every new law. Every time the Vampires are released into our home we fight them. We have no weapons, and we die beneath their fangs. But we fight."

"Good," the Gryphon said, her tail smacking Drake against the side of the face as a flame similar to Ellie's surrounded her, melting the creature into the woman he had seen before. Both in a mural and pulled out of one.

Rana.

Gasps filtered through the Forgotten, the lingering fear twisting into awe as the power and light that twisted around her pulled them into her. It was as though they couldn't stop themselves. Even the ones who had run away returned, the few that had been hiding behind buildings and down darkened streets emerging.

"They recognize their creator," she whispered, turning to

Jarron and Drake and waving them closer. Drake wasn't quite on board for that, but Jarron had rushed to her, like some lost dog looking for scraps of food. He half expected his brothers tongue to be hanging out.

"Just as Jarron recognizes the only thing that can heal him," she continued, patting Jarron on the head like a dog. It was beautiful imagery. "You all recognize the power, as I recognize yours. As I can return it to you. As I will, but on one condition."

The murmurs had stopped, whispers silenced. No one moved. Even Drake was holding his breath, his dragon tense against his chest as smoke built in his throat.

"Anything," A woman at the front finally said, her voice barely more than a whisper.

The quiet goddess's face spread into a smile, her hands extending toward them as pure light dripped from the tip of each finger. Mesmerizing every one of them.

"You must fight with us. Fight the monsters above. Fight the vampires that seek to destroy everything. Fight with the power that will be returned to you, and it will be yours to keep. Will you fight?"

"Yes!"

There wasn't even time to draw breath before the answer exploded over everything. Before light filled the cave.

24

ELLIOT

"Finally, we can finish this. Henry, why don't you round up the rest of the dragons. Find the Goddesses, I would rather do this in one shot. End you all so that true power can take your place."

Oh great, here we go: Villain monologuing. I folded my arms over my chest, content to prod and poke him into a long tirade. Not that drawing out the start to the battle was smart. But it definitely gave Zoe, Drake, and Jarron time to finish up their escapes.

"Really? You are sending Henry to do your dirty work, like he is some kind of servant," I prodded, giving Killian another look as the two of us stepped forward, closer to my sisters and Xi's puppets. I glanced back at Henry, the guy was already seething. Gad, he was so easy to prod. "I mean, even I know he's better than an errand runner and I hate the guy."

"You have hundreds of vampires at your disposal," Killian piped in, "and you chose to send the demon? I mean, I've only been leading dragon battles for a hundred years or so. But even I know better than that."

Henry looked furious. Mattia, however, was smiling like a devil who was handed the soul of an angel.

Hmm, that might have backfired. I hadn't meant to send a legion of Vampires after an injured Dragon and his brother. Both of whom happen to be my mates.

Great.

"Henry!" Mattia yelled, his eyes still on us. "The Dragon warlord is right. Why don't you take the Vampires? Fetch the stragglers, and while you are at it, make sure you find Rana. The others are here, so she must be around here as well. It's been centuries since I have seen her smiling face." Mattia's eyes still bored into mine, his dark scowl making it clear he knew he had made things a million times worse than I expected. A million and one seeing as he chose that moment to pull the knife out from wherever he had been hiding it. The silver blade gleamed, the ruby glinted and my stomach might as well have dislodged itself in the heart of the city that was a thousand feet below us.

I wish I had never lost that. The knife in his hands spelled death to all of us, and he was the one who was outnumbered. Task one: get the damn knife away from the damn warlock.

"Oh, I will find her, but I can't guarantee any of them will come back in one piece. Their power, their blood, all mine." Henry stepped up to Mattia, glaring darkly at us before he took off through the opening in the cave, the vampires following behind him, leaving Parris to look pathetic and withered without his army.

"Ripped them to shreds," Mattia called after him, still flipping the knife.

I didn't know how it was possible to make four words sound like a mixture of lust, malice, and constipated fury all at once, but Mattia managed it. It oozed from him like a puss filled boil that you can't stop picking.

It simultaneously made me want to cringe, punch him in the face, and squeeze the last of the puss filled boil out of him. Like he was one giant zit. The thought twisted my face and I made a sound that sounded like my stomach was turning itself out, retching over and over again.

Everyone turned to me, silence ticking through the group that had been seconds away from battle, faces twisted up in confusion. Well, all except Hilda, who was back to giggling.

"Sorry," I said to Mattia, swallowing another stomach twisting vomit noise. "I just had this image of you, with puss flowing out of your head."

"Like a volcano zit?" Hilda asked, unable to control the level of her giggling anymore.

"Oh god, that is so much worse," I gave her a wink and heaved again. Everyone still staring at me as I pulled my fire into my throat. Hacking, coughing, and spraying it right at Mattia.

The fire was useless, but it did give me the cover I needed to rush him, swinging wide and right to where he was dodging vomit fire, Fallon shifted and took off like the wimpy kid she was. Screaming with her hands in the air.

I came in from one side, Hilda from the other, both of us flanking him in an attempt to get the knife, magic already sparking everywhere as he countered, and the battle exploded.

His hands spread, smoke and sparks flying toward me and my sister in an attempt to keep us away. I dodged, although barely. Hilda was not so lucky, her body flying back in a tumble that could have ended badly if she hadn't shifted into her true form, the massive cat landing lithely atop the rubble of the buildings that littered the city.

The impact thundered through the ground, the crater that was opening up on the other side of the city shaking everything as more buildings disappeared into the giant hole.

Pumping my feet faster, I rushed toward Mattia, Suvi appearing through the black smoke he had coated everything with and hitting him with something that looked like a bowling ball made of light. The man went flying, the knife went flailing toward a mountain of loose stone, dust, and shards of glass. I ran to reach it, only to find myself blocked by a pale faced idiot, fangs protruding, grey marks lining his marbled skin.

"God, Parris. You can't keep hold of anything can you?" I taunted as I jumped over him toward the city graveyard that had swallowed the knife. "First you lose your girl, then the knife. Bet you lost the kid too."

Parris pushed me out of the way as we lunged for the hilt of silver that was clattering against stone, falling deeper into the still shifting ground.

I could barely keep my footing and track the knife, let alone attack the bastard. All I could do was get to the knife first and stab him into oblivion. Which would be great if I wasn't trying to outmaneuver a freaking fast Vampire who kept popping in and out of existence with how fast he was moving. I was a damn Goddess; this shouldn't be so hard! Luckily, it wasn't just me, Callay and Killian had joined in on the search.

My foot slipped against yet another stone as it slid out from underneath me. The second I caught sight of the knife, something else would shift and the massive boulders and pieces of buildings would swallow the thing again. My

Phoenix was screaming in my head, desperate to melt the rock into molten lava and pull the thing out as easy as I was bobbing for apples. But with Killian and Callay searching alongside me I didn't see that ending well.

"Not that you cared for her. You created her." I yelled as the ground rocked again, the flashes of light from high above a dark omen to the battle that Suvi and Mattia were locked in. I could have sworn I saw one of them fly overhead like a badly thrown paper airplane. I would hope that Xi and Hilda would step in and help, but knowing them...

"You lost her too, didn't you? The demon's wanted her for themselves." All I could really do was taunt him. Try to throw him off track enough that we could get in front of him.

"I may have lost her. But I wasn't the one to kill her." He smiled, his greasy grin spreading as he shifted his hand, reaching for the knife that I hadn't seen settle on a massive boulder right beside him.

He never made it.

"You fucking bastard!" Callay screamed, lunging at the guy with all her power and strength. Magic exploded everywhere, rocking the ground, exploding rocks in a shower of rubble. And, unfortunately, collapsing the ground below us.

The city could not take any more. The massive cave gave one last heave, rocks falling from everywhere as the abyss that was swallowing Rydaim spread right underneath us, and everything crumpled into whatever was below. I tried to grab Callay as I shifted, wings frantically flapping, talons reaching, but she slipped away. Her and Parris screamed as they fell, the knife glinting in the last of the light.

I kept myself above the vanishing world, fruitlessly trying to dodge all of the boulders and buildings that were tumbling down around me. Killian shifted with a growl, his dragon shrouded by a black smoke as he too tried to grab her, but she was gone. Zoe's dragon screamed as she returned, her roar the last thing I heard before a boulder slammed into the dead center of my back and sent me hurtling down with the rest of the stone, into the world below.

Into the city I had destroyed centuries before.

25

ELLIOT

SOMETIMES BEING IMMORTAL SUCKS. That fall should have killed me.

I should have been a red smudge on the grey ash world of the City of Soot. Like Ceres and all other tyrants who get overthrown. Instead, I was blessed with a mind-numbing pain that made me sure I had fractured every bone in my body. Skull included. Which would make sense seeing as the world was full of sparks of every color, the pops of light prodding against my skull and mixing with the sounds of the marching band I had landed in. A marching band that had a bass drum that was being played against the broken pieces of my skull.

Screaming out in agony, I pulled myself to standing, the world buzzing and shifted as rock settled, as dust continued to kick up. But not because the ceiling had fallen in. But because I had fallen from one battle, into another.

The marching band turned into fireworks, the sounds of battle everywhere as the sparks of color came into focus, and the magic that I hadn't seen in centuries came to life. It was everywhere, mixed with screams of death, fear, and power as The Forgotten fought the Vampires that Mattia had sent down here.

"Ellie!" Jarron's familiar scream ripped through my head with thankfully less pain than the firework parade. I must be healing, although perhaps still hallucinating. Jarron was looking at me with his usual fiery eyes, the gold blazing behind human pupils. "Ellie! God, are you okay?" His hands were everywhere, his big mitts having multiplied as I could have sworn his hands were everywhere. Pressing against everything. Holding me up, forcing me down. Maybe both. Considering I was really struggling trying to tell which way was up it could have been both.

"What happened?" Drake asked. That explained the hands.

"The knife," I gasped out, my head still spinning as the words slurred. "The floor gave out. Callay attacked. Oh god... Callay."

I spun on the spot, trying to peer through the dust, through the firework show that was everywhere, desperate to find her. She wasn't a goddess, I wasn't sure if she could survive...

I saw her hand first, the fingers curled around the handle of the blade, all of her smothered by what must have been a metric ton of rock.

"Oh God, no."

I stumbled through the debris from two cities, every joint screaming as I forced them to move, unable to get them to move fast enough. I need to get there. I needed to save her. There was still a chance. I knew there was.

There had to be.

My Phoenix's scream, however, was a mournful song that I didn't want to hear, I didn't want to acknowledge. I clawed at the stone that covered her for only a minute before I got my wits about me, my magic humming as I picked up the massive amount of stone, throwing it into what appeared to be a dark forgotten corner of the city.

It crashed with a boom that mixed with all the other attacks, mixed with the scream of Killian's dragon as he landed behind us, Zoe not far behind. It was all sound, it was all a world that was shrouded by sound. By the screaming that was ripping from my Phoenix, bleeding through everything.

Callay lay, one hand wrapped around the knife, the other around the neck of the vampire who had used her to create one of his many experiments. No, not an experiment, a child who never had a chance.

A child that she never got to meet.

A child that was gone. Just as she was.

Blood was everywhere, dripping from the crushed bones of the powerful girl, and from every cut that she had given the vampire from the knife. Every cut that she had used to end his life. I hoped he died before they had landed. I hoped she got the reward of beating the Vampire who had used her. Who had tried to destroy her.

Judging by the smile, I think she had. Still didn't make it fair.

"No!" I screamed alongside Killian's roar, alongside Jarron's sob, the roar of agony adding to the bass drum of pain.

Something that grew even worse by the familiar laugh that pulled my focus, all of us turning at once. Henry laughed with a sound from a nightmare, the tones pulling from heaven and hell as he heaved, the battle raging behind him. Each flash of light illuminated his true form, his long limbs, his dislocated jaw, his clothes that were ripped and covered with the blood of The Forgotten he had already slaughtered.

I had only seen his true form once before, when I had first pulled him from heaven and the strength of the underworld still flowed through him. When we had flown side by side and destroyed this city, the demon so strong that no one could stop us.

So strong I had never been able to face him since. It was why I had made the blade. Part of me wasn't sure he could be killed without it.

"Henry." I bent over and grabbed the knife. "What do you say we finish this?"

"I would care for nothing more." He smiled, his eyes flitting from me to my entourage, waiting for me to excuse them. This time I smiled, like hell if he thought that was going to happen.

The forgotten appeared to be kicking some vampire ass. Suvi and Mattia were going at it. Fallon had probably hightailed it into oblivion. This one was ours.

"Wonderful." I said, flipping the knife once as we all raced toward him, claws and knife and flame at the ready.

He looked like he was going to shit his pants.

Good.

I lunged for his neck with the knife as Killian swiped with his front claws. Zoe came in from the top with her jaw open so as to snap him to bits. Jarron and Drake rushed to either side, human arms ready to hold him down. One swipe of the blade, that's all it would have taken.

One swipe to end him.

Inches from grabbing him, however, he flashed in a white light and vanished from our grasp. His twisted body moved from one spot to another, looking over us from a pile of stone and ash.

I knew that light. I knew what it meant.

"Is that what you did before you let the vampires have her?" I asked, my phoenix screaming as my heart pulled uncomfortably. "You sucked her power away?"

"Naw," he said in that horrific voice, elongated face twisting into a smile. "I sucked her life away too. For a child, she sure tasted good. I knew I was raising her for something. With her power, it will be no problem to destroy you. To destroy all of you."

Jarron screamed as the words struck home, his agony pulling through the sounds of battle as he took off after the demon. Henry smiled, vanishing in another pop of light, this time appearing at top of Zoe. Her dragon screamed as he laughed and stroked the brilliant red of her scales.

"Let's start with this one," he taunted, his long fingers digging into her neck and sending her howling. Sending her blood dripping over her neck, the demon twisting to lap it up like a dog.

"No!" Everyone shouted at once, Killian's dragon bursting from him as he moved to snap at the man, but he vanished right as Killian's jaws would have closed around him. Zoe thrashed in pain, Killian roared in anger. Drake, Jarron and I spinning in place as we searched for him. It would be so easy for him to vanish and be gone. But I knew the bastard. He wanted our heads, and he couldn't fit dragon heads in a jar.

"Move out of shift," I hissed toward Zoe and Killian, the two of them doing so without question, although Zoe immediately fell to her knees, clutching her neck as blood poured from multiple wounds.

We would have to find Rana after this was done.

"I thought we were going to end this!" I called into the rumble of battle, a loud bang echoing from overhead as Suvi and Mattia collided in something that looked like a nuclear blast, mushroom cloud and all. "Are you really so much of a coward?"

"No," his voice came out of the burst of white light overhead, his twisted outline darkening as he stepped closer, as the dozens of others behind him stepped out of the ash filled air right behind him. "I needed to get some backups."

Well, shit.

"Really? You need backup? You can't take us all on your own." I said as I rushed him. The man smiled as the vampires around him swarmed toward the dragons, blocking us in until it was just he and I. A shield of blood-sucking undead. I would be impressed by his ingenuity if he hadn't totally miscalculated who I was with.

"Fitting that your last minutes would be with you and I. Alone," I smiled, flipping the knife as a dragon screamed over the war, sucking the sounds of battle away for one tiny breath.

It was enough.

"Vampires stop," Drake boomed, his dragon's growl freezing all of the blood-suckers in place. "Demon freeze."

And one demon.

I already knew it wouldn't hold. Henry may have looked scared, but he was already pulling his foot closer, he was already starting to glow.

I had one chance.

I rushed him, blade sliding through the air as I sent a javelin of my phoenix's fire right to his head. A fountain of wet sprayed over me as the knife sunk into his neck, hitting against his spine. I leaned into the weapon, pressing it against bone and flesh as my fire hit him right in the face, drowning out his scream as the knife cut and sawed, and his head fell away.

The war behind us might have gone silent with the sound of his head as it hit against the stone floor.

Blood was everywhere, I was covered with it, and the vampires who had begun to fight against Drake's power were turning toward it, hungry for a taste of the blood that had fallen from heaven, that should have come straight from hell.

"Shit." I threw Henry's body as high up as I could, Killian's dragon exploding into the air and catching it, ripping it apart and showering us all with blood. The drops of demon blood were like alcohol against the flame that I was already sending toward the vampires, the dripping lava hitting against their greedy faces and turning them all to ash.

Screams echoed around us, the smell of burning flesh everywhere as the monsters dissolved into nothing and left us standing in the darkened city, standing beside the head of a demon, in a circle of vampire dust.

The Forgotten ran toward us, Drake's command having spread through the cave and allowed each and every one of the monsters to fall. The vampires were gone.

The demon was devoured.

The vampire was crushed.

A celebratory shout lifted through the crowd, only to be silenced by a flash of black and white, and a bang of power that reigned down and smothered us into silence.

Mattia and Suvi were still going at it. The last two warriors in the war that I had started long before. Light and dark.

Opposing forces.

We were only half done.

"Isn't it beautiful?" Xi said as she and Hilda wandered into our observatory, eyes toward the sky as yet another blast illuminated the blackened city. "Good and bad. Light and dark. I wonder who will win. I wonder who will build the new world?"

"And you say I caused all the havoc in the world," I hissed, flinching as Suvi stumbled.

"You may have been the one to start it. But I have been working to finish it for ages. It's all as I have planned. They will be the ones to decide."

"You have already sacrificed so many lives, Xi," I said with a nod toward where Callay still lay, covered in blood and death. "If he wins, there will only be more."

Another explosion, this one sending rock and sparks dripping over us, and many of the Forgotten running. I did not move, I let the magic pool around me, burning away some of the stone near my feet.

"Then he better not win," Xi turned toward me, smiling demurely before returning to watch the show, her eyes glittering with the color that had driven me mad for so long. "And don't worry about Callay. I made her a deal, and she has already been returned to where she asked, although what good it will do her, I have no idea. She was a child when she made her choice, and children are fools."

I wanted to rage at her, but a scream from above pulled my attention. Suvi screamed as she was thrown away, Mattia soaring after her with a look of success on his face. The two of them were out of sight, but it didn't matter, everyone knew what was coming next.

"You can stop this, Xi," I pleaded, turning to face her, grabbing her arms with the full intent to shake her back into sanity, instead all I got was a glare. Like she thought that would work with me. I was as powerful as she was, I could take her, but I could not stop this. I was not their creator. It was not my power that could stop this.

"This light and dark nonsense. It doesn't have to happen. Just stop it."

"Light and dark, someone said from behind me as Xi laughed with a low dark chuckle that made it clear that she had wanted Mattia to win all along.

She wasn't saving Suvi for a battle she would win, she had been saving her for slaughter.

"No! You bitch."

"Light and dark. Good and bad," the voice came again, even through the fog of shock I recognized it as Zoe that time. "Killian we could end this."

"Oh my god," I gasped, turning to her, a smile already overtaking my face. She was right.

Xi turned, her face falling from victory and twisting into a snarl. The two barely registered her outburst, and they sure didn't see her try to lunge after them because both I and Rana had tackled her to the ground.

"Only a light can kill a dark," Zoe continued, blood still pouring from her shoulder and she stepped closer to Killian.

"Only a dark can kill a light," Killian responded. "I don't want to kill you Zo, but I would like to end this nonsense."

"You are going to kill me just to end a war?" Zoe snapped, the waves of rainbow tinted magic rolling over her skin.

Great, they were so close and they were going to head right back into this nonsense.

"Oh, this is even better," Xi said. She stopped fighting me to clap in glee, just like a child in a candy store. Like she inevitably was.

"No, Zoe," Killian snapped through a clamped jaw, he

was still trying to control his temper. "If Mattia wins..." the dread lingered in the air, Xi's chuckle turning to a yell of protest that I muffled by shoving her face into the dirt. "Do you think you can take him."

"I'm not sure how strong the power is after what happened before, but I can try. And even if I fail, at least I tried." she shrugged, wincing in pain at the motion.

"Well, let's give you the best shot," Rana said, leaving me to wrestle the unicorn as she stood, placing her hand on Zoe's shoulder.

Brilliant yellow light flooded around us in an orb, shimmering from Zoe's shoulder as Rana healed her. Zoe didn't even so much as wince as the light faded, my sister leaning in to whisper something that even I couldn't hear.

The two of them didn't wait, the second Rana's hand had left Zoe they took off, Killian clutching the knife in his hand as they scaled over rubble and raced toward the twisted sound of Mattia's laugh.

"What did you tell her?" I asked as I released Xi, knowing even she was foolish enough to try to stop them. She liked mischief, and part of her wanted to see this through.

"To kick him in the balls. Because he fucking deserves it."

26

ZOE

"So, how do you suggest we do this?" I asked as we stumbled over the last of the rubble and onto the roof of one of the soot covered buildings.

We could see Mattia and Suvi better from here, the two twisting over each other as fire, smoke, and flashes of light mixed with the old woman's lightning. Mattia hurdled his body through the air, soaring after Suvi who appeared to be hovering unassisted. The man's black smoke swelled everywhere, stretching away from him in frightening greedy arms.

Suvi twisted through the air, her lightning snapping after the black smoke, eliminating the reaching fingers one by one, but not quite enough.

It wasn't quite lights out, but Suvi wasn't going to be able to hold out much longer.

"You go to the left, I'll go to the right," Killian said, cringing as Suvi took another hit. That one had to hurt. "I can't end him. You have to do that. But I can help you get close enough."

"As long as we don't start fighting each other." Standing this close to him was becoming more trying by the moment.

"Fight it, Zo. We have to do this." He was clenching his jaw as tight as I was, the line in his scruff making me want to punch him.

First, he tried to take my crown, and now he... No. I need to focus. I nodded as another flash of light smothered everything. Ripples of screams echoed from below, Mattia's laugh smothering from above. It was like a god damned death tunnel.

Guess we needed to add a corpse and make it a reality.

"Let's go," I said, running toward Mattia before Killian responded.

"Is this why you hid so long, sister?" Mattia's voice echoed through the city as I scaled up what looked like a twisted fire escape to another building, his voice booming through my bones the closer I got to him. "Because you knew you would fail?"

He laughed again, the sound banging against my magic, the hot electric rage behind it flooding through my veins. The same hatred, the same vile want of blood that I felt for Killian was pulsing back into existence. While not as strong, and definitely not as deranged as what I felt for my true nemesis, it was enough.

If I could focus on it, I might have a chance.

"I will not fail," her voice was old and frail, it warbled in what could only be pain, pulling me forward as I jumped from roof to roof, pulling myself closer to the man that was still hovering in the air. Same as Suvi had done, same as I should be able to.

Not that I had any idea how, but you don't know unless you try. And, it's not like I was going to land flat on my face. Worst case, nothing happens and I shift into my dragon, distract him with fire while Killian ties him up or some shit. We really should have thought up a better plan, not that we had time, or the ability to plot without killing each other.

Actually, going in blind was probably better.

"Seems to me that you already have," Mattia taunted, the words meant to be the death knell before the final blow. It was now or never.

I threw myself off the side of the building.

Trying to figure out how to fly as a human was much harder than it should be. My dragon was screaming, her wings pressing against my spine as they tried to start the shift and save me from smacking against the carved stone road.

"Fly, damn it, hover, do something!" I hissed to myself as Mattia laughed, as the road came closer, as the wings pressed harder, exploding from me second before I hit the ground.

Agony ripped over me as I hovered there, wings flapping against my spine, blood pouring over my back, and my very human hands stretched toward the ground as if they would catch my fall.

Well, this wasn't normal. Who was I kidding? This wasn't fucking possible! Partial shifts were not uncommon, Drake had even been able to accomplish it as a child. But that was scales, and talons, and maybe a forked tongue. Not massive Dragon wings protruding from a very human body. I sure as hell didn't expect this. Or to expect it to be as painful. I wanted to scream with the agony that was ripping over me.

Unfortunately, Suvi did that for me, the blood curdling sound inches from death.

"Damn it." I barked, putting the wings to action and launching myself into the air.

He had already started. I needed to focus, I needed to end this.

I soared around the buildings, closer to Suvi's scream, to Mattia's laugh, and to Killian who was hovering there as though this whole half magic thing was normal. Except he didn't have dragon wings ripping out of his spine. Bastard.

God, I wanted to kill him.

No, not yet. Not now. Mattia. Focus on Mattia.

Ignoring the shock on my brothers face, I sped toward Mattia, Killian following as we both plunged toward him, ready to take the bastard down.

The writhing witch was screaming from the stone roof of one of the many buildings, Mattia's eyes trained on the white magic that was seeping into him as though he was inhaling it from her. He didn't even notice us coming for her. We could do this, one shot, Killian grabs left I grab right and we rip him apart like a bag of potatoes chips, rotten contents showering us like confetti.

I was ready, hands extended, both of us soaring towards him. And then I looked at Killian and everything inside of me went haywire. That thirst for irrational blood screaming as my hands turned towards him, lightning and whatever else I could control ready to explode right at Killian.

"It's time to end this," Mattia pulled my focus at the last second, snapping me out of the delusions. I smacked some sense into myself and shifted my hands one inch, sending the powerful attack right into Mattia instead.

The man howled, losing height as he tumbled down to the darkened cityscape below. Killian changed directions, grabbing him before he got too far. He held him by the scruff like a naughty toddler, dragging him back to meet his fate.

"Don't do it," Suvi gasped from the top of the building he

had been torturing her on, her arms shaking as she pushed her way to stand.

Oh god, she was covering blood and sweat, one of her arms sagging as though it was dislocated. Wings moving, I darted toward her, her eyes terrified as she tried to stop me. Any words were drowned by an otherworldly scream that bounced off the stone buildings, freezing us both in place as hell opened up all around us.

Literally.

Fire exploded through every street, it ran up the sides of the already ash covered buildings, it exploded through the windows so covered in soot that I hadn't noticed they were there. Soot and charcoal burned from every surface, filling everything with smoke and turning the world to fire and brimstone. And we were caught in the center of it. Mattia had turned into a full-on psychopath.

"Do you really want to fight me, Killian?" Mattia broke away from my brother, soaring around him and smothering them in a globe of smoke. "You know you will lose, you lost before, and you will lose again. You can't face me; your magic is equal to mine. I will only devour your power and become stronger!"

Shit. So much for a quick in and kill. Suvi's blue eyes dug into mine, the powerful light that had protected me for so many years having faded. She didn't need to say it for me to know. She was spent. She could run back up, but this bitch was mine.

"You can't even hope to face me!" Mattia said as the dark smoke closed, flashes of fire coming from inside as I assumed Killian began to attack. A swipe, a bit of flame, hopefully it was enough to keep him distracted from what was coming.

My wings narrowed, shooting me down to them, and through the wall of black like a drop of light in the dark.

"Maybe he can't," I said, as I quickly caught my bearings and turned toward the man. "But I can."

I hit him again, a second attack, this one right to the face. This time he flew backward, a short scream pierced by cheers from somewhere below.

Don't rejoice yet, he was quickly recovering and sending so much black smoke my way that if it wasn't for the roar of Killian's dragon and the faint crackling of the burning world I might have thought he had cast me down to hell.

"Well, well, what foolish little dragon brat do we have here?" He stroked his chin, licking his lips as he watched me in all the wrong ways, his eyes sparking against my need for blood and death again.

I let it take me, with his black smoke obscuring everything there wasn't a Killian to redirect the murderous rages. This time it could all be for him.

"The rightful queen," I said confidently, the power zipping stronger at the admission, at the image of the crown atop my head. It was beautiful, it was glorious and... "and you're in my way."

I smiled as he did, our matching malicious grins growing as I let sparks of light flicker from my fingertips, and he let fire burst from his. The same fire demons I had seen Killian conjure before burst to life, the tiny gnashing things running around the inside of the smoke prison like they were on some kind of hamster wheel.

The guy really had another thing coming if he thought that would scare me.

"Is that some kind of threat?" Mattia asked, the fire twisting back into smoke.

"No. Just an observation." Screw this banter. I attacked

him again, putting the full brunt of my power against him. Well, not against him, against the smoke that was flowing out of him, using it as a conduit to push the power the Unicorn had cursed me with right into him.

He was laughing at me for missing, smiling with the illusion of how easy this would be. And then he felt my attack inside of him, he felt the bubbling burning energy that popped and exploded like those little fire demons.

I kept my focus on him, knowing that Killian's dragon would be on the other side, waiting. Waiting to finish him off, waiting to protect me, waiting to devour me. I had no clue. But I didn't dare look away as the massive scaled beast burst into being and Mattia screamed, as his skin boiled.

"I don't need to threaten you." My voice was as dark as the black smoke that was nothing but a trickle out of him now. "Why threaten when I can just end you?"

The magic continued to pour through him, bubble against him and devour him from the inside out. The black smoke vanished as he sucked in his last breath, the dark veil falling away to reveal the massive shimmering black scales on my brother.

Killian's dragon flapped its massive wings, the maw of his beast opening until each of his razor-sharp teeth glinted in the all-consuming fire, until even I could see the bubbling black flame of his beast choke at the back of his throat, ripping out of him.

With a roar, the deep ebony flame that devoured everything in its path. It swallowed what was left of the man, drenched his bubbling skin and melting bones in black so deep that not even the light of the fires could reflect off it.

There was nothing to reflect anyway, I may have killed him. But Killian's fire had swallowed his soul.

The haunted echo of Mattia's scream rumbled over

everything, lingering long after Killian had devoured him. The scream was one final knell, growing farther and farther away as it traveled over the city, as it echoed the end of whatever war we had been sucked into.

And then there was silence.

Silence that stretched on as everyone waited, as everyone watched the blackened body of the monster fall to the ground. He hit against hard stone with as much glory, and as much blood, as the King before him.

It was then that the crowd broke out into cheers. It was then that the hurrahs of victory broke over everything and Killian and I looked at each other, Suvi already pulling herself to standing, ready to pull us apart if need be.

Like we were dogs in a cage fight.

Except when I looked at Killian and his ugly dragon eyes, the slits falling away as the dragon withdrew and the two of us hovered in the air together, I didn't want to kill him as bad.

Well, maybe a bit. But I could control it.

"Should we go down?" I asked, suddenly wondering if I was even going to be able to put the wings away.

"After you, your majesty," Killian said with a nod of his head, extending his elbow towards me.

I wasn't about to fight him, although I might have been scared out of my mind to touch him, I took his arm anyway, the two of us descending toward Jarron, Drake, Ellie, and a very pissed of Xi.

"I knew you could do it!" Ellie squealed throwing her arms around my neck and pressing her lips against mine for a brief moment, the tiny touch sending my dragon into a fury. I was going to have to get her alone later, it seems.

If only to figure out what the hell was going on.

"I knew you had it in you," Drake said, nearly ripping me

out of Ellie's arms in a move that might have been possessive, but I didn't care. The energy of this moment had wiped any of the irritable burning away.

The magic was still there, the power was still there, but I was just me. Albeit, I was me with giant wings protruding out of my back. But still me.

The cheers mutated, the Dragons that I had hid from the fighting before peeking around buildings, scattered amongst The Forgotten as they were drawn to the sound. Their dragons were drawn to this moment.

To me.

All of them were staring at me.

All of them were chanting my name.

Chanting what I had waited my whole life to hear.

"All hail Queen Zoe! The Dragon Queen shall take her throne!"

27

ELLIOT

"Isn't it like a told you, a little bit of soap and everything washes away." Rana smiled, hands shoved deep in her pants pockets as she walked beside me, ignoring the throngs of people that were heading in the same direction.

"Are you talking about the city or the 'sins of my past'? Because if you are going to go on another rant about my sins and recovering my soul or whatnot, I will not hesitate to put you back in the mirror." My phoenix laughed at that, the chortling sound pulling her focus and she rolled her eyes, burrowing her hands deeper into her pockets. It was amazing the things didn't go down to her knees.

"I would be fine with that, less people to stare at me." She immediately moved closer, forcing a smile and a wave at the Forgotten who were rushing to the giant building at the end of the cobbled street we were walking towards. "Perhaps I could not be an old man this time as well. Or even better, you could give me normal eyebrows?" She gave me a shy smile, her long afro of curls bobbing around her face.

"I dunno, you keep lecturing me about the cleansing of my soul and those eyebrows are a guarantee," and also the perfect revenge. I gave her a smile and she sighed, making that half caw, half purr sound she always did.

It was loud, twisted, and if you had never heard it before could easily be the most terrifying thing you had ever heard. No wonder the dragons that had been walking too close took a mighty step back.

"I wasn't talking about your soul," she snapped over my snicker, and I rolled my eyes. That would have been a first. "This time I was actually talking about the city."

She gave a grand gesture to the glittering buildings and sparkling cobbles, like she was displaying the prize on a game show.

The soot covered buildings were gone, the charred remains of my lust driven fire had been scrubbed away with nothing more than a little magic. Everything glistened in the ever-burning light of the ceiling, white stone, ruby accents, diamonds and emeralds and everything else inlaid into the stone that was carved so intricately it could only be done by magic.

The City of Soot was what Rydaim had tried to be, and the building before us what that damn mural had pretended to stand for.

White stone towered over everything in dizzying spires that might as well be dripping from the ceiling. The front of the spires were encased with diamonds that sparkled until it looked like the whole thing was made of glass. White glittering glass that seamlessly blended with the gold inset stained glass windows, colors and designs twisting into pictures and scenes that I knew all too well. I didn't have to go up the steps of burnt sapphire to see the four panels of me and my sisters along the far wall, our thrones right before.

Or they had been. I had crushed them to dust once upon

a time. Who knows what Hilda had replaced them with, she was in charge of this ceremony and I had stoically stayed away. Not because I didn't support what was going on, but because being in the cathedral was going to be exactly what Rana kept teasing me about.

A spiritual rebirth.

It was the last step. Now it was me who was plunging my hands in my pockets, grateful I had opted for the fancy dress pants and not the feathery dress I would usually wear to these things. Except this one wasn't for me and I wasn't about to steal her thunder.

"I was starting to worry you were going to miss it," Jarron said, breaking through the crowd to sweep me off my feet, planting multiple kisses along my jaw until I was passed to Killian, the two sandwiching me between them as Killian kissed the back of my neck.

"God damn it you too," I hissed, well aware that I had started to smoke and the fancy pant suit I was wearing was in real threat of turning to piles of ash. "Will you knock it off, haven't I told you I will never be in the mood for a public orgy."

Killian chuckled, Jarron moaned and continued to kiss my jaw. Thank god the knife concealed there one of my mates could control himself. Drake wrapped his hands around my waist and pulled me out of my dragon sandwich, holding me against him as he backed us toward the stone sentinels that stood in the courtyard, glistening water pouring from the fountain again.

I would be sad at the loss of two warm bodies, but Drake was as warm, his hands as firm against my hips.

"Back off boys," Drake said, a laugh clear in his voice. "You heard the lady, hands off, or I am going to stick the nice stone lady behind us on you."

He nodded to the fountain, to the three dragons, and the carved woman that once upon a time had meant nothing more than a reminder of the dragon's place beneath us. The fountain had been recreated, some weird prophecy born out of nothing. I guess in a way it had come true after all. A woman and her dragons had saved them all.

"Yeah right," Killian laughed, Jarron rolling his eyes. "You are going to make the stone come to life? I thought that childhood fear was long gone."

Oh boy. I knew that Drake had seen the sentinels before, but these two had not. Note to self: have fun with that later.

"Hey! Will you guys hurry your asses up! We are about to start!" Hilda yelled from the wide-open door of the cathedral, her voice echoing over the empty courtyard like a blast from a cannon.

Oh god. Empty courtyard.

We all looked around in shock, before taking off toward the door, Hilda chuckling as we plunged ourselves into the darkened space, the door slamming behind us.

"You should have left them out there. They could have barged in like the lost love at a wedding and destroyed everything. It would have been wonderful," Xi sighed from where she was leaning against one of the twisted vines carved into the pillars, hand folded over her waist as she stared at the other side of the cathedral, right at out murals, and thrones, and everything that was about to happen.

Guess there is no time like the present. I turned, ready to face my spiritual awakening, or some video playing all of my sins or some shit. Instead, I faced a single throne placed between the murals of me and my sisters, the massive stone seat could have easily fit five grown adults wide and at least ten tall. Our glassy serene faces looked down on the stone seat, and the woman who sat in the center of it.

Zoe looked as salivating as she always did. Chestnut hair waving over her shoulders, her eyes pure red from the dragon that was peering through them. The color of her flames reflected the same shade of ruby in the massive ornate dress she wore, and in the wings that extended from her back, stretched from her spine to spread nearly the width of the side of the cathedral. Suddenly, the size of the throne made sense.

"Dragons! Forgotten! Fae!" Zoe bellowed the moment the doors to the cathedral closed. Her voice echoed over the stone buttresses; it ran along the edge of the massive room until it sounded deep, powerful. Like the queen she was. "The tyrant who lorded over us for hundreds of years has fallen. We fought together to defeat the others that came to upset our home. We joined together to defeat an enemy we didn't even know existed. I fought beside you, with you, and together we restored our kind to what we once were. We restored our heritage. Our traditions."

She paused, the hundreds if not thousands of people who had crammed into the cathedral shifting their weight as they waited, everyone holding their breath. I leaned closer to Drake, Jarron and Killian flanking my other side as she stood, taking one step down, her dress dragging behind her, her wings stretching even further.

"We restored our prosperity," She continued, her voice cracking. "And with that, you have chosen me to lead you. You have called for me to take the throne as your Alpha. Is this what you wish? Is this the future that you wish for our people?"

The question lingered in the air, the building itself seeming to hold its breath before everyone before her lowered to kneel, heads bowed, dragons growling in submission. The seven of us were the only ones who still stood. We remained huddled at the back of the cathedral, pressed against the door, watching as she took another step forward, closer to the small table that I had missed in the crowd, and the massive crown that sat in the middle of it.

"Then I accept," She whispered, her voice barely carrying back to us as she lifted the crown, standing straight and tall as she placed it atop her head. The fiery red of her eyes boring right into mine, glistening with fire, with tears.

My own emotion pooling to match it. Yes, I was crying, and I wasn't even ashamed.

~

"THESE ARE BEAUTIFUL," I WHISPERED, RUNNING MY FINGERS through a bin of rubies so deep that there must have been thousands there. Zoe smiled, even though her dragon was growling, the low menacing sound rattling the gems, reminding me exactly who they belonged to.

"Thank you," Zoe said, leaning back on the upholstered sofa we sat on, the crown still perched on her head. I had a feeling neither her nor her dragon were going to take it off soon.

Hilda had made the thing completely encrusted with rubies, which happened to be what her dragon hoards. That crown may never be set down. Let's hope that she had some stellar neck muscles, she was going four hours strong now, and I happened to know that Jarron and Killian had a bet.

"You're lucky that she's letting you touch them, let alone see them," Jarron chuckled. "If it were me, I would be ashamed that my dragon picked something so cliché to hoard. Jewels that just so happen to be the color of your beast? You can do better, Zoe."

Zoe jerked forward, growling at Jarron who chuckling

and leaned back, hands interwoven behind his head, his button up shirt falling open. I swallowed and looked away. Being in the same room, alone, with all four of them was trying every last bit of my patience.

"Oh, you're one to talk," Zoe snarled, the heat in her voice acting like ice water against my bristling mating instinct. The term was suddenly making more sense than ever. "You keep your junk in a shoebox under your bed. But seeing as Ellie blew up your house..."

Zoe smiled, waved her hand, and Jarron about lost it, his dragon going into a full rage and shooting him across the coffee table towards Zoe. Luckily, he never made it, both Drake and Killian lunged into action, Zoe continuing to laugh as I sat, shaking my head.

Damn my Phoenix for bonding with ALL of the siblings. You would have thought she had realized that I had my hands full with the three, but no. She needed my best friend too. And there, she goes snickering again, although that might have been more from the wrestling dragons and rippling muscles in front of me.

"Hey now. It wasn't just your horde that was destroyed in that blast," Killian said, wrestling Jarron back into his seat. I probably would have helped if I wasn't so lost in the fact that I had blown up not one, but two dragon hoards.

Good god, it was a miracle the two haven't beheaded me.

"Of course," Killian continued when Jarron appeared to have calmed down. "Mine wasn't tucked in a shoe box..."

And they were back at it again.

"Stop!" I bellowed, glad it took me only one try to calm them down. "If it helps I did it to save your life, and I will help you to replenish it. What did you horde anyway?"

Jarron immediately turned a shade of pink so bright that

his blonde hair was almost orange. He sat back in his chair, lips parted as everyone else began to laugh.

'Yes, Jarron, tell your mate what you hoarded," Zoe goaded him on, I would have given her a look, but all the others were still laughing, staring at him expectantly.

"Do I want to know?" I asked, my stomach officially in my stomach. Jarron was furiously shaking his head no, while Killian prodded his back.

"Tell her, bro. Get it over with."

There wasn't a drop of gold in Jarron's dark eyes, his lip twitching into a tiny bit of a smile as he mumbled something I wasn't sure that anyone could understand. Killian and Zoe broke out into larger fits of laughter anyway.

"What was that?"

"Panties!" Jarron suddenly roared, jumping to his feet and throwing his hands in the air. It didn't miss my notice that he wasn't looking anywhere at me. "I hoard women's panties. Are you happy now?"

Everyone was laughing. Jarron was officially tomato red and I was frozen in shock, confusion, and I have to admit: the tiniest bit of intrigue.

"Do you mean like used..."

"We don't have to get into this," Jarron interrupted, still not looking at me.

"Oh yes we do," Killian chuckled, throwing his arm around Jarron's shoulder. "Tell her about the red ones with a bow..."

"Wait. I don't want to know," Thank god my Phoenix was chuckling at the ridiculousness of the situation, because I was sure my jealousy meter had hit an all-time high. "Please tell me you hoard something normal, Drake. I would even take a horde of cats at this point."

The laughter slowly died off, Drake's smile fading as he

stepped closer, kneeling on the other side of the table to produce a battered cardboard box.

"Kittens then?" I asked, he only shook his head, lifting the flaps of the box and pulling out stacks of what at first appeared to be old yellowed paper. It wasn't, it was thousands of pictures, taken over hundreds of years. He and Zoe when he was a kid. Drake teaching what looked like a climbing summer camp. Climbing over some frightening mountain, not a rope to be seen. Drake and about fifteen other climbers. A picture of Killian and Jarron taken from a distance. A picture of him and I that he had taken back when the circus still stood and we were practicing the routine we never got to do.

Picture after picture or moments. Of life.

"Memories. That's what my dragon hoards. I used to say it was in search of family, but I found that now. Now there is only memories to hoard. Memories to make." He was growing closer, so close, all I could see was the melted honey in his eyes, the round lips that I had wanted to kiss from that very first day, when his hands grazed my hips.

"You are my family, Ellie. You all are."

I closed the gap between us, kissing the lips that I had waited so long to make mine. Taking the dragon that I wanted just as bad. I didn't care who else was here, who else saw, they were all mine, and I would have them all.

Forever.

28

CALLAY

WELL, damn it all. This time I knew I had honest to god died.

I had been falling. Stabbing the bastard as much as I could in pure rage-murder need. Even I knew I could not survive a fall into the abyss below the mountain.

All I could do was take Parris with me into the grungy afterlife. Make him pay for what he did to me. To what he did to the child he put in me. The child he had been responsible for. The child who had died because of him.

Every stab had been for her.

My death was all for her.

Standing here, however, was making me wonder if it was all in vain. Fucking Unicorn had tricked me, just like all the others I had watched her toy with over the years. Even I wasn't exempt. Which was why I was here, in the middle of the forest I hadn't seen in centuries, standing yards from the quaint little house that had protected my family for so long, the one that we had all died in eventually.

Like a fool, a fool who didn't think it was possible to live a few hundred years, I had asked to come back here. To save them all from the cold winter and the starvation that would one by one take us all.

Now that I was here, however, I realized how pointless it all was. I couldn't force myself to take a single step forward. All of this had happened hundreds of years before. The universe and the world had gone on without them. And everything had survived.

Even if they hadn't.

Raised voices boomed through the heavy log walls of the single room cabin, the oiled paper windows rattling as my parents yelled and screamed inside. I had forgotten how much they used to fight. Hearing it again was like reliving a bad dream.

Maybe I would have been better off dead. Why had I even asked for this? Starving in the middle of a barren wilderness must have addled my brain.

Screw this shit.

Before I could turn around, the front door creaked open, my little sister stomping her way out, cursing under her breath. I had only seen Lilly for a moment, and even then, she had been unconscious and thrown over Parris' shoulder. But the blonde hair, the tiny frame, my sister looked exactly like her.

Maybe it was here. For all I knew I had died, frozen to the forest floor, trying to catch a goddamned fish and hallucinated my entire life. I was sure that was a thing.

Seeing her was nearly proof.

Except that seeing her also brought back the buzzing energy of the magic that the Unicorn had given me, the power I hadn't been fully able to explore. Now, there was no one stop me.

"Lilly." I gasped as my kid sister caught sight of me

standing there, I was sure beyond a doubt sure that they looked the same now. Hallucinating or not, I didn't care.

"Callay?" she asked, looking me up and down curiously. It was only then that I realized I was wearing the same jeans and jacket I had died in, you know, a few hundred years in the future. I definitely looked like a freak against her traditional peasants' clothes of the mid to late 1600s. Or, that's what a textbook had said when I had researched it once upon a time.

"Callay? What are you doing? What are you wearing? You were supposed to be collecting wood..." Her eyes grew with each question, the superstitions that we had been raised to believe starting to take hold. I half expected her to ask if I was a witch.

I would have asked if I was a witch.

"Did you run into the magician in the woods? Did you get away or did he steal your soul?" Close enough. I mean, she wouldn't have been wrong with the witch either.

Just a different soul sucking villain.

"No, Lilly." I shook my head, bending down until I was looking her in the eye, her dark brown eyes. I wondered what color Lily's eyes had been.

"Lilly? My name is Danna... who is Lilly?"

"No one." Forget falling to my doom. I had stabbed myself right through the heart. I shook my head again, trying to dislodge the pain. "But Danna, there is danger coming, we need to get ready to leave.'

"Leave?"

"We have to leave, you and I so that we can save our family. I know someone that can help, but we have to find her before it's too late." I wrapped my hand around hers, her tiny palm warm and sweaty against mine.

"What danger, Callay?"

"The soldiers..." I began, but Danna was already narrowing her eyes at me in confusion.

"No. The soldiers are nice, they brought us pies last week." It took all my effort to keep my lips sealed. I had almost forgotten how nice the soldiers were in the beginnings. Before they stole our food. Before they stole and used everything.

"Yes, but the danger is coming for them too. We have to be ready. Will you help me get ready?" I held on to her hand tighter. I wasn't going to let her go, although it would probably make this whole thing easier if she chose to come with me.

She pressed her lips together, looking from my weird clothes to the tiny house behind, the paper window still shaking with the screaming that was going on inside. Danna let out an exhale and turned back to me, nodding once before she stepped closer.

"We have to hurry, then," I whispered, pulling her away from the house and into the sparse forest. The same forest I had died in.

Or hallucinated in.

Who the fuck knew anymore?

"Where are we going?" She asked as she tugged on my hand, her fingers digging into the back of my hand in fear.

"Do you know what a Unicorn is?" I asked as I led her deeper into the woods, closer to the pond that I knew would change everything.

"No," Danna whispered, afraid now. We weren't supposed to venture into this part of the woods that soul eating Witch was supposed to be here, and by the width of her eyes that that was exactly what she was expecting.

"Don't worry. I will show you. I will keep you safe." I gave her a smile, but the poor kid was shaking so much now that she looked like she was made of paper torn in the wind.

"Do you promise?"

"I do." I also promise to help the kid find a bit of a backbone before all of this was over.

"And we will find this unicorn?"

"Yes, and when we find her, we will kill her and steal her horn." Power buzzed through me, igniting everything until my hair began to glow and lift the same as it had done for centuries now. I have expected Danna to scream and run away, like a good superstitious peasant, but she stared at me, jaw dropped, awe bright in her eyes.

"Is it the Unicorn that did that?" I could only nod in answer, scared that I would say the wrong thing. I was amazed that hadn't scared her. If the kid saw the murderous rage that was pumping through me we might have a problem. "And if we kill her, that will save our family?"

That time I smiled, wide and menacingly as the power picked up and the girl tried to pull away, my hand wrapping tighter around hers.

"It will save everything."

ALSO BY REBECCA ETHINGTON

THE WORLD OF IMDALIND

THE CIRCUS OF SHIFTERS

ABOUT THE AUTHOR

Rebecca Ethington is an internationally bestselling author with almost 700,000 books sold. Her breakout debut, The Imdalind Series was cited as "Interesting and Intense" by *USA Today's Happily Ever After Blog*.

From writing horror to romance and creating every sort of magical creature in between, Rebecca's imagination weaves vibrant worlds that transport readers into the pages of her books. Her writing has been described as fresh, original, and groundbreaking, with stories that bend genres and create fantastical worlds.

Born and raised under the lights of a stage, Rebecca has written stories by the ghost light, told them in whispers in dark corridors, and never stopped creating within the pages of a notebook.

Find me online
www.rebeccaethington.com
contact@rebeccaethington.com

www.ingramcontent.com/pod-product-compliance
Lightning Source LLC
Chambersburg PA
CBHW022031240626
47154CB00007B/2352